The
Game
Runs
Deep

The Game Runs Deep
Copyright ©2019 Deon Wright Publishing

ISBN: 978-1-7328607-2-8
Library of Congress Control Number: 2019917822

www.authordeonwright.com
Facebook: Facebook.com/authordeonwright
Instagram: @author_dw
TikTok: @authordw

PRINTED IN THE UNITED STATES OF AMERICA

Acknowledgements

First and foremost, to God I give all the glory. Courtney, thank you for putting up with all those late nights. It's going to pay off. I love you. Mom, thank you for your encouraging words. This book would not be if it weren't for your support. Thank you for always pushing me. You were preparing me for this. To the rest of my family, friends, and supporters I love every single one of you.

I dedicate my first book to my Dad. I will always honor you. You gave me life and for that I am forever grateful. God bless your soul and may you rest in peace.

Broke As A Joke

The rats ran through the attic, scratching the boards like a DJ putting on a show. Quinn lay on his back in the half-dark, staring at the water stain spreading across the ceiling. It was Friday, the last day before spring break, and all he could think about was how badly he wanted out of The Jungle, out of this house, out of being broke.

"Quinn! Boy, get outta that bed and get ready for school! Don't make me come in there again!" Teresa's voice tore through the thin bedroom door. She always yelled like the walls were soundproof.

He swung his legs over the side of the mattress, careful not to knock over the milk crate he used as a nightstand. Same clothes from yesterday, same busted sneakers. It wasn't like there was much else to pick from. Grabbing his backpack, he headed for the door only to find his mother blocking the way.

"I'm proud of you, my future brain surgeon," she said, her voice softening. Tears welled up as she looked at him like he was still the baby she'd rocked back when she was a young girl. "Three more months, Quinn. You'll walk that stage, go to college, make something of yourself. I worked too hard for it not to pay off."

He shook his head. "Ma... look around. We're six months behind on the mortgage. Me graduating ain't gonna change that. I'm eighteen now. I gotta start bringing in money."

"Just because you eighteen don't make you grown," she snapped. "Stay focused on them books. The Lord will provide."

"Ma, if God was gonna help us, He would've done it already. I'm tired of watching you struggle. I can't sit back and keep watching without doing anything. I want to take care of us like Pop did."

"Do you want to end up like your father, in an early grave?"

Quinn shook his head and looked at the floor.

"Your father was a conman who only knew how to sell drugs or rob somebody. Your father was in out of jail and always caught up in some mess. That's what got him killed."

"Pops had us living comfortably. You must have forgot all the shit he did for us."

Teresa slapped Quinn across the cheek, and he held his hand on the spot where it stung.

"You better watch your damn mouth!"

"What if I don't want to go to college?"

"Oh, you're going!"

"That's what you want me to do! What about what I want ma?"

"This is my house, and I make the rules in here! That means you're going to take your ass to college and get a degree so you can get a real job!"

"This isn't even your house; this is Grandpa's house."

"No, this is my house! I pay the bills here!"

"Ma, you can't even afford them bills. The bank is about to take this house away from you!"

Teresa grabbed him by the collar and shoved him against the wall, her fist cocked like she was squaring up with a man on the street.

"If you don't like my rules, move out! Until then, I don't want to hear another peep about getting a job or paying bills. What kind of job are you going to get with no diploma? Tell me that? And I'll be damn if you get out here in these streets and sell drugs for a living! No, you're going to stay in school get a diploma then go to college. Like it or not that's your only choice. Now hurry up and get your behind to school before you're late!"

She shoved him toward the door.

Quinn stepped off the porch, taking in the block. Broken bottles, cigarette butts, and bullet casings glinted in the morning light. The Jungle wasn't just a nickname. It was home to hustlers, junkies, and enough rats to make you wonder who really owned the place. Six months behind, a bank breathing down their necks, and his mother still talking about college like it was a golden ticket.

Quinn knew better. In The Jungle, respect wasn't handed out with diplomas. Quinn shook his head at the living conditions that most of his neighbors considered normal. He looked up the street, past the dope dealers and junkies making drug exchanges. The block he lived on had been an infamous dope strip for years. It was streets just like the one he lived on, that Quinn's father used to sell dope.

Quinn's main man Roc was waiting on the corner by the stop sign as usual.

"About time you brought your ass out the house!" Roc said once Quinn made it to the corner.

"What's up fool?" Quinn said giving his boy a pound. "Are those the new J's?" He noticed the new kicks on Roc's feet. "Those joints are fresh."

"Yeah, you know me. I got to stay fly for the honeys. But aye, you're lucky I didn't leave your ass. You're about to make me late for class."

"Nigga, stop lying," Quinn said knowing Roc skipped almost every class. "Shit, do you ever go to class?"

"Hell nah, but there's this fine little honey in my first period that's new to the school and I'm trying to tap that."

Quinn laughed. Sometimes he wondered if Roc ever thought about anything else besides pussy. Roc was a real knucklehead and had no interest in school at all. To him, it was a waste of time. He didn't see anything in a textbook that would change the fact that he was poor and black. Quinn didn't blame him because he felt the same way.

Quinn zoned out through all his classes, hardly able to focus on anything that had to do with schoolwork. His

4

mind was stuck in a daydream. All he could do was imagine how life would be if his pockets were fat.

"Can anyone give me the answer to the problem on the board? What about you, Quinten?"

"Huh?" Quinn responded as his daydream was interrupted.

"The answer to the problem on the board, do you, have it?"

"Uh uh…I'd like to use a lifeline," Quinn answered, trying to make light of the fact that he had been startled.

The class chuckled.

"Since you find Algebra amusing, I want you to meet me after class." Ms. Hanson snapped back.

"*Oooooh*!" most of the class said mockingly.

"Jennifer, can you let me, Mr. Walters, and the rest of the class know the answer to the question on the board?"

"Yes, the answer is X equals two."

"That is correct. I'm glad someone is paying attention in my class."

The bell ended the last period of the day. All the students rushed to gather their books and backpacks.

"Don't forget your homework for chapters three and four! There will be a quiz on Tuesday!" Ms. Hanson spoke quickly before any of the students slipped out the door.

"Mr. Walters!" Ms. Hanson snapped, reminding Quinn of their little meeting before he could sneak out of the classroom. Once they were standing in the classroom alone, she began to lecture him.

"Your grades are starting to slip. You have gone from an A+ to a B- in one month. What is causing you to lose focus?"

"It's nothing. I'll do better, Ms. Hanson, but I really need to get home," Quinn lied. He was just uninterested in anything she had to say.

"I hope you get it together fast, Quinten. Graduation is only four months away and you don't want to lose your perfect G.P.A. You're a very good student and I'd hate to see your hard work go down the drain. I'm willing to give you some extra credit to keep your 4.0 grade point average but next time you're in this classroom, please keep yourself alert. I have faith in you Quinten, so please don't disappoint me."

"Can I go now?" Quinn asked, letting her know he was uninterested.

"Have a good evening, Quinten," Ms. Hanson stated in frustration.

Quinn walked out of the classroom letting Ms. Hanson's words go in one ear and out the other. He wasn't trying to hear any of that, *'I have faith in you. You're a good student'* shit. He had always been a good student but that hadn't gotten him anywhere. School was a joke. It wasn't helping him make any money and he was starting to realize just how much of a waste of time it was. He was still stuck in the ghetto.

He had sent scholarship applications to a dozen different universities but each time he received a letter in the mail, it was a rejection. Quinn was going to school in a non-accredited district which meant universities had no respect for the education that his mother thought would magically change his life. He knew for certain that he would have a full ride scholarship if he was attending school on the suburban side of town.

When Quinn reached the outside of the school building, all his homies were hanging out. His homies Lavere, Quik and Terrance had already dropped out of school, they just showed up afterwards to mingle and socialize. Most of the freshmen students loaded their bus in the bus line located in the school parking lot. A select few of the students had cars and the rest proceeded to walk home like his crew did since their neighborhood was only a five-minute walk from the school.

It was Friday however, so instead of heading back home, everyone headed straight to Glenn Park to watch the car show that would be on display. It was a weekly event that occurred at the same time and place every Friday. Hustlers from every hood throughout the city would drive their cars through the main street that ran through the middle of the park. They would drive throughout the streets with excessively loud music blaring from amplifiers and bass booster stereo systems. Several young brothers drove through in the latest sport car models, SUVs, and luxury coupes. Only the street elite could stunt on the main street. If you didn't have a fly car, you had to park on the side streets then walk over to Glenn Street.

It was the time and place where the young hustlers who were getting the most money got the chance to show off, usually before everyone migrated to Club Live later in the night. Even though it was the beginning of March, the temperature outside was about seventy degrees. The weather in the Midwest was always unpredictable no matter what the season. Some of the ladies were already dressed for the nice weather in what would be considered summertime clothing and every groupie and gold digger in town flocked around the ballers. It was the perfect recipe for chaos because hundreds of people were all packed in a place where jealousy, egos and hormones were all mixing.

People danced to the music blaring from the car stereo systems. A large crowd of fellas were engaged in a game of basketball on the Glenn Park court, and everyone else just walked up and down the street and admired the different cars. Quinn set his eyes on a bad-ass convertible Bentley Continental GT that was parked on the street. The navy-blue exterior was glistening against the sun rays, the inside was a cream color and plush. Twenty-four inches of chrome added even more luxury to the British engineering.

A light skinned brother with long cornrows under a New York Yankees fitted cap occupied the driver's seat. Quinn recognized the man as Brooklyn. He was well known throughout the city. Quinn had heard about his crew, the Midwest Connection, moving heavy weight throughout the entire Midwest region.

As Quinn was eyeing the Bentley, he spotted Jayla. From head to toe, she was drop dead gorgeous. There wasn't one nigga in town who didn't want to knock her socks off. She was walking in his direction, and he was almost hypnotized by the sway of her hips moving. Jayla was a senior like Quinn, and he had wanted to hook up with her ever since his freshman year. Without any hesitation he stepped up to get her attention.

"What's up, Baby Girl?" Quinn said trying his best to be smooth.

"Excuse me," Jayla said harshly, then tried to brush past him but he stood in her way.

"Hold up a minute. Why you moving so fast, Gorgeous?" She blushed slightly. "To keep it real, I been feeling you and I can tell you're feeling me too."

"Boy stop! What makes you think that?" Jayla said shifting her weight to one hip and placing her hand on the other.

"If you weren't, you wouldn't have stopped where you were going to be standing here with me. You need to quit playing hard to get and let me make you mine."

"Sorry, not interested. Plus, I have a man, okay."

"I hope you don't mind that I ask but this man of yours, how serious are y'all? Do you love him?"

"Hell no" was Jayla thought. She didn't love her man, just his money. In fact, she loved *any* man with money but the main cat she fucked with was Damon. Quinn knew exactly who he was, the right-hand man to Brooklyn, and they were the richest hustlers in the city. They supplied every territory in the town.

Damon kept Jayla's nails and hair done along with spending money to shop all day. All she had to do was let his fat ass lay on her and pump his penis while she faked an orgasm to stroke his ego. If he handed over a stack of bills afterward, to her it was worth it.

"All you need to know is that I got a man that takes good care of me, something you can't do for me."

"What your man got that I don't, Baby?"

"No, what do you got that he doesn't?" Jayla asked knowing very well Quinn was completely lacking in the economics department.

"Why don't you find out?"

"There's nothing for me to find. I can look at you and tell."

Jayla would never give Quinn the time of day even though she had to admit, he was cute. Quinn's chocolate complexion, deep waves and perfect set of teeth made his smile contagious. As far as looks, she would say he had reason to be cocky but that didn't mean a thing to her because he was broke as a joke. Jayla viewed being handsome as just a bonus not a necessity. *"Broke niggas are only good for dick."* Jayla was thinking.

Jayla looked down at Quinn's dirty busted up Air Force Ones that told his whole story. Quinn was so broke that he only had one pair of shoes that he had been wearing every day for the past year. He wouldn't get much more wear out of them before the toes started talking. If he didn't get some money for some new shoes soon, he would be walking around in his socks and all those joints had holes in them.

Quinn followed Jayla's eyes and looked behind him. That's when he noticed Damon pulling up to the curb beside where they were standing. *"Shit, I hope this nigga don't start tripping."* Jayla thought to herself, but it was too late. Damon had already spotted her talking to another guy behind his back and by the look on his face, he wasn't happy about it. Quinn couldn't care less about Damon because no man ever put fear in his heart; therefore, he was ready for a confrontation.

The fat sloppy man in his early thirties marched toward Quinn with fury written all over his face. Other than the diamonds on his neck and wrist, nothing stood out about Damon to Quinn. He wasn't fly enough to be with a lady as fine as Jayla.

"Get your own bitch, Little Nigga," Damon stated then wrapped his arms around Jayla and aggressively squeezed her breast with both hands.

He grabbed her chin then forcefully stuck his tongue down her throat. The gesture made Quinn sick even though Jayla was Damon's woman and not his.

"Ugh, stop it, damn!" Jayla hissed.

She hated when Damon acted so unruly. He was extremely possessive and acted like he owned her.

"What're you doing talking to this dusty bum, Jay?" Damon barked. Quinn knew the comment was intended to indirectly disrespect him.

"Can't you see that I'm getting my own chick right now?" Quinn replied slickly to Damon's insult while looking him square in the eye.

Damon got up in Quinn's face then looked him up and down with disgust. "My girl ain't feeling your thirsty ass so bounce before you get fucked up."

"Who's going to make me?" Quinn challenged. He had never been one to back down even though the man was almost twice his size in weight.

"This Glock on my hip will handle you and the rest of them lil' niggas with you."

Quinn's homies were standing right behind him ready for a fist brawl that would only end with Damon getting stomped out. However, when Damon flashed the weapon under his shirt that was resting on his waistline, Quinn reluctantly eased back.

"That's what I thought, pussy."

Damon was feeling powerful knowing he could easily stop the little nigga's heartbeat. Quinn's crew backed off knowing the confrontation was a battle they wouldn't win.

"Uh huh yeah, you right." Roc said. He was just as agitated as Quinn, but he knew better than to jump stupid with Damon.

"Get in this car bitch!" Damon ordered Jayla then yanked her arm in the direction of his Jaguar. Jayla kept her head down as she walked away and got in the convertible with Damon.

"Don't even sweat it, Q." Roc said in low tone.

"You trying to play me bitch!" Damon yelled as he and Jayla both got in his car.

Before they pulled off, Damon snatched Jayla up by her weave then wrapped his fat fingers around her throat. He choked her until her skin flushed purple. Tears came rolling down Jayla's cheeks as her eyes were pleading for someone to help. Quinn was hotter than fire and even thought about risking his life on some, Captain Save a Hoe, shit. His better judgement told him to chill. Word on the street was that Damon had shot a man in the face who owed him money and it was in broad daylight. As Quinn watched Jayla get a severe chastisement, he stayed calm but inside he felt rage.

Damon had slapped her across the face several times causing her high yellow cheeks to bruise to a purplish tone.

"I'm sorry, Baby! I didn't mean to disrespect you!" Jayla yelled out while she was begging and pleading for him to discontinue his trouncing.

One thing Quinn hated was a male who had to enforce his power over a female by putting hands on her. Several people began to stop what they were doing to witness the drama unfold.

"Ooooh shit!" or *"Damnnnn!"* were most of the comments that could be heard as spectators instigated Damon's inflicted abuse like it was a heavyweight showdown. As Jayla continued to plea, cry and duck from the blows, all anyone could do was watch until Damon was satisfied that she had begged enough. He released his hold around her weave and Jayla held her head in her hands, obviously feeling embarrassed and humiliated.

Damon looked over at Quinn and smirked with a cocky grin. He pulled the gun from his waist and aimed it in Quinn's direction. Damon chuckled as Quinn froze in place, bracing for impact. After seeing how ruthless he was on Jayla, Quinn wasn't sure what the man was capable of. He looked Damon in the eyes like he always said he would whenever his killer took his life.

"Bum!" Damon yelled then sped off up the street stopping next to the Bentley that Quinn had been admiring not too long ago. Damon exchanged brief words with Brooklyn before they both sped off into the distance.

13

Mostly everyone in the park had stopped what they were doing to watch the altercation that had quickly escalated and nearly ended fatally. Quinn's blood was boiling with rage so extreme that he could hardly control himself. Quinn told himself he shouldn't be angry, but he was. It was all a part of the game.

Quinn hated that Jayla put up with a man who was laying hands on her. That pissed him off even more. Quinn knew Jayla was only with Damon because he was getting money, and Quinn wasn't plain and simple. Quinn vowed to himself that it would be moments like these that he would remember after he came up. One day, the tables would turn, but for now he needed to come up with a legit plan that would put him on top. Everything after that would come full circle.

"Ayo, I'm out," Quinn said to his homies who had already brushed off the incident.

Quinn stormed away from the park, heat in his chest with every step. The more he replayed Damon's disrespect, the tighter his fists curled. Dude had punked his whole crew in front of everybody and made them look soft. That wasn't something you just let slide.

But as the anger burned, reality crept in. Going after Damon wasn't a fight, it was suicide. The Midwest Connection wasn't some corner crew; they were heavy. Quinn didn't have the paper, the firepower, or the soldiers to even the odds. Hell, he didn't even own a gun.

And after staring down the barrel earlier, he'd felt that cold truth, guns carried weight. The man holding one owned the room, the street, the situation. When people knew you were willing to pull that trigger, they gave you a different kind of respect. The kind that made even your enemies think twice.

But Quinn also knew money alone didn't keep you alive. He'd seen plenty of cats in the hood get rich quick, flashing cash without backbone, only to end up in a casket. Without respect, money just made you a target.

"I've been chasing the wrong thing," he muttered, jaw tight. All this time, he'd been blinded by dollar signs, forgetting the foundation, power and respect. It was like someone had just wiped the fog off his vision.

If he wanted to level up, he had to earn his stripes. And that meant nobody could keep sleeping on him. Respect wasn't given. He had to take it.

His first step. Get a gun.

Nothing More To Lose

For weeks, Quinn buried himself inside his room with the door shut. He hadn't stepped foot in Glenn Park for the past several Fridays.

He hardly even came out of the house, opting to stay home and plot ways to get his hands on some serious money. The only time he came out of his room was to eat, drink or release his bowels. Quinn had already figured that crime would be the only way to make a large sum of cash in a short amount of time. Hours that turned into days had gone by. He had exhausted his brain, and he still hadn't come up with a good plan that he thought would get him paid. Quinn stared at his ceiling feeling hopeless. All his homies were out hanging and making the most of the little they had to look forward to. Quinn had no enthusiasm. Small things didn't excite him and life without an abundance of money just wasn't a life worth living. He wanted the world and everything in it.

"A broke nigga can't accomplish shit," he mumbled to himself in frustration.

"Oh! Praise the Lord! Hallelujah! Thank you, Jesus!"
Teresa shouted.

Quinn sat back trying to remain undisturbed by his
mother's hooting and hollering. He thought she was just
having another one of her praise antics. He couldn't
understand why she was praising God every day and He
hadn't done anything to get them out the situation they
were in. Teresa came busting through her son's
bedroom door. Quinn lay on his bed with a pillow over
his face.

"Get up boy! I need you to go somewhere with me."
Quinn tried to ignore his mother's request not wanting
to be bothered. She snatched the pillow off his head.
"Boy, put some clothes on so we can go!"

Teresa had noticed for the past few days that Quinn
had been locked inside his room from sunrise to sunset.
Several times, she asked her son what was on his mind
but each time he insisted that he didn't want to talk
about it. Quinn knew his mother couldn't understand
what he was going through so there was no need to talk
about it. She said he was going through one of those,
'teenage phases', whatever that meant. Quinn got up
and threw on some clothes but took his sweet time to do
so. Quinn wasn't in the mood to leave the house. He was
too focused on coming up with a hustle plan. That's all
he had time for.

"Boy, hurry up. I don't have all day!" Teresa came
back in her son's room, yelling as always.

After Quinn finished getting dressed, they took the
city bus over to the Community City Bank. When they
stepped off the Metro in front of the large glass building,

Quinn immediately thought about all the money that was locked away somewhere inside those four walls. When they reached the teller's desk, a rude Caucasian male treated them as if they were lost and weren't supposed to be there. When Teresa told the teller she wanted to cash a check, he sarcastically asked if she had an account and told her that it would be a thirty-dollar fee to cash the check.

"I don't have an account here but the check has this bank written on it so I know I can cash it here for free," Teresa stated.

The teller looked surprised when he saw the amount of the check and even started to treat them differently. Quinn thought it was funny how money could make a person change from rude to polite. Quinn was even more surprised when he caught a glimpse of the ten thousand dollars that was written out to his mother. He was curious about how she'd gotten that kind of money. The teller cashed out Teresa with one hundred c-notes and placed them in a large envelope.

After leaving the bank, their stomachs were growling so the two headed over to The Cafe where they enjoyed lunch. Teresa told her son about how her job had mailed out settlement checks for years of ripping off the workers. She said that she was going to pay off a few bills and put some money away for his college tuition. Quinn didn't tell his mom that would be a waste because he had no intentions of going to college. They ordered two appetizers, two entrees and two desserts enjoying the best meal they'd had in a long time. The waitress was very polite and friendly, so Teresa left the server with a nice tip.

Just a block over from The Cafe was the Palazzo Shopping District. Teresa told Quinn that she would buy him two pair of shoes of his choice from the Foot Locker located in the shopping district. Quinn was excited to finally get some new kicks, he chose a pair of retro twelve Jordan's and a new pair of Nike Air Force Ones. Teresa also bought him a Nike tracksuit, some denim jeans and fresh white T-shirts. Quinn changed into some of his new gear in the dressing room and threw his old clothes in the shopping bags. The fresh gear had Quinn feeling like a different person. It seemed like every female he walked past greeted him with a smile rather than the frowns he was used to receiving. Quinn followed his mom around until she bought herself a few items too.

They walked toward the bus stop with a few bags apiece, having spent several hundred dollars in just a few hours. Quinn couldn't wait to get to school and rock the rest of his new gear. It felt good to him, knowing he had money to spend and the ability to get the things he wanted. It was a feeling he longed to have all the time.

After walking into the bank earlier, he got an idea of what his next move would be. It seemed crazy at first, but he knew it could be pulled off. The ten thousand dollars was just a taste of what having a pocket full of money felt like. When the Metro pulled up, they boarded the public bus and headed back home. With all the shopping bags, they stood out amongst the mostly poor people who rode the bus. Quinn looked around the large city bus and noticed a group of four grimy looking men who had their eyes on him. One of the dudes tapped his partner's shoulder and they both took note of Quinn.

As the bus made its route, several passengers exited the bus, but the group of four stayed put. The driver was making his last stops and Quinn's stop just so happened to be the very last. With just one more stop left, the driver opened the bus doors and called out for any passengers to exit. Quinn stayed put. He just sat there waiting for them to exit the bus first, but they didn't move.

"Come on, Son," Teresa said, trying to ease the situation but Quinn didn't feel comfortable. He knew these cats had ill intentions.

As soon as Quinn got up, they decided to rise to their feet too. They all pulled out guns, aiming them directly at his temple.

"Y'all are going to have to get off this bus or I'm calling the cops!" the elderly bus driver threatened.

"Call the cops and you won't live to see another day," one of them threatened.

"Give us the bags," said the one who had tapped his partner. He looked like Meek Mill with nappy braids and a long scar across his cheek.

Quinn was enraged but he handed over the shopping bags out of fear for his mother's life. The Meek Mill lookalike's partner started going through their belongings and pulled out Quinn's new pair of Jordans.

"Damn homie, these are fresh! Too bad they ain't my size," he said examining Quinn's new kicks. Next, he snatched Teresa's purse and went through all her belongings until he came up empty.

"I know one of y'all got some loot on you. How else y'all afford all these new clothes. Quan, check his pockets," Meek Mill said to the biggest one in the group who began to pat Quinn down.

"What are you doing? Strip this nigga out his clothes." Quinn was stripped out of his shirt and pants until he was standing in nothing but his boxers.

"He ain't got nothing," Quan said once he didn't find anything.

"Strip her out of her clothes too."

"Y'all soft without them guns in your hands," Quinn said unable to hold his tongue out of anger.

Quinn tried to lunge at the ringleader who had his gun pointed at Teresa, but the young goons put him in a choke hold.

"What the fuck you say?" The Meek Mill wannabe asked angrily but he knew Quinn's words held truth. Before Quinn could speak again, cold hard steel smashed against Quinn's mouth causing his lip to swell and bleed.

"Shut up you little punk or next I'll put a bullet in your mouth."

Quinn watched them violate his mom in front of his face, stripping her of her clothes and dignity. Teresa still had the face and physique of a woman in her twenties. The fat pervert felt her up with lust. Her eyes were filled with water, but a tear never fell from her eyelids. She stood while he went through every pocket that she had worn. Still, they came up empty. He ripped her underwear completely off then snatched at her bra until she was completely exposed. That's when the envelope of money fell onto the bus floor. He opened it up and his eyes widened at the small fortune.

"Jackpot! It's even better than I thought. Just for being generous, I'm going to be nice and let y'all keep y'all little shopping bags."

The ringleader ordered the rest of his goons to let them go and they proceeded to exit the bus. Except for some new clothes, Quinn and his mother were back to having nothing. Just like that their blessing had been turned to a curse. The way the young goons had humiliated his mother, Quinn could never forgive. If he ever saw their faces again, he was going to get revenge.

Teresa and Quinn put their clothes back on and stepped off the Metro bus. At that point, Quinn was beyond angry. He thought about the ten thousand dollars that came and went in less than a few hours. It wasn't the type of money to change your life drastically, but they needed it.

Quinn had reached his breaking point. He was tired of men pushing their weight around while he sat back and did nothing. His ego had taken a beating, and his pride had literally been stripped of him. In his mind, he had nothing more to lose.

Plotting And Scheming

Quinn picked up his phone and dialed Roc. If there was anyone who'd be down for his latest scheme, it was him. Roc was always ready to move, no questions asked, exactly the kind of soldier Quinn wanted on his team.

"What's up, Fam?" Roc picked up.

"Aye bro, I need you and gang to come by my crib tomorrow. I have some business to discuss with y'all. I'm working on a plan that's all about getting this paper, you feel me?"

"Yeah, yeah, I feel you. Aye, you know the Midwest Connection are throwing a swimsuit party at Club Live tomorrow. It's going to be ass and titties bouncing and shaking all over the place, plus everybody on spring break too. It's about to be lit! I know you're going to bring your lame ass out the crib for that."

"I'm not worried about no stupid party right now. I'm trying to get my money up. I got a plan that could bring us some dough. I'm serious, Fam. We can really get money."

"Ok money man. What's the scoop then genius?"

"Look, it's too much to talk about over the phone that's why I want to round up the gang, it's serious what we about to get into and I need to know everybody is on board."

"Whatever it is, I'm with it as long as it's going to make money like you say."

"No doubt. Just come thru after y'all leave that stupid party."

"Yeah, whatever, lame ass dude. I'll holler at you later."

"Bye, fool."

Quinn hung up, irritated at Roc's short-sightedness. His boy was so focused on chasing booty that he couldn't see how backwards he was moving. Parties could wait. There'd be plenty more with the same girls from the last one. Quinn knew that once he got his money right, those same women would flock to him like pigeons to bread.

The next night, Quinn sat in his room, sketching out a plan in his head. A bank robbery. Risky, yes, but it was the most lucrative idea he'd had so far. One mistake could be deadly, so he was determined to map it out perfectly. He figured they'd need weeks of surveillance before making a move.

A small rock tapping against his window snapped him out of thought.

"Bring yo ass outside fool!" Quik called from below.

"Alright, keep it down!" Quinn hissed back, mindful not to wake his mom, who would lose her mind if she caught him sneaking out after midnight.

He slipped into his Nike sweatsuit and fresh Retro Jordans, then climbed out the window. Outside, the crew huddled together, passing around a bottle of Hennessy bought by Roc's girl, Vanilla. At just twenty, she had a fake ID and could score liquor for the underage crew.

Vanilla was bad. Every guy Quinn knew wanted her, but since she was with Roc, she was off-limits. Short, curvy, with long blonde hair, green eyes, and a mix of white and Hispanic features, she carried herself with the ghetto-fabulous attitude that earned her the nickname.

They were still buzzing about the party Quinn had skipped.

"You missed all the fun," said a girl standing next to Vanilla.

Quinn recognized her from school, one of Vanilla's friends.

"I'm Tanisha," she introduced herself. She was just as petite as Vanilla, with smooth brown skin, dark eyes, full lips that reminded Quinn of Meagan Good, and natural jet-black hair grazing her shoulders. Her black two-piece bikini peeked through the straps of her jean shorts, which clung tight to her hips. Her figure made it hard not to look.

"What's up?" Quinn said with a slight smile.

"It's about time you got out your feelings and brought your crybaby ass out the house," Quik teased.

"I thought we were going to have to kick in your crib and pull you out," Roc added.

"Man, fuck y'all," Quinn shot back, knowing he hadn't been around much lately.

"Where you get the fresh gear? You ain't dressed like a homeless person for once," Roc joked, eyeing Quinn's outfit.

"Why don't you get off my nuts?" Quinn replied, shutting down the subject.

"You going to let him talk to you like that?" Quik egged on.

"Shut up before I beat yo' ass," Roc snapped back.

They all laughed, strolling down their beat-up block, ignoring the poverty around them. By the time they reached Roc's house at the end of the street, they were ready to settle in his basement. Roc's mom worked nights, so they could chill without disturbance.

Inside, Lavere sparked up a blunt of Reggie weed, taking long pulls before passing it.

"Nigga, puff-puff pass!" Quik barked. "You know the rules! You always hogging the damn blunt. And quit wetting the end of it. It ain't a dick!"

Everyone cracked up as Quik snatched it, took two hits, then passed it to Terrance.

Quinn glanced around at his boys, the only thing he truly loved about the hood. Terrance was the muscle, tall and built like a linebacker. Quik was the reckless jokester. Lavere, the light skin, tatted pretty boy. Lastly, Roc, the brown tatted dread head, and slick-tongued charmer.

"This nigga is high as a giraffe pussy," Quik said, staring at Quinn. "Nigga, are you sleep?"

Quinn had been lost in a daydream of the crew iced out in diamond pendants and watches, speeding exotic cars through city streets. He snapped back.

"I'm wide awake, y'all the muthafuckas that's sleep! When y'all going to wake up and get y'all shit together!"

"Fool, you trippin!" Quik shot back.

"What I'm saying is we all are sitting here wasting time. The whole reason I wanted us all to link up tonight was to discuss some money moves we need to make. They say time is money, so we should be plotting how we are going to get paid."

"Yeah, I'm with that," Terrance said.

"Okay, Genius. What is your plan?" Roc pressed.

"Look, I been thinking for a while, and I got the game all figured out. Out here it's all about money, power, and respect. Well flip that backwards and it works the same way. First you get respect, and then you get the power, then the money. Now let me break it down a little further. When people respect your gangster, you got the power to make them do whatever you want. Then you take their money plain and simple. I realize the only way for broke niggas like us to get money is to take it from the people who have it."

"I'm with that. Let's break in one of those mansions in Madison Hills," Quik said.

"That's not what I'm talking about. Those cribs have gates with guards, surveillance cameras, and alarms that will pop off and notify the cops as soon as you trespass on somebody's property. The police will be outside, ready to arrest you as soon as you step one foot toward a house."

"So, what do you suggest then?

"Who knows somebody that has some guns that we can get for cheap?" Quinn asked.

"My grandpa is a Vietnam vet. His old ass got weapons of mass destruction in the house," Lavere joked.

"Nigga, I didn't know your grandpa was in the military but that's perfect. I just need you to see if you can get us each a gun then my plan can go into motion. We can't make moves in the streets without protection."

"You still haven't told us what exactly your grand plan is?" Roc pushed.

"I think we need to rob a bank," Quinn said flatly.

"A bank? Dude you must be high. That ain't no good idea," Lavere said.

"I know it sounds crazy but it's the fastest money we will ever make. I was thinking about the Jewelry & Loan store around the corner. I know there's some money inside that joint. All we have to do is get in and get out before the cops show up."

From there, Quinn laid out his plan in detail. Masks, gloves, time limits, control over the crowd, teller compliance, and weeks of casing the spot to learn its traffic patterns and blind spots.

"Vanilla, we're going to need you to be in on this too. If you help us, we'll make it worth your while."

"Whatever y'all need, I'm down," she said.

"Count me in too," Tanisha added. Quinn didn't fully trust her yet, but he figured she could be molded into an asset.

Looking around the room, he asked, "Who's in and who's not?"

"You know I'm in," Roc said.

"I'm in too," Quik said. Terrance nodded in agreement.

Everyone looked to Lavere, who was still hesitant.

"It's too risky."

"If you don't take risk, you'll stay broke. I know you ain't drop out of school just to work with your grandpa cleaning those damn, old fart homes. What do you get, a few hundred dollars a week? You probably make the same amount selling this Reggie weed. All your money goes to gas for that beat-up Firebird."

"At least I got a car, and since you want to talk, don't smoke no more of my weed."

"Look bro, I'm not trying to clown you but you ain't ever going to get no play pushing that old beat-up piece of junk. You can make a quick ten thousand or more in less than five minutes. I know this can work."

Lavere took a moment, then finally said, "Ok, count me in too."

"Good," Quinn said, nodding. "Let's drink to it."

The Hennessy went around the room until it was gone. The blunt followed, smoked to the nub. Quik passed out drunk on the basement floor, and Roc marked his face with a permanent marker while Lavere snapped pictures.

Eventually, the night wound down. Quinn, tipsy and ready to crash, got up to leave. Tanisha brushed against him.

"So, you going to leave without telling me goodbye?" she whispered.

"I'll hit you up," he told her, though they hadn't even exchanged numbers yet.

He slipped back into his house, crawled into bed, and drifted off dreaming of the boss life he craved only to wake up to the same depressing reality.

The Come Up

Not long after Quinn finalized his plan, he stumbled upon an abandoned garage, a perfect hideout for the crew's upcoming missions. Inside, the place was bare except for an old table and some mismatched chairs that had clearly been scavenged from a curbside down the block.

Pulling out his prepaid phone, Quinn sent Lavere a quick text:

Where you at?

He waited. Ten minutes passed with no response. Growing impatient, he tried calling. Still nothing. Twenty minutes later, the garage door creaked open, and Lavere stumbled in, half-toppling under the weight of a massive duffle bag.

"Can one of y'all niggas help me? This bag is heavy," Lavere complained.

The five-man crew rushed over, grabbing the handles and setting the bag onto the wooden table. When Lavere unzipped it, the contents glinted under the dim light. An

AK-47, Glock .45, 9mm, Mossberg shotgun, and an AR-15.

"This is exactly what we needed," Quinn said, inspecting each weapon carefully. "Are these joints loaded?"

"Duh, Nigga." Lavere handed him the Glock.

"Good. I think we're ready."

POW!

The shot echoed in the garage, sending everyone ducking for cover.

"Quit playing around before you hit somebody!" Lavere barked.

"Shut your scary ass up," Quik wheezed between laughs.

"We need to get these guns back the same way they are now. I took these from my old man's gun case."

"He's right. We need to focus. We're about to do something serious and we don't have time for games right now."

Quinn shrugged off his backpack, unzipping it to reveal five black ski masks. He tossed one to each man.

"I can't keep skipping class just to ride around and go look at the damn building. We need to go in there. We've been scoping it out for a week. We're ready to clean out the place."

"What're we waiting on then?" Roc asked.

They filed out of the garage and piled into Lavere's two-door Pontiac Firebird. Ten minutes later, they rolled into the lot of a neighborhood Jewelry & Loan shop. Quinn scanned the crew, then slipped on his ski mask and gloves.

"It's time to get this money," he said, stepping out and sprinting toward the entrance.

Roc, Quik, and Terrance followed, bursting through the doors like a SWAT raid. Quinn fired two shots into the ceiling—*POW! POW!*—making customers drop in fear.

"Everybody get on the ground and put your hands on your head!" Terrance shouted.

The terrified crowd obeyed instantly.

"As long as you muthafuckas cooperate, nobody will lose their life today!" Roc roared.

Quinn vaulted onto the clerk counter, pointing his Glock at the first teller. "Open the drawer!" He gestured at the other two. "Keep your hands up until I tell you otherwise."

The teller's hands shook as she fumbled through the keys.

"Don't make me kill you!" Quinn snapped, agitation rising.

"I'm sorry just please don't shoot me," she begged before finding the right key.

"Fill it up."

Quinn tossed her the black duffle. She dumped in the cash with trembling hands. Now show me the safe. She walked nervously toward the back of the store while Quinn followed, gun pointed to her head. The black steel safe was in the corner of a small office. The woman's hands trembled as she twisted the knob until it clicked then opened revealing more money stacks and a few expensive jewels.

"Toss that Rolex in too." Quinn barked. After the bag had been filled, Quinn zipped it quickly then slung it over his shoulder moving swiftly toward the exit. Gun still raised.

"Good job, y'all didn't make me have to shoot somebody," Quinn state right before he exited the shop. Quik, Roc, Terrance walked out behind him.

"Two minutes flat. Perfect timing." Quinn said checking his watch. He bolted toward the getaway car, the others close behind. They all piled into the Pontiac.

"Step on it, Nigga!" He ordered Lavere.

But Lavere just sat there, the car's engine dead.

"Shit! Why'd you even turn the car off, we were coming right back out?" Quinn snapped, panic in his voice.

Lavere twisted the ignition. The engine sputtered.

"Fuck! Start!" Lavere slammed his fist on the horn.

Beep!

Clank! Clank! Clank!

Sirens wailed nearby. Police were closing in fast. Lavere kept trying.

Several cruisers skidded into the lot, officers charging into the building. They hadn't noticed the Pontiac yet.

The engine coughed back to life. Lavere didn't hesitate. He backed out sharply and sped down the main street, vanishing. Seconds later the cops rushed out the Jewelry & Loan and realized their suspects were gone.

"Sheesh. That was close!" Terrance exhaled.

"I can't believe we just got that off!" Shouted Lavere.

"We almost didn't, fucking around with your old raggedy car," Quinn said, still on edge.

"How else was we going to get there then? None of y'all got wheels."

"I know we got to a lot of loot! Let me see that." Quik reached for the duffle.

"Hold on, Dawg. Wait until we get back to the spot then we can count this paper." Quinn reassured him.

Minutes later, they were back in the garage. Quinn dumped the duffle onto the table, bills spilling everywhere.

"You're going to have to dump this old clunker. It's time for a new ride anyway," Quinn told Lavere.

He started counting. Two hours later, bleary-eyed, he finally stopped.

"Taking money is the easy part. It's the counting that's hard!"

"I know most of your bright ideas seem crazy, but this really was genius!" Roc said.

"You won't believe how much we got on just one lick."

"You finally done counting?" Roc pressed.

"Yep."

"Well, how much is it, Nigga?"

"Over seventy-five thousand. That's fifteen thousand apiece for each of us!"

"We got to celebrate," Quik said, already planning his purchases.

The garage filled with talk of cars, clothes, and jewelry—plans to burn through the fast money.

"Don't get too comfortable, that's not a lot of money, that was just the start up. I've seen ten thousand go in one day."

"Man, what are you saying? We good! We just got fifteen thousand dollars apiece. That's more than any of us has ever had."

"Do you want to be small time or big-time? Real ballers are sitting on more than fifteen thousand dollars. This was a small lick just to show that we could do it and we executed to perfection. We were in and out within two minutes. Nobody got shot, nice and clean. But we can't stop here. Our next hit, we can double up but in order to do that, we need to rob a real bank."

"Man, forget that. Let's enjoy this money."

Lavere had no interest in pushing their luck again so soon. Quinn, though, was already plotting the next score in his head.

A few nights later, they were back in the garage, ski masks and gloves on. Quinn gathered the crew for a quick talk before their next move.

"I know y'all spent most of the dough that y'all made from the first hit, judging by everything y'all been buying. L'z, you got that Mustang you always wanted I know that took damn near your whole fifteen thousand to get. I told y'all that money wouldn't last long. It's cool though because what we did last time was the just the beginning. It's time to start getting more paper."

Their second target: a small neighborhood bank.

"If we can do it once, we can definitely do it again and again," Roc said with arrogance.

"That's what I like to hear. Let's drink to that."

Quinn took a swig from a bottle of Hennessy, then passed it around.

Busy Getting Money

Naomi hated having to borrow money from her Big Mama, but desperate times called for desperate measures. Rent was due, and if she wanted to keep a roof over her head, she had to swallow her pride. Naomi approached the front door of her Big Mama's house. As soon as she knocked, her sister Alexis flung it open. She didn't speak; she just stood there with her arms folded.

"Hello to you to," Naomi greeted.

"Girl you ain't nobody," Alexis said, rolling her eyes.

"Whatever, excuse me." Naomi bumped her sister's shoulder and pushed her way inside. Alexis always carried an attitude for no reason Naomi could understand.

"Where's Big Mama at?"

"In her room."

Naomi made her way to the back of the house. Big Mama lay in bed, watching television. Her health had declined over the past few years, battling both lung cancer and arthritis, which kept her in bed most of the time.

"Hey, Big Mama. I just got off work and figured I would stop by on my way to school."

"Hey baby, the money you need is right here on my nightstand."

"Thank you so much, Big Mama, I will pay you back as soon as I can I promise."

"Don't you worry about that child, just get your business taken care of."

"I know, I just had to get my car fixed and pay for books this semester. I don't have any money until I get paid, and I couldn't ask Michael for it because he doesn't have it."

"You tell that young man of yours I said hello. How is school going?"

"It's good but just between books and bills, I can barely afford to make ends meet."

"You know you can always ask me if you need help. I understand you're trying to do something with yourself, and I don't mind helping any way that I can."

"Big Mama, the whole reason why I moved out is because I didn't want to be another burden on you. I promise I'm going to pay you back."

"I don't want your money, just come see your grandma sometimes baby."

"I'm sorry, I just been so busy working overtime and trying to keep up with school."

"Oh girl, that reminds me, now that you say that. You be careful. The reporters have been talking about those bank robberies on the news and I would hate for you to get caught up in any of that foolishness. I hope they catch whoever those damn hoodlums are. Pray over that job every day you go into work. With all this crazy mess going on you, need the Lord's protection."

"I will Big Mama; I will come by this weekend, I promise. I'm off this Saturday and I just have one class in the evening."

Naomi kissed her grandmother on the cheek and left, heading to the library to catch up on her homework before class. Midway through studying, she received a text from her manager:

MANDATORY MEETING THIS SATURDAY

"Great, I can't get a break," Naomi muttered.

She managed to finish her assignments just in time for class, then speed-walked across the community college campus. Two hours later, she arrived at her apartment where Michael was still glued to his PlayStation.

"How was class?" he asked without looking up.

Michael had been home all day, still in the same spot since Naomi left that morning. She wanted to see him productive, but didn't feel like starting an argument.

"I've been running all day. I got the rest of the money to cover our rent from Big Mama and I dropped the check off at the office. Anyway, I'm tired so I'm going to bed."

Naomi went straight to her bedroom and crawled under the covers, falling asleep almost instantly.

The following Saturday, Naomi sat through the mandatory town hall meeting.

"Okay everyone! Your branch manager has some very important information that needs to be shared with all employees that is why we called this town hall meeting. If any of you have been paying attention to the news, you should know there have been a lot of bank robberies lately and everyone will be required to undergo new employee training to help us all be prepared if a robbery were to occur here in our own branch. There will be a test after the training to ensure you all have retained the knowledge."

Naomi wasn't happy about giving up her day off, but the overtime was worth it. She sat through the presentation, fighting off sleep. The branch manager flipped through slides explaining security measures and employee responsibilities in the event of a robbery. Everyone, including Michael, took notes, then received a test sheet and a new employee handbook.

"You all should be knowledgeable of the information in the employee handbook but just in case you need a refresher, it has been provided to you again. Remember, you all are our best defense when it comes to preventing robbery, saving our assets, and keeping our customers protected. In order to leave the meeting, you will need to complete the test with a score of one hundred percent. Good luck."

Afterward, Naomi planned a quick Starbucks stop. She had another test later, but her body was exhausted. She'd studied, though, and she remembered her promise to Big Mama. Life had been busy, seeing her grandmother only two or three times a month. Naomi was determined that once she graduated, things would slow down and get easier.

Devante! You got company at the door! And open a window. I can smell that damn weed all the way up here!"

"My bad, Mama. I'll be up there in a second!"

Roc took his time climbing the stairs. He'd been smoking a spliff and counting the cash from the last three robberies. Most of it he'd saved, though he recently splurged on his first set of wheels, a baby blue Lexus with twenty-two-inch rims that cost around three thousand. Carefully, he stashed the bills in Nike shoe boxes under his bed, then went upstairs to answer the door.

Vanilla was waiting, her eyes roaming over his shirtless body and gold Jesus Piece. Roc nodded and motioned for her to follow him to the basement.

Once downstairs, he opened the shoe boxes and resumed counting. Vanilla relit the spliff and inhaled, then exhaled a thick cloud.

"When am I going to get in on this?" she asked, eyeing the money.

Roc took a couple puffs before responding. "I got a plan for you, shawty. That's why I told you to come over."

"What's the plan? I'm ready. Y'all been doing the damn thing without me. I know you can use my help.

The more people y'all got to control the crowd, the easier it is to make the process go smooth."

"Nah, Baby. I got a different plan for you."

Roc counted through the last bill, totaling just over one hundred thousand. He stacked the cash neatly and slid the boxes under the bed. Then, leaning over Vanilla, he placed a firm hand on her throat.

"You want to be down with the crew?"

"You know I do, Daddy," she replied.

"If you want to be down, then show me," Roc said, kissing her roughly. Vanilla responded eagerly, hands on his chest, rolling on top of him.

Roc reclined, and she slid her fingers down to his waist, pleasuring him expertly.

"Take them clothes off. I want to see that body," he commanded. She obliged, slowly shedding her skirt, tank top, bra, and panties.

"Bring that pussy to Daddy."

Vanilla mounted him, moving like a dancer, wet and inviting. Roc devoured her juices, then shifted her around his mouth, using his tongue skillfully. Afterward, he kissed her, then positioned her on the bed for intercourse.

Midway, his phone rang.

"Please don't pull it out," Vanilla whined, nearing climax.

Ring! Ring! Ring!

"Baby…Don't stop please."

Vanilla squirted, and Roc climaxed inside her. He checked his phone: Tina had called five times. He blocked her number for now.

"Who was that baby?" Vanilla asked.

"It was Quinn," he lied.

"What he want?"

"He was probably checking to see if I ran the plans for our next lick by you yet. The guard at the bank will be able to spot us before we come through the glass doors. We need you to distract him long enough for us to make our move."

Roc lit another spliff, and they went over Vanilla's role in the next robbery. Hours later, their plan was complete.

"I'm so hungry," Vanilla said.

"What you want to eat, Babe?"

"Ugh, I don't know but I'm starving?"

"You never know what you want."

Roc laughed. "C'mon, let's go. Maybe by the time we get in the car, you'll know what you want."

As they stepped out, the doorbell rang. Tina stood on the porch.

"What is this bitch doing here?" Vanilla asked.

"Who are you calling a bitch?" Tina snapped.

"I'm talking to your thirsty ass! Now stay away from my man! I already told you before, stupid ho." Vanilla punched Tina, breaking a nail in the process.

"Man chill!" Roc intervened.

"What you doing here, Tina? Don't just be popping up at my crib."

"Why you acting brand new? You've been ignoring my calls, now I see why."

"Are you fucking this Bitch, Devante?" Vanilla cut in.

44

"And if he is, you ain't going to do shit!"

"Tina!" Roc snapped. And Baby, you need chill too.

"Answer my question. Are you fucking her or not, Devante?!"

Vanilla only called Roc by his government name when she was mad. Both Vanilla and Tina looked at Roc, waiting for his confirmation or denial. Roc kept his mouth closed, figuring silence was the best response.

"I can't even believe you. I'm done with you."

"Baby, why you assuming something you don't even know?"

"Fuck you, Devante! You ain't shit!" Vanilla shoved her hand in his face and stormed off up the block, but he followed her.

"So, you really going to chase after her!" Tina yelled after him.

Roc waved her off. "Don't pop up at my house again!" he barked.

He caught up to Vanilla, trying to smooth things over. "Baby, just stop and talk to me for a second!"

"I'm tired of your shit, D! You always playing me like a fool and then you go and fuck a bitch I don't like!"

Vanilla and Tina had been best friends until Roc came along. Both liked him, but when Roc and Vanilla became a couple, Tina couldn't control her jealousy. Eventually, their friendship completely soured when Tina started talking to Roc behind Vanilla's back. She wouldn't stay away, trying to be the one he chose, but Roc was only loved Vanilla.

"Baby, you the one. I love you. These other bitches don't mean nothing to me."

"Then why do you keep playing me like a fool? Huh? You don't love me if you did, you wouldn't keep cheating on me. And don't lie and say you not fucking her because if you weren't, she wouldn't be popping up on you."

Roc had been caught red-handed. He couldn't lie; he had to admit his wrong.

"I'm sorry, Baby, but just hear me out."

"I don't want to hear none of your apologies and excuses. Just leave me alone. You're dead to me!"

Vanilla stormed off, and Roc let her go. There was nothing he could say to calm her down at the moment. He returned home to his mama, who immediately gave him an earful, but thankfully she was about to leave for work.

"I've done told you about those fast ass girls, Devante! Now if y'all going to do all that fussing and fighting, make sure it's not at my house!"

"I didn't make them start fighting, Mama."

"I don't give a damn. You either learn how to control them little tramps or I'll put your ass out!"

Roc went back to the basement and smoked another blunt. The altercation had killed his buzz. He knew he had to let Vanilla cool off before trying to apologize. She had given him too many chances, and yet he continued to cheat and lie. He knew he wasn't shit like she said, but he hoped she wasn't done for good.

Even though Roc was a player, he really wanted to be faithful. He just wasn't ready to settle down. Too much ass was being thrown his way for him to turn it down. He had plans to get his act together and settle down with Vanilla. One day, they would even have kids, and he would be a faithful father and husband. Right now, he was young, still trying to get lust out of his system.

Roc wondered if Vanilla would still be around when he was ready to be the man she deserved. She had been his rider, and he wasn't about to lose her. He called her cell phone and went straight to voicemail. He typed a long text about how much he loved her, pressed send, and set his phone down. He knew she would read it, even if she didn't respond. He had to get back on good terms with her, especially since she was key to the next robbery. Roc decided he would try his best to be faithful if Vanilla gave him another chance.

Roc watched Vanilla Walk toward the bank. She wore white skinny jeans, a red blouse, and black five-inch pumps. Every step turned heads, and men driving by slowed down to admire her. Her booty swayed with every stride, heels clicking on the concrete. Roc was seduced.

Vanilla hadn't given him any action in nearly three weeks. She was punishing him for cheating. He had passed on other women just to stay faithful and wasn't getting rewarded for it. He leaned against the building; face hidden behind a newspaper. He lifted his sunglasses and winked as she entered the bank.

Brushing past the security guard, she looked back and smiled when she caught his attention, especially his eyes on her plump booty.

"I'd like to open a new account," she said firmly.

"Certainly Ma'am, have you ever banked with us before?"

"No, I haven't."

"Not a problem. Have a seat and one of our advisors will be with you momentarily," the teller said, pointing toward a white leather sofa.

Everything in the bank was white—walls, floors, furniture, and patrons. Vanilla blended in with the upscale crowd despite her ghetto roots.

This bank is wide open, she thought. There was no bulletproof glass; the staff were too comfortable. She studied the seven cameras on the ceiling, one guard, and two tellers. Today, she wore a brunette bob wig and oversized sunglasses as a disguise. Nobody expected what was coming.

A few minutes later, the advisor approached. Vanilla pulled out her phone and texted: *Ready.*

"Excuse me, Ma'am, how can I be of assistance to you today?"

Her phone rang. "Sorry, I have to take this," Vanilla said, answering quickly.

"Hello. What? Are you serious! Why didn't you tell me you didn't have a ride? No, I can make it there now. Don't worry, I'll be there soon."

"Sorry, my sister just got in town and is stranded at the airport with no ride. I need to head over there now. Can we schedule this for another time?"

"Sure, just give me a call and we can set up an appointment," the advisor said, handing her his business card.

"Thanks so much," Vanilla said, faking it well.

She sashayed toward the exit, smiling at the guard. He couldn't help but stare.

"How's your day going so far?" Vanilla asked, sparking light conversation.

The guard's attention was fully on her. Little did he know, the distraction would cost him his job.

Pow! Pow! Pow!

Shots from a rifle shattered the bank's glass doors. Roc entered, AR-15 aimed at Vanilla. She froze, hands in the air. The guard attempted to draw his gun but was stopped cold. Roc covered Vanilla's mouth and pressed the gun to her head.

"Y'all know what this is! Drop your gun!" Roc yelled. "If you even think about it, I'll blow her brains all over your pathetic uniform!"

Vanilla cried, forcing out a few tears. "Please don't hurt me!"

"Shut up bitch! Now drop that shit unless you want to be the reason she dies today."

The guard dropped his weapon. Roc snatched it in one swift motion.

"Good choice," he said, smiling beneath his ski mask.

Terrance and Quik controlled the crowd, forcing everyone down.

"Hands on your head!" Quik yelled. "If you even think about doing anything other than what I just said, I will blow a hole in the back of somebody's head! Everybody got that!"

The teller slowly stuffed money into Quinn's black duffle bag, sweat dripping.

"Two minutes!" Terrance yelled, glancing at his watch.

The safe was only half-empty. Quinn punched the teller in the nose when he stalled, blood gushing, then kicked him in the ribs to hurry things along. Quinn grabbed the cash himself, filling the duffle bag.

"Two minutes and thirty seconds!" Terrance shouted. They had thirty seconds left.

Every dollar went into the duffle. Quinn jumped over the counter, duffle in hand, nearly overflowing. The teller hit the alarm.

"Let's go, Nigga!" Roc yelled, pulling Quinn out.

Outside, cops were closing in. Roc released Vanilla, and they dashed toward the getaway SUV. Lavere waited, door open, engine running. Quinn tossed the duffle inside, spilling bills. Vanilla, Roc, Terrance, and Quik piled in.

"Go! Go! Go! Go! Go!" Terrance screamed.

The SUV tires screeched as Lavere sped out, topping seventy-five in a thirty-five zone. He hit the highway, blending with traffic. Minutes later, they reached their safe spot.

"We just cleared that hoe out!" Roc said.

Roc and Quinn slapped fives; Terrance and Lavere laid out the cash while Quinn set up the money counter. Hundreds, fifties, twenties, fives, and tens covered the old wooden table. Over an hour later, they tallied the sum.

"What we lookin' like?" Quik asked.

"One hundred thirty-eight thousand," Quinn replied.

"That's what I'm talking about! Easy!"

Vanilla hovered over Quinn. "Make sure you separate my cut!"

"I got you, Sis. Don't even trip!"

"You deserve an Oscar for the way you performed today. That was golden, Baby!" Roc kissed her in appreciation.

After counting, everyone collected their cut.

"I'll catch y'all later. We're about to go celebrate," Roc said, thinking freaky thoughts.

"I don't know what kind of celebrating you think is going down, but it won't be that kind, you still on punishment, boo," Vanilla said.

"Ha! Nigga you gonna get blue balls!" Quik laughed.

"Whatever. She just fronting for y'all. She knows that's all me."

"Nigga, you know y'all about to go home and cuddle," Quik joked.

"Damn, baby. How you goin' to embarrass me like that?" Roc kissed Vanilla again, then shook hands with his crew.

"Stay up my brother," Quinn said as Roc dapped him.

Vanilla and Roc walked out to his Lexus. Roc unlocked it, and Vanilla hopped in while he tossed the money bags in the trunk. Seconds later, they peeled off. The robbery was their third in three weeks, each racking up over seventy-five thousand dollars. Money was flowing faster than they could spend it.

A Night To Celebrate

The summer heat came to an end, and Quinn's school days were over for good. He didn't miss them one bit. He wasn't worried about getting a college education because he was getting paid.

It was another Friday and the ballers both big time and small time had brought out their cars to stunt on Glenn Street. Quinn and his crew parked along the curb with all their cars lined up next to each other.

Quinn began to think back to the days when he used to walk to the park. It was crazy how now they were the ones with nice fly wheels parked on the street. People surrounded them coming up to their cars, engaging in small conversation. Quinn was puffing a spliff and bumping Lil Wayne as his little homies, Tank and Slime approached his Benz. They were a couple years younger than Quinn.

To the young cats, especially those two, Quinn was a ghetto superstar. Tank and Slime walked up and

admired his black S550 AMG and the chrome rims it
was sitting on.

"What up, Big Dawg?" Tank asked, walking up to
the driver's window.

"What's the deal homie?" Quinn replied.

Quinn took a deep inhale on the spliff he was
smoking then passed it to Tank.

"Same old thing, getting tired of school. I need to be
getting money like you. My teacher wants me to learn
about World War II but niggas like me is at war in the
streets. Just teach me how to get the money because
that's what it's all about. You feel me?"

"That's real."

"I need to get me one of these," Slime said after
circling the Benz and checking out all the details.

Quinn liked Slime and Tank because they reminded
Quinn of himself. They were hungry and ready to
make big money.

"You'll get one of these just get on your hustle,
that's all it takes. By any means, do what you have to
do for the loot."

"Why don't you let us run with your crew? I'm
down for whatever," Tank said.

"You ready to put in work?"

"Hell yeah."

"Okay, bet. I'm going to remember that. When the
time is right, I'm going to get at y'all. Don't even trip."

Slime and Tank hung on to Quinn's every word.
Quinn knew the right thing to say would be to tell them
to stay in school and go to college, but the truth was

that was a path he didn't follow, so he would be a hypocrite to tell someone else to do it.

Roc was leaning against the hood of his Lexus handing out flyers to Quinn's party that he was co-hosting later that night. His cousin Randy was a bouncer at Club Live and Randy had all the connections to the owners and promoters. Once Roc put the word in Randy's ear he was able to contact the promoters and set up a birthday bash event for Quinn. Almost everyone knew about it already, but Roc wanted to make the word spread as far as he could. As nighttime approached, Glenn Park began to clear out.

"Aye I'm about to go get fresh. I'll get with y'all later," Quinn yelled, sticking his head out of his driver's window.

His crew was posted around the trunk of Roc's Lexus. Roc had a liquor bar inside his trunk and was passing around shots to everyone.

"Meet me at my spot around eleven," Roc said.

A few minutes later, Quinn was parking his Mercedes down the block before he went home like he had been doing for the past few months. His mom was clueless about everything he was into and the amount of money he had been reeling in. He made sure to finish out his last semester of high school and graduate only for her sake. It would have broken her heart not to see him walk across the stage. Now that it was over with, he was ready to come clean about his decision not to go to college. He was a grown man getting his own money so there was nothing she could do to stop him. He was glad to know he was finished with school for good. Now that he was a graduate on top of being eighteen and paid, he no longer needed to answer to her.

Quinn had found a penthouse loft downtown. He paid the rent off and didn't have a bill due for a while. Only a few hours away from turning nineteen years old, he was holding a stash of two hundred thousand dollars. He walked toward the door, ready to come clean about his decision to move out and not go to college. As far as how much money he had and what he'd done to get it, he decided it was best if he kept that a secret. He would just tell her that the summer job had given him a raise and he now had enough money to move out. The truth was he never got a job never even applied for one. He planned to give her an envelope with ten thousand dollars as a moving out present.

As soon as he stepped inside the house, the smell of soul food took over his nostrils. That made him decide their conversation was going to have to wait until after he ate.

"How are you doing, Son? My sisters from church will be over for our fellowship meeting tonight. I just finished cooking. Do you want a plate before they all get here and start eating?"

"You know I want a plate, Ma. You don't even have to ask that question. Why you always inviting them over here and they don't bring no groceries?"

"Boy, this is my house. I can invite who I want."

"Yes, Ma, I hear you, but I'm just saying."

"Don't, 'but me', boy. You heard what I said. Here you go, now eat up," Teresa said, putting a plate down in front of Quinn at the table. Quinn wasted no time chowing down on the catfish nuggets, spaghetti, collard greens and cornbread.

"Slow down boy. You're going to choke eating like you never ate before."

Quinn chuckled with laughter. "I'm sorry but it's good. You know you got the best cooking in the neighborhood. That don't mean you got to feed everybody in the neighborhood though."

"Boy, what did I just say? Don't make me have to tell you again."

"I'm sorry, Ma," Quinn said laughing.

"Have you enrolled in your fall classes yet? You know you are going to get the run around if you don't do it by the deadline."

Quinn swallowed hard knowing the conversation he dreaded having with his mom was about to happen. He finished his food and got up to put the plate and eating utensils in the sink.

"Don't worry about washing your dishes. I'll do it later."

"Mama, there's something I been meaning to tell you," He blurted out. "I got a job, and I found a nice apartment near where I work. I don't want to be a burden on you anymore and now that I'm eighteen and I've graduated, I think it's time that I take care of myself."

"Boy, what did you just say? You don't need to be worried about no petty job. You need to be focused on starting college and getting your degree. Do you know even know what field of study you want to go into?"

"Mama, I'm not going to college. It's just not for me." He pulled out the envelope with money inside of it. "Here's a little moving out present. It's ten thousand dollars."

"You must think I'm stupid, huh? Where'd you get all that money from? That job didn't get you that much money that fast."

"I saved all my checks this past summer," Quinn lied.

"I know better than to believe that. Since you're going to lie to me, you might as well get out!"

"What?"

"I said get out! Don't ever bring any dirty drug money in my house!"

"What are you talking about, Mama? I worked for this money."

"That's a damn lie! When did you start selling drugs, Quentin?"

"Mama, I haven't ever sold any drugs."

"You must think I'm stupid. I see those damn drug dealers at the end of his block every day. I didn't work this hard to let you turn into one of these hoodlums running up and down these streets. I told you about those boys you hang around. You get out of this house right now! I will not have a drug dealer living under my roof! If you're going to stay here, you're going to work and go to school. I can't believe that after all I sacrificed; you're going to throw it away!"

"Mama, I'm sorry. I'm just trying to help you out! I'm tired of seeing you struggling, seeing us struggling."

"I don't need you to have any sympathy for me and you ought not to have any for yourself." Teresa was heartbroken and felt as if she had failed Quinn as a parent assuming he was involved in the streets. She had done everything in her power to steer him in the right direction, but he still chose the wrong path. All she could do was pray he'd turn around and go the right way before it was too late.

"Get the hell out my house! I'm not going to say it again!"

Quinn walked out of the house, upset that his mother didn't support his decision even though he was prepared that something like putting him out might be her reaction. However, he didn't feel guilty and was relieved that he didn't have to hide it anymore. He was a few hours away from turning nineteen. He had a big birthday bash and was going to live it up.

Life was good at the moment, and he was happy. He pulled off, heading to his new spot. It reminded him of a five-star hotel, and he liked that it was highly secured. If someone was there to see him, they would have to get clearance from the front desk first. He didn't plan on having any visitors, but it was a nice feature.

Quinn decked out his new condo by getting pool tables delivered and then setting up a bar with two sixty-inch flat screens to watch mounted above. It was the perfect bachelor pad and chill spot that only his

homies knew about. It was also personal safe spot
where he could relax and keep his valuables hidden,
including his stash. When he got to the spot, he took a
shower and dressed into a new Gucci outfit that he
purchased from the Palazzo shopping district. His GG
supreme shoes matched his belt and the collar on his
black Gucci polo shirt. His white denim jeans pulled
the outfit together perfectly.

For accessories, Quinn put on a gold rope with a
diamond medallion that read *Mafia*. Each member of
his crew had their own chain to symbolize their
affiliation. He had to be extra fresh for the party so to
complete his outfit, he opened the box of a new bust
down Cartier and slid the timepiece on his wrist. It was
a gift to himself, a trophy for his accomplishments. He
had moved himself from the hood to a nice loft that
overlooked the city. He thought about how most
people where he was from would never experience the
finer things in life. He had reason to celebrate.

"Pull up to this gas station on the corner," Quik
said, talking on his cell to Terrence.

Quinn and Quik followed Terrance and Lavere into
the gas station parking lot. Quinn was driving his black
Mercedes while Lavere was in his cherry red Mustang
with the off-white leather interior showing since he
had the top down.

"I need to cop a pack of Cigarillos and some breath mints out of here," Quik said once all four of them exited the two vehicles and entered the gas station.

"Man, the honeys are out tonight," Lavere said while looking across the street at the long line outside Club Live's entrance.

All Lavere could see was booty and breast as he scanned the line filled with females dressed in their tightest and most revealing outfits. Quinn walked up to the counter and bought two packs of Cigarillos so he could roll up a spliff and get high before they entered the party.

"Spark up that La," Quinn said to Quik before he pulled out of his parking spot.

"You always trying to smoke up somebody's weed," Quik said as he pulled a bag of blue dream out of his pocket then proceeded to break the weed down into the Blunt shell.

"I left my smoke at the crib. Plus, I need to be high before I step in this joint, you feel me?"

Quinn turned up his stereo and let the bass vibrate their bodies and proceeded to pull behind the club in the employee parking lot. His boy Roc was good with the bouncer who was connected to the owner so he knew his car would be ok. Quik lit the freshly rolled spliff between his lips and took two puffs then passed it to Quinn. About twenty minutes later, his doors opened, and a cloud of creamy white smoke exited into the atmosphere. They met up with Terrence, Lavere, and Roc, then walked to the club entrance passing an even longer line than when they first pulled up.

61

"What's popping?" Roc said to the bouncer who was also his older cousin.

"What's up, Family?" Randy said as he handed each one of them VIP cards before they entered the club.

There were a few slick comments and mean mugs from the people still waiting to get in the club as they watched the Mafia members cut the line. The party was in full effect when they entered the building.

"Everybody make some noise for my boy, Quinn!" said the DJ as Quinn walked up to the VIP lounge.

The whole crowd cheered at the DJ's command. Quinn gave a nod to the DJ who was his homie, Jazz, from high school. The Mafia's crew walked up a flight of stairs to the private section that overlooked the club and plopped down on the red leather sectional. A cute young bartender brought over a tray of champagne glasses with two bottles of Ace of Spade. The Mafia had bought out the bar. Even though they were underage, a thick stack of cash to the bartenders made that issue go away.

After popping the cork on a bottle of Ace of Spades, champagne suds overflowed and fell to the floor. Quinn took a sip straight from the bottle. He then sat back and vibed to the music and atmosphere of the club. Honeys all around were looking up, with their eyes on him. He was unfazed by the attention. He looked up into the mirror on the ceiling and was reminded why the honeys couldn't stop staring. He was wearing Gucci from head to toe and rocking an iced-out Cartier. The half karat studs in his ears along

with his Mafia charm twinkled even brighter than
usual in the dark club.

Meanwhile, Jayla was on the dance floor getting her
groove on with her two friends. They began shaking
their behinds on each other when the DJ had played
"Back That Thang Up" by Juvenile. Several men were
walked up trying to get their junk twerked on but got
shot down.

DJ Jazz gave Quinn another shout-out and played
Lil Wayne's joint, "Money on My Mind," a special
request for Quinn. Quinn got up and instantly began to
feel the music, rapping the lyrics as he grooved to the
beat. Jayla looked up while she was dancing and
noticed Quinn standing on the couch in VIP.

"Damn he is fine. He looks so much different," she
thought to herself but was referring to the jewels on his
neck and wrist. Remembering how he used to try to
holler at her, she was determined to get his attention.
She walked toward the VIP rope that led up the stairs.
There was a bouncer guarding the section and he'd just
sent away three ladies trying to get in.

"You got a pass?" was all the bouncer said when
Jayla got up to the rope.

"No, but how about we exchange a favor for a
favor," Jayla said seductively, leaning her hip to the
side so the bouncer could get a view of her banging
body.

The bouncer was practically having sex with Jayla
as he looked her up and down. She was the finest
female in the entire joint and there were mad cuties in

attendance. The bouncer felt as if he had to shoot his shot.

"Give me your phone number and I'll let you past this rope."

Jayla smiled and pulled her cell out of her Fendi clutch and sent him a text, so he had her number.

The bouncer lifted the rope so Jayla could pass. "I'll call you." He said between winking his left eye.

"Can't wait," Jayla said with a smirk. His number would be blocked before the end of the night.

"Hello stranger," Quinn heard a familiar voice say.

Quinn turned his head to see who the greeting had come from. He was surprised to see Jayla standing over him. It had been almost a year since their last encounter, one that he still remembered vividly. He damn near sobered up after thinking about the situation almost getting pissed off all over again. He studied Jayla, noticing her skin glowed with more vibrancy but her hazel brown eyes contained less innocence. He had a feeling that her man still wasn't doing his job, and she was getting around on the low. Her body was womanly as a generous amount of breast and booty filled up her black and white dress.

"So, you don't remember me now big time?"

"Of course I do." Quinn scooted over on the couch and patted the cushion for to Jayla to take a seat next to him. "You want a glass of champagne?" Quinn offered.

"That's cool." She responded.

Quinn poured Jayla a glass and she sipped. They chatted but didn't bring up their last encounter at Glen Park.

"Hold on, this is my jam!" DJ Jazz was playing Chris Brown.

"C'mon let's dance!" Jayla said pulling Quinn to get up.

Jayla led Quinn down to the dance floor and began to grind on him matching the rhythm of the beat. Quinn matched the rotation of her hips and pressed against her ass. Quinn wondered how Damon would feel if he knew his woman was on the dance floor grinding on another man.

Quinn knew feeling up on Damon's woman was dangerous, but his ego wouldn't let him fear another man. Jayla was attractive to him, and she represented an itch that he never got to scratch. Now that his money was up, he didn't feel as if Jayla was out of his league. He was just the type of man that she wanted, a baller.

"What are you getting into later tonight?" Quinn pressed.

"That depends on what you're trying do."

"Why don't you roll with me?" Quinn's thoughts were filled with visions of him between Jayla's thighs.

"Hmmmm…" Jayla said as if she was carefully thinking over his offer. Quinn figured she couldn't stay out too long without her man inquiring her whereabouts.

"Hey, let me see your cell."

"My cell? You already acting insecure and we ain't even made it official yet."

"Whatever. Just let me see it big head."

Jayla wasn't trying to lock Quinn down or nothing.

"Here," Quinn said licking his top lip before biting down on his bottom one."

"Damn he's sexy," Jayla thought to herself. *"And he got a little money now. Maybe I can squeeze him out of a few dollars."*

Quinn hoped Jayla didn't see the gang of freaks he had in his contacts and text message log. Jayla went straight to the dial screen and entered her phone number before handing his iPhone back to him.

"When you don't have an entourage with you, call me and maybe we can hook up."

Jayla sashayed away as Quinn's eyes followed her voluptuous booty. He was upset that she up and left so quickly but didn't mind the nice view of her backside. Especially since he just got her digits. In due time, he was going to tap that and when he did, he was going to put it down. Jayla turned around to stop and see if he was still watching. Quinn bit his bottom lip in a seductive way, and she smiled back before finally drifting away.

"You still trying to get at that?" Roc asked.

Roc had been noticing Quinn and Jayla conversing for several minutes. Vanilla was with him, glued to his hip.

"Happy birthday, Quinn!" Vanilla said while hugging him.

"Thanks, Sis. I appreciate it."

"If you had game like your boy, you would have been knocked them boots. If you need some tips, I got you," Roc joked.

"Boy please, you don't have no game!" Vanilla snapped.

"My game got you!" Roc shot back.

"Don't even trip; I got that on lock. Trust me, you'll see." Quinn said.

"Yeah, we will see. Now which one of these other honeys are you taking home because we know it's not going to be that one."

"You got jokes, huh?"

Quinn shook his head then scanned the crowd checking out the many honeys in the building. Almost every honey in attendance was making eye contact whenever he diverted his attention on her. Quinn spotted Tanisha at the bar. He watched the bartender sit two drinks in front of the cat who was sitting next to her. The dude slid one of the glasses toward Tanisha ignoring the orange wristband on her wrist which meant she wasn't old enough to have alcohol.

As Quinn looked at Tanisha from head to toe, he had to admit she had sex appeal. She rocked her hair in box braids that were pulled up into a big bun and her short red dress made no effort to cover her thick brown thighs.

"Didn't I say I got it under control? Watch me work." Quinn left Roc and Vanilla behind and approached the bar where Tanisha was sitting.

"What's up, Ma?" Quinn walked up from behind Tanisha and stood in between Tanisha and the cat that was in her ear. Quinn gave him a mug then tapped his waistline to let him know he was carrying inside the club. The punk ass dude put his hands up and walked away without protest.

"Is that what you say to all your different girlfriends?" Tanisha replied to Quinn's greeting.

"I don't have any girlfriends. You know that."

"Yeah, okay."

"You're looking sexy tonight, Baby."

"Thanks. You don't look too bad yourself."

Tanisha checked out Quinn's neck and wrist that was glowing in the dim club. His waves shined from the fresh haircut he had gotten earlier. Quinn had the good looks and swag that every girl wanted, there was no way Tanisha could deny his charm.

"C'mon, Ma. Let's shake this joint."

"Isn't this your party, Birthday Boy?"

"I'm not much of the party type plus I'm kind of hungry, you down to grab some grub, my treat?"

Before Tanisha could respond Quinn was pulling her out her seat toward the exit. Quinn motioned with his hand for Roc to follow them as they made their way out the club. Vanilla was all over him not letting him breathe with all the different ladies surrounding. Quinn laughed as Roc and Vanilla left out behind him and Tanisha.

They headed to the 24-hour breakfast joint. When Quinn walked in, he saw Jayla at a table with her two friends. Playing it cool, Quinn nodded when Jayla winked at him. They sat down, ordered breakfast, and began to chit-chat. After a while, Jayla and her friends got up and left, while Quinn's party was still waiting on their food. Quinn locked eyes with Jayla as she purposely brushed past him, letting her booty graze his shoulder.

"So, you're going to keep flirting with another bitch in my face?" Tanisha snapped, unable to tame her jealousy.

"Calm down. You're getting upset over nothing," Quinn responded while waving her off.

"Uh, hello...You just disrespected me having another bitch wink at you, then let the bitch rub her ass on you in my face and you didn't check her ass!"

"Chill, Ma," Quinn said nonchalantly. Tanisha wasn't his girl; in fact, he was one hundred percent single, so he didn't know why she was tripping. "It's not like you didn't have dude pushing up on you at the bar in the club," he reminded her, which made her get quiet.

The nerve of these chicks, he thought. *They already know the game but still try to bend the rules.* Quinn shook his head.

Vanilla stared at Roc, waiting for him to chime in, but he just shook his head and laughed. Their waitress came to the table with their food, and they all dug in like it was the last supper.

Ring! Ring! Ring!

"Hello?" Roc said, picking up his cell in between bites of his pancake.

"Yo! Where y'all at?"

Everyone could hear Quik's voice on the other end of the phone.

69

"We're at the breakfast joint. Pull up, Nigga."

"Okay, bet that."

Shortly after they finished eating, Lavere, Quik, and Terrance showed up outside the restaurant. Next thing you knew, Roc was zooming through the streets in his Lexus as Lavere kept pace in his Mustang. Quinn's Mercedes trailed behind. They all pulled up beside each other at a red light.

Vrrrm...Vrrrm...Vrrrm! Roc revved his engine. Lavere responded by making his Mustang roar. The traffic light turned green, and Lavere floored his Mustang, reaching sixty miles per hour in roughly six seconds. Roc tried to keep pace, but Lavere slowly pulled away.

"Suckas!" Lavere yelled, laughing hysterically.

"Slow down! One-Time!" Terrance yelled.

Roc and Quinn had already hit their brakes and turned off the highway after spotting a squad car on the side. Looking in his rearview, Lavere saw the cop pulling onto the interstate. He thought about taking the officer on a high-speed chase, but since he had no warrants and was driving clean, there wasn't much the cop could hold against him besides speeding. Lavere decided to pull over, knowing he could handle whatever ticket came his way.

"Stay calm and act normal," Lavere said to Quik and Terrance.

"Toss that Blunt out!" Terrance said to Quik.

Lavere cracked his window, and Quik flicked the Blunt onto the highway pavement. Lavere was shaking inside, remembering too many interactions with police

70

that hadn't ended well. He sprayed his car with air freshener to mask the lingering smell of weed smoke.

"All he going to do is write me a ticket for speeding, just act normal."

"Put your hands out the window!" the cop yelled through a speakerphone.

Lavere followed instructions, sticking both hands out where the officers could clearly see he didn't have anything. His eyes darted to the side mirror as two officers approached, one with his weapon drawn, walking cautiously toward Lavere's window.

"Is this car stolen?" the cop demanded.

"No, it's mine, Sir."

"Sure it is," the cop replied sarcastically. "Where's your license and registration?" Lavere began to reach toward his glove compartment.

"Hey! Don't move!"

"I apologize, Sir."

"I asked you, where is your license and registration? That was a question, not an order to move."

"It's in my glove compartment, Sir."

"Keep one hand raised and with the other, slowly reach over and grab your information."

Lavere did exactly as instructed, handing over his registration. The officer took the license and insurance to his partner, who went back to the squad car.

"I'm going to need all of you to step out of the vehicle now."

"Sir, why are you asking me to exit my car?"

"I ask all the questions here, Buddy! Now all of you get out of the car slowly or I swear I will put a bullet in one of your smart-ass mouths."

They all slowly got out as instructed.

"Up against the guardrail and hands on your head." The cop commanded, and they complied.

"Now get on the ground and keep your hands above your head."

"Sir, what did I do besides speed to warrant all this?" Lavere asked, irritated.

"If you say anything else, I will put a bullet in your got damn head!" the cop shouted, spittle flying from his lips.

Lying face down on the pavement, they prayed silently, hoping God would get them out of this alive. Too many times, Lavere had seen young men shot by cops for nothing. The aggressive officer dug through their pockets and pulled out Lavere's stack of cash.

"This is a lot of money for a young kid like you to be walking around with. Where'd you get all this money from? Are you a drug dealer?"

"No Sir."

Lavere watched helplessly as the cop stuffed the bills in his uniform pocket.

"Yo, why you taking my money?" Lavere snapped.

"Quiet, you little punk! I'll take more than your money. I'll take your worthless life if you keep at it," the cop spat back.

The second officer returned with Lavere's license and insurance.

"His information checks out and the car is registered in his name," the second officer stated.

"Let me see this," the aggressive cop said, grabbing the license from his partner. He studied it for several seconds.

"Lavere Collins, you're free to go, and next time, slow down or I'll write you a ticket."

Officer Moore was frustrated he hadn't found drugs or paraphernalia but knew the kid had just gotten lucky. The cops got back into their car and sped off, faster than Lavere had been driving.

"Fucking pigs. I can't stand those muthafuckas," Terrance said.

"How much did he take from you?"

"A little over three stacks."

"Man, that's some bullshit!"

"Hell yeah. But it's ok. I'll bounce back from that."

Lavere wasn't sweating the money; he was just grateful they didn't shoot him and make him another news story.

"Ooooh yes! Just like that!"

Tanisha's moans echoed through the suite, loud enough that anyone in the next room could probably hear. Quinn had booked out the entire Presidential suite at The W Hotel for the night, making sure they had privacy.

"Damn!" Quinn grunted, feeling himself reaching the edge.

"How does that feel, Daddy?" Tanisha gasped, her voice thick with pleasure.

Quinn closed his eyes, letting his imagination drift. For a moment, he pictured Jayla instead of Tanisha, and the fantasy fueled his rhythm as he moved into her doggy style.

Tanisha arched her back, throwing her hips in time with his movements. Quinn couldn't deny it, she could take pipe, no question.

"Fuck!" Quinn moaned, spilling into the condom just as Tanisha hit her climax.

After the intense birthday session, Quinn called room service, ordering the most expensive champagne on the menu. He sank into the oversized Jacuzzi tub, letting the bubbles wrap around him as he sipped and puffed a Cuban cigar filled with top shelf weed.

He felt like the man, untouchable in the glow of the suite. But even in that moment of luxury, his thoughts drifted to Jayla. He wished she was there instead of Tanisha. He thought about Damon, the level he was operating on, and realized how far he had to go. Since the day their paths had crossed, Quinn had been planning to take Damon's spot and soon, he would.

Caught Up

Got any good leads yet?" Officer Moore asked casually as he stepped into Detective Stephens' office. Stephens had been glued to his computer for eight straight hours.

"No, still the same bullshit," Stephens replied. "I've been studying the same tapes for weeks and can't find anything pointing to the identity of these assholes. Dead ends everywhere."

Moore noticed the frustration etched across Stephens' face. He remembered pulling over a kid the night before, a new car and wad of cash in his pocket. Something didn't add up. He pulled out the note he'd written with the kid's info.

"Hey, I think I might have a suspect. Someone you should investigate. I pulled this kid over last night. He's nineteen, driving a spanking-new Mustang, and had more cash in his pockets than I make in a month. I don't get it. I work hard and barely make ends meet while these street thugs live like rock stars. Anyways, here's his name and address. Run a background check and see what comes up."

"Who's the kid?"

"Uh... Lavere Collins," Moore said, passing the note to Stephens.

"Never heard of him, but I'll look into it," Stephens said, scanning the information.

"Let me know what you find," Moore added before leaving.

Stephens returned to the surveillance footage, still coming up empty. He logged out and decided to take a rare weekend off, hoping some rest would bring clarity by Monday.

When Monday arrived, Stephens followed his routine, reviewing tapes and records. He felt the weight of the case pressing down. No lead meant no raise, and failure was not an option. He recalled Moore's tip and pulled the note from his drawer:

Lavere Collins. 19 years old. Check criminal history.

Using the Police Department's Records Manager, Stephens scanned Lavere's file alongside his partner, Cindy.

"Hmmm... Any relatives?" Stephens asked.

"A grandfather and grandmother. Same address as his ID. He must live with them."

"What about the grandparents? Criminal history?"

"The grandfather's a retired vet, clean record. The grandmother's deceased."

"Should we bring him in for questioning?"

"I don't see anything tying him to the robberies. Just a kid with a nice car his grandparents bought him. Pretty typical," Cindy said.

"Yeah, but I've got a hunch about this one. Hold onto his file," Stephens said. Cindy printed it out.

Stephens poked his head into her office. "Coffee run, want anything?"

"Black, no sugar," Cindy replied, smiling.

"Ugh, how do you drink that?"

"Raw caffeine keeps me alert," she shrugged.

Stephens stepped out, tired and frustrated. He dialed Moore.

"Stephens! Just the man I've been meaning to talk to," Moore shouted.

"Talk. I'm listening," Stephens said.

"You and Cindy have been getting closer than usual. How was it getting between those tight little cheeks? I know you're fucking her."

"Jeff, she's married and so am I."

"What's that mean? She's smoking hot; I'd bang her."

"I bet you would," Stephens said dryly.

"Everyone's noticed the flirty behavior. Coffee runs, little gestures…"

"She's my partner. We're just friends."

"Fine, Buddy, cut the bullshit. You've got to live a little outside this case," Moore teased.

Ignoring him, Stephens got to the point. "Remember the kid you pulled over?"

"Yeah, asshole. Guys like that are scum, lowlife pricks getting over on the system."

"I want us to pay him a visit tomorrow. See if we can find any dirt."

"Good idea. The more of those assholes off the streets, the better."

"Three o'clock after lunch. Doughnuts nearby. Best in town."

"Doughnuts? Count me in."

In one of the city's roughest neighborhoods, Moore and Stephens arrived at Lavere's address. The cherry-red Mustang sat in the backyard. Moore knocked three times.

"Uh... Hello Officers. Can I help you?" Lawrence Collins, Lavere's grandfather, said, clearly surprised.

"Detective Stephens. Mind if we come in and ask a few questions? Won't take long," Stephens said.

"Alright," Lawrence replied, opening the door.

"Have a seat," Lawrence directed them to the couch.

"That's a nice car you have," Moore said.

"Oh, that's my grandson's," Lawrence said.

"Where'd he get it?"

"Bought from a car lot," Lawrence explained. "He's also working a better-paying job now, helping out with bills. He's grown. As long as he's working, he's fine."

Stephens leaned forward. "Your grandson Lavere here? We think he might be involved in recent bank robberies."

"What would make you think that?" Lawrence asked, wary.

"We're questioning everyone nearby."

"Lavere!" Lawrence called.

Lavere walked in, confused. "Detective, why are you here?"

"Where'd you get the money for that car?" Stephens asked.

"I've been saving."

"And your job?"

"That's personal," Lavere said.

Moore scowled. "Not how you talk to a cop, boy."

"It's fine. He doesn't have to answer that," Stephens interjected.

"Mind if I look around?" Stephens asked.

"You don't have a warrant," Lawrence said.

"I can get one, or we can do it now. Your choice," Moore threatened.

Lawrence hesitated, then nodded. "Fine. Look around, but you won't find anything."

Stephens walked through the house, Lawrence hovering. In the basement, he found a glass display case with multiple guns, the same models used in the robberies. He snapped a picture.

"First big break," Stephens said to Moore.

"Quite a collection," Stephens remarked in the living room.

"I'm an ex-Marine. I respect the Second Amendment," Lawrence said, staring down Moore.

Stephens stepped forward. "Mr. Collins, you and your grandson are under arrest. You have the right to remain silent. Anything you say can and will be used against you in a court of law." Stephens pulled out to handcuffs.

"That's absurd! We didn't do anything!" Lawrence shouted.

Moore spat, "We've found evidence. You're coming in."

Back at the precinct, Lavere sat nervously inside the interrogation room. White walls. A wooden table. Four chairs. Lavere sat twitching, trying to read what the cops knew. Cindy entered, her eyes piercing.

"I'll be blunt. You're being charged with serious crimes."

"I don't know what you mean," Lavere said.

"Are you sure? Four weapons found in your basement match the Fast Cash Jewelry & Loans robbery. Your grandfather isn't taking the fall."

"I don't know what you're talking about."

"Cut the bullshit. I know you and your four accomplices did it. What's their names?"

"I don't know."

"Twenty-five years to life. You want to sacrifice yourself for your friends?"

Cindy pressed. "Your grandfather has an alibi. You quit your cleaning job. How can you afford a $20,000 car?"

Lavere stayed silent.

"Work with me. Keep your freedom. Snitch, and you're free. Don't, and you're looking at years."

Lavere thought of his crew and the tight bond they'd built. But jail loomed. An angel and demon sat on his shoulders, each tugging a different way.

"I know you didn't do this alone. First to get caught, first to save yourself," Cindy said.

Lavere stared at her, weighing loyalty versus freedom.

"What do you want from me?"

"The names of your accomplices."

He paused. Too much love for his homies to rat them out. But freedom was priceless.

Roc inhaled deeply as he took a long toke of his spliff. Tina's head bobbed between his lap while he palmed the back of her head with one hand. His phone began ringing and he reached for it to hit the ignore button without even checking to see who was calling.

"Don't stop, keep sucking it."

The ringer on his iPhone blurted out again. *Who is calling my line back to back?* It was obvious the person calling him didn't get the memo that he was busy after the first ignore. He reached for his cell again to find that it was Lavere calling him.

"What up? -- Keep going, don't stop."

"What?"

"Nothing I was…never mind what's up? Why you keep blowing up my line?"

"I need to meet up with you Quinn, Quik, and T. I'm on my way over there right now."

"Can it wait?"

Roc was in the middle of getting one of the best blowjobs of his life.

"We need to talk ASAP, it's an emergency."

"What is this about?"

"It's too much to talk about over the phone, when I see you, we will talk. Make sure T, Quik, and Quinn meet you there too." Lavere hung up before Roc could even respond.

Roc focused his mind back to his pleasure. He guided Tina's head back and forth as she made his flesh disappear then reappear until he released in her mouth. Roc grunted loudly then exhaled heavily after coming down from his euphoric moment of bliss.

"You have to go Baby, I got some business to take care of," he pushed Tina off him and tossed her clothes to her.

"That's it?" She questioned expecting that they were going to have sex, but it wasn't going down. The only reason he let her suck him up was because Vanilla was still holding out from having sex with him. It had been two months, and he was too horny to wait until she was ready to give it up again.

"I got something to do. I'll call you," Roc said pushing Tina toward the door.

"All right, it's done," Lavere said to Stephens after hanging up the phone with Roc. He hated himself for what he was about to do.

"Congratulations, Dirt Bag, your first honest deed is almost done. Now I want you to wear this and record everything that is said," Detective Stephens handed Lavere a tiny microphone connected to a tape recorder. "If you want to stay out of jail, bring me back the tape with everything that is said during the conversation. Get them to talk about the robbery. I need evidence of them admitting to the crimes." Stephens tapped Lavere's shoulder and walked back to his undercover car.

Lavere had already formulated a lie that would get him out of his bad predicament. Having to choose between his boys and freedom was a hard decision to make. *I have to do this*, he thought left with no choice but to cooperate with the cops in order to save his own ass. He felt like a puppet under their control. *Soon this will all be over with.*

Lavere checked to make sure the mic wasn't visible before he knocked on Roc's door. Immediately, it opened.

"Where you been? We been waiting on your ass. You the one who called this meeting so, what's up?" Roc said to Lavere.

"Something bad just happened, and I don't have no bread."

"What, Nigga? What do you mean you don't have any bread?"

"I got robbed."

"How did you get robbed for your whole stash of money?"

"Some niggas ran up in my crib and stole everything. They must have found all the cash because I went to check if it was there, and it was gone."

"Who the hell was it?"

"I don't know. Nobody was home. My old man came back to everything rummaged through, then he called the cops. That's why I've been calling you all day," Lavere said looking at Roc.

"How much did they get you for?"

"A hundred stacks."

"Why did you stash all your money in the same place? I can't believe how dumb your ass is."

"Look, we need to do another hit. I need y'all to just help me out. Y'all act like y'all done forgot all the licks we done hit. All the money that we got we wouldn't have if not for my contributions to these missions. One mission and I'll be back straight that's all I'm asking for."

"We done hit a lot of different spots to get the cheddar we got. How is one mission supposed to make up for all that?"

"We can hit the Community City Bank downtown."

"You're talking about the big one on Thirteenth and Main Street? Hell nah, that's the biggest bank in the city."

"That would be a big lick, but the problem is there's too much traffic down in that area." Quinn stated.

"And there's a police station right in that area," Terrance added.

"That's why it would work, with so many people we can go in unnoticed. They'll never expect one to happen right under their nose."

"You might be right; we could use that to our advantage." Quinn said. He was now thinking it over.

Realizing that he was starting to reel them in, Lavere needed to press the record button on the tape in his pocket, but he couldn't bring himself to do it.

"We could definitely make that work to our advantage," Quinn said as he began to plot the heist in his mind.

Quinn rubbed his fingers through his neatly cut goatee. He was seriously contemplating robbing the biggest bank in the city. It was risky but had the potential to make them some major dough.

"I estimate we could get five hundred thousand, that's enough to replace my entire stash" Lavere was luring him in with numbers.

"Okay, let's do it. For now, we'll each front you twenty stacks apiece to put you back on your feet."

"I'm not giving this nigga no money, it's not my fault he got robbed." Roc said

"This is a brother ship, when one of us takes a loss we all take a loss."

"Community City Bank is a level we haven't touched yet," Terrance said.

Quinn didn't care about risk, he always focused more on the reward aspect. He was the most addicted to the fast money lifestyle they were living. He was a junkie for cash and the more money they made, the more he wanted. Five hundred thousand dollars was too much for him to resist.

"We can do it. We didn't get this far for nothing but we're going to have to be on point with our plan. Let's set this up but since it's a bigger bank, it's going to take some time. We can't go in our regular black attire. We have to blend in, there are too many people around. Somebody will spot us running in. There's a lot of construction going on downtown, so I think that's how we should disguise ourselves. We need to wear some overalls, construction gloves, orange safety vests and hard hats over our ski masks, all construction related, so we blend in with the workers. Only handguns since they can be concealed much easier.

Lavere listened to Quinn map out all the intricate details of the robbery. He still hadn't recorded anything. Sweat was dripping down his palms as he held his finger on the record button in his pocket. *Press it.* That was his thought, but he just couldn't bring himself to do it. It didn't feel right to be the only one to walk away clean because he was just as guilty as any of them.

"What's our time limit?" Roc asked.

"Three minutes and that's pushing it. The station is right around the corner, so we have no time for slip ups. If we get caught on this one, we will go down hard but we won't worry about that because we won't get caught." Quinn was feeling cocky.

"This is going to boost all of our pockets."

"Hell yeah, now let's start casing this joint, nah-mean? Time is money," Lavere said reciting one of Quinn's favorite quotes.

"You got that right, Fam. I'm going to check some different resources to see if I can find out who ran up in your crib. One thing that I know for sure is that word on the street gets around. For now, just keep your ear to the streets and keep your eyes open. If you see any random cats flexing, then you know what's up."

"I really need this lick, Fam. Once we hit the Community City Bank, I'll be right back like it never happened."

"No doubt, Fam. You will be back in no time. Just let this be a lesson to never keep your whole stash where you rest at."

"Collins! Get in the car now!"

Lavere approached the undercover car that was parked across the street from his house then got inside.

"Do you have the tape?" Detective Stephens questioned.

"Yeah, it's inside."

"Well go and get it."

"I wasn't able to record anything."

"What do you mean you weren't able to record the conversation?"

"I couldn't press record. They would have noticed."

"That's why you press record before you go to meet with them! Are you stupid or what!" Detective Stephens was shouting in Lavere's ear.

"You're screwing up, Collins! You remember what we talked about? Do I need to remind you of the time you're facing? You got one last chance. When this robbery is going to happen, you let us know and we will be there to listen in on the conversation. All you have to do is press record and we can hear everything. This is your last chance, and I mean it, Collins! Now get out."

Lavere planned to take the money and get out of town. He didn't know who to fear more, his homies finding out about him snitching or the cops and their threats of burying him under the jail. His decision was either risk his freedom or his life. It was a hard choice to make. He would either get labeled as a snitch and have to hide his face in the streets for the rest of his life or spend most of it locked up in a cell.

Lavere thought about how he could avoid both snitching and jail. He had nearly a hundred thousand dollars. With each of the Mafia giving him twenty stacks apiece, he was about to double his fortune plus what he was going to make from the robbery. With a little more than a quarter million dollars, he would have enough for him to relocate to another city where no one knew him. He could change his identity then start over. He had a plan to purposely lead the detectives to the wrong location because after this bank robbery, he was going to get out of town and disappear without a trace.

"What's the info?" Moore asked sternly.

Lavere was sitting in the back of Stephens's undercover car, yet again. Moore was in the passenger seat.

"The next heist will be at the Green Ridge Bank."

"It's going down next Tuesday at noon."

"Good, we'll be in position and ready to go. You just see this thing through, no screw ups. You get this thing done and you won't have to worry about me any longer. Now get out."

Showtime

What are we going to do, baby? We're sinking deeper in debt. I can barely keep up with my books and classes, let alone most of the bills. I need your help holding this household together. You're supposed to be the man." Naomi's voice cracked, frustration spilling over.

"Our lights are past due, my car note's three months behind. They could repossess any day. I can't even afford insurance. Every time I drive, I'm praying I don't get pulled over. But how do you dodge the cops with expired tags for a year?"

Naomi ran her hands through her hair, feeling the weight of it all. She loved Michael, but his lack of ambition was suffocating. Unlike him, she was hustling. Twenty credit hours completed in her first year toward her accounting degree. At this pace, she'd be certified in four years. Four years to get the future she wanted.

But Michael? He was stuck. Lazy, content with a petty security job, distracted by video games and weed, reliant on Naomi's connections to get by. After he lost his warehouse job, she practically had to force him to find another gig. His priorities were skewed, and hanging out with his friend Jacob often came before her. Dates were a memory, the last one a cheap buffet. Romance, attention, and intimacy were also drying up.

"You must think your shit don't stink," Michael snapped. "You're not perfect, Naomi."

"There he goes again," she thought, rolling her eyes.

"I never thought my own woman would talk down on me. At least I have a job. A lot of guys are worse off," he countered.

Working together didn't help. Their schedules now overlapped completely, leaving no space between them. Michael put on his freshly starched uniform, pinned the security badge to his pocket, and strapped on the holster with his gun and billy club.

"You act like I don't have responsibilities! Lawyer fees, fines... I need you to hold me down," Michael said.

"If it wasn't for you partying with Jacob, we wouldn't be in this mess. Driving drunk was your choice," Naomi fired back.

"I only had two drinks! I wasn't even drunk!"

"You failed the Breathalyzer, Michael."

"How can I move past my mistakes if you keep holding them over me?"

"You need a plan for your life. I've finished a year of school, and you haven't even tried enrolling or finding a career. Sitting at that petty security job won't get you far. It's time to grow up. Be a man. We're not in high school anymore."

"So now you're attacking my manhood? I'm a grown man! Never thought my own woman would judge me like this. You ain't real. As soon as times gets hard, you start flaking."

"I could've left when you got locked up for a DUI, but I bailed you out. I'm pushing you to do better because I love you. Appreciate that!"

"There you go, always painting yourself perfect," Michael muttered.

"Whatever. I'm done with your shit. When I'm gone, you'll realize what you had."

"You can bounce. I don't need you. I'm a grown man!"

"Okay, then walk to work!"

"Fuck you!"

Naomi stormed out, slamming the door. Michael followed, but she was already in her car before he could lock the door. She backed out almost hitting him. He banged on the passenger window.

"Open the damn door!"

Naomi rolled it down just a crack, glaring. "So now you need a ride?"

"I don't have time for this! Unlock the door!"

The twenty-minute drive to work was silent. Naomi blasted music, almost blowing out his eardrums, singing along obnoxiously, every lyric a jab. Michael seethed quietly, knowing exactly what she was doing. She wanted to get under his skin, and she was succeeding. By the end of the shift, he hoped the tension would ease, but neither of them was holding much hope for that.

"Man, I got a bad feeling about this," Lavere muttered, his eyes glued to the white van parked across the street from Community City Bank. The winter sun reflected off the glass façade, painting sharp streaks across the asphalt.

"Look Nigga, I don't have time for you to be flaking out. Are you trying to do this or not?" Quinn's voice was sharp, slicing through the tension like a knife.

"I don't know, Fam. Something just don't feel right."

"Let's run in, handle our business and get out of here. It's that simple. Stop making it complicated."

"I'm telling you; something just doesn't seem right."

"Yeah, something definitely ain't right," Roc interjected, glancing at Lavere with icy eyes. "It's your scary ass that's going to get us caught up. And why are you sweating so damn hard? It's thirty degrees outside and you sweating like it's the middle of July."

Quinn didn't have time for hesitation. "You know what, switch positions with Quik. I can't have you getting us caught up."

It had been Lavere's idea to hit the lick. Now, as adrenaline twisted in his gut, he was frozen like a deer in headlights. Quinn tossed him the gun. "After we get out, you get in the driver's seat and wait until we come out. If you see anything suspicious, honk the horn. You know the signal. And don't turn the engine off this time."

Sweat drenched Lavere, dripping onto the wire-taped device strapped to his chest. If the cops couldn't hear him, he'd have an excuse. Shame gnawed at him. These were his brothers. They'd grown up together in the Jungle, called themselves the Mafia, and now fifteen banks later, they were about to see a million dollars vanish in smoke...or worse, themselves behind bars.

"Our time limit to execute is two minutes. Enough to get in, handle business, and get away before the cops arrive."

Quinn checked his watch: 12:55 p.m. Guards were switching for lunch. Traffic was light. Pedestrians hustled past, oblivious. Perfect.

"Collins, where are you? We've been in position for over an hour."

Detective Stephens's voice blasted through Lavere's earpiece. Infuriated. He knew something was off. The wiretap he had given Lavere included a tracker. Stephens had already prepared for disaster.

Quinn sized up his team. Ready.

"Let's go."

Lavere stayed behind. The other four bolted across the asphalt, disappearing into the bank.

Inside, Michael shook off lunch, ready to take over. His security job was routine, but he took it seriously. Work was simple, paychecks steady, and life was...messy. Naomi's complaining, their financial strain, he shoved it from his mind just as Quik slammed through the doors, weapon raised.

"Everybody get on the floor!"

A gunshot cracked like thunder. Customers froze. Some at teller windows, others in line, all staring at the masked intruder.

"Everybody put your hands up!" Terrance barked, shoving the hesitant to the ground.

"Don't move," Quinn snapped, Glock pressed to a teller.

"O... O... Okay..." Naomi stuttered.

"I need all the money in the bag unless you want me to shoot you too. Don't make me have to do it."

Quinn shoved a balled-up trash bag onto the counter.

"And don't give me any marked bills. Open up that safe and if you even think about pushing that emergency button, I'll pop yo ass."

He noticed pretty the teller. Brown-skinned, long black hair. She was unlocking the safe, shaking.

"Hurry up!" Quinn growled, cocking the pistol.

Naomi feverishly stuffed cash into the bag.

Honk! Honk! Honk! Honk!

Lavere's signal.

It was time to go.

"Y'all heard that! We need to get out! That's the signal!" Terrance warned.

"Keep emptying the drawer," Quinn insisted, still pressing the gun to her temple.

"C'mon man, let's ditch this muthafucka before the cops show!"

Sirens erupted, tires squealed, and chaos collided with adrenaline. Terrance bolted to the door.

"Fuck!" Quinn cursed, snatching the cash.

"Don't fucking move!" he barked, firing at a security guard who tried to reach his weapon. Blood spurted from a graze. Quinn followed with two near misses.

"Anybody else want to try to be a hero!"

Michael stayed down. Others cowered. One guard's desperate attempt to stop them turned the bank into a warzone. Glass exploded; papers fluttered like wounded birds.

The robbers ran out, firing at the building, shattering the glass.

"Drop your weapon and put your hands on your head!" shouted officers, blocking streets, guns raised.

"Fuck, we're surrounded!" Terrance froze.

"Get to the van," Quinn commanded.

They sprinted, bullets whizzing past, doors slammed. To their shock, the cops stopped firing.

"If you try to escape, we will open more fire!"

"What the hell are we going to do now?"

Quinn's mind raced.

"Me and Roc are going to shoot out the window to hold them off. I'll shoot out front, you bust out back," he instructed Roc. "On three, step on it full speed L'z. You ready, D?"

"Ready."

"One…Two…Three."

Gunfire erupted from the van. Lavere floored it, smashing through streets. Shots tore through windows, bullets whizzed past. Quik was hit in the throat and arm;

Terrance grazed. The van rammed three cop cars, spun 360 degrees, barely upright. Over twenty bullet holes, yet they pushed forward.

Two cops chased as Lavere swerved onto the interstate. Quik's blood poured.

"Don't do this to me, man! Please don't!" Roc screamed.

Quinn turned away. Quik was gone.

"You've got to keep fighting! We're getting you to the hospital!"

Quik's body went still.

Lavere's hands gripped the wheel, tears mixing with sweat, as he maneuvered through traffic, narrowly avoiding collisions. A helicopter joined the chase, lights scanning the streets like a predator.

"They got the chopper on us!"

The engine screamed. Flames licked the hood.

"This van is about to catch fire!"

Lavere stopped. Police shouted commands.

"Why are we stopping!?" Terrance snapped.

"This muthafucka ain't going too much further," Lavere said.

"We in the middle of traffic!"

"I'm getting us off the freeway, then we run," Lavere said. He gunned the van, U-turning through lanes, weaving through honking cars, finally pulling into a quiet street.

"We need to split up. The chopper is on us. I'll lead them so y'all can escape."

"I'm not leaving him here," Roc said, holding Quik.

"He's dead! There's nothing we can do! Y'all get out and run in different directions. I'll keep driving north."

"You sure?" Quinn asked.

Lavere nodded. Roc and Quinn pulled Quik's body out, laid him in the grass. Quinn closed Quik's eyelids; Roc whispered a prayer.

"We'll keep it lit for you. I love you, bro," Roc said, tears running freely.

"Meet us back at the spot," Quinn told Lavere. He hoisted the bag and vanished into the shadows, taking the long route to the hideout.

Lavere urged Terrance and Roc.

"I love y'all niggas," Roc said, they split off into different escape routes.

The van stalled. Flames erupted. He vomited the adrenaline and guilt coiling in his stomach then jumped out. He ran through alleys and hopped fences. Inside a random backyard he dug a hole and buried the wiretap.

As he continued his escape down a sidewalk the chopper's spotlight now glowed on his every move.

Cop cars swarmed in. He was cornered. Officers jumped out; guns raised. Sweat, blood, and fear slicked his skin. Raising his hands above his head, he surrendered.

The chaos inside the bank had finally quieted. The smoke hung thick in the air, acrid and heavy, mingling with the metallic scent of blood. Glass crunched beneath the feet of officers moving cautiously among the overturned desks, scattered papers, and shattered teller windows. Several were too consumed with assessing the damage and the casualties to notice Naomi sprinting through the wreckage.

"Call an ambulance!" Naomi screamed, her voice slicing through the tension as she dropped to her knees beside Michael.

He was slumped against a desk, blood seeping through his uniform. His eyes, bloodshot and glassy, rolled painfully into the back of his head from the stray bullet that had struck his rib. His breathing was ragged, shallow, like each gasp cost him more than it should.

"No!" Naomi panted, clutching him as if sheer force of will could keep him alive. Her chest heaved, tears streaking her face, mingling with the grime and blood.

"Baby, I love you. Stay strong for me, please. I need a paramedic over here now!" She pressed her hands to his chest, trying to feel his heartbeat, her fingers trembling as the pulse wavered beneath her touch.

"Please, Baby, be strong for me. Please. I need you. I can't do this without you."

For a fleeting second, Michael's eyes flickered with clarity. He fixed her with a gaze heavy with love and exhaustion.

"I… love… you," he rasped, every word a battle against the pain.

"I love you too, Baby. Help is coming, Baby. You're going to make it. Just be strong for me," Naomi whispered, her voice breaking, trembling with desperate hope.

Michael's chest heaved violently, each breath shallow and ragged. He tried to speak again, but all that escaped was a weak gasp. Naomi's fingers clutched his wrist, checking his pulse with mounting panic. Then came the hollow silence.

It was gone.

"No... no, no, no!" Naomi screamed, collapsing over him as the paramedics burst through the debris-strewn doorway. They worked swiftly, lifting him from her arms, but Naomi's hands clutched his shirt, refusing to let go.

"Ma'am, we've got him! He's coming with us!" one paramedic said, gently prying her hands away.

Michael was loaded into the ambulance, the siren wailing as it tore through the streets. Naomi stumbled beside it, reaching out until it pulled away, her sobs mixing with the echoing chaos of the city.

Inside the ambulance, paramedics worked on multiple victims from the robbery. But for Naomi, the world had narrowed down to the empty space Michael had left behind, her heart breaking in a way that no siren or chaos could reach.

Two detectives were seated across from Naomi staring in her face. Next to the detectives were her supervisor and branch manager.

"Hello Ms. Simmons. I am Detective Duncan Stephens," said a quirky, white guy in his early thirties. "My partner and I have a few questions we'd like to ask you regarding the bank robbery that occurred here earlier today."

The last thing Naomi wanted to do was answer any questions. It was an hour after the robbery. Her work uniform was bloody, she had make-up smeared all over her face and not to mention, the big knot she had on her forehead.

"Ms. Simmons, I know the perpetrator had a concealed identity, but we'd like for you to give us the best description that you can give us."

"I couldn't see their faces. There's no way I can describe them."

"Did you recognize the man's voice from anyone you may know?"

"Of course not. I don't know that man. I've never seen him before in my life."

"You know, Ms. Simmons, we have to ask questions in order to solve a crime. A large percentage of successful bank robberies have an inside source."

"Are you trying to insinuate that I had something to do with this?"

"Ms. Simmons, we have a standard protocol for all employees just in case this type of event was to occur."

"I know the damn protocol."

"Ms. Simmons, your bank supervisor who was present at the time informed me that you failed to follow that protocol."

"Can you explain why you failed to comply with the company policy that is clearly stated in your employee handbook, and we just had a town hall meeting going over that protocol?" Her manager asked sarcastically.

"He had a gun to my head. I just froze up."

"We need our employees to be fast on their feet. There's no room for slip ups when in that situation. As one of bank tellers, you have a huge responsibility. The lives of our customers are in your hands. Because you failed to follow the protocol, we took a big hit today and two of our security officers and one customer was killed."

Naomi couldn't believe it. She felt like Frankie in Set It Off. However, this wasn't a movie. This was real life.

"My boyfriend was just shot! He was one of those security guards. I just experienced the most traumatic event in my life! Are you seriously questioning me about company policy? You're keeping me here to tell me this? If you had a gun pointed at your head, what would you do? Would you sound an alarm and get you're your head blown off!" Naomi couldn't hold it together any longer.

"I'm sorry, Ms. Simmons, but we are going to have to suspend you pending further investigation. Charges may be filed against you if we can link you to the perpetrators. Please hand us your badge."

"Charge me? I didn't do anything. Have you ever been held at gunpoint?"

"You breached company policy that is grounds for immediate termination. Someone will notify you within the next eight to twelve weeks informing you of our decision of whether or not to file charges against you."

Naomi threw her badge in the branch manager's face and stormed out of the office. As she walked out of the bank, she picked up her cell phone then saw that she had twenty missed calls. Big Mama accounted for almost all twenty of them. Naomi pressed the speed dial number to call her grandmother back.

"Hello Baby, I've been worried sick about you are you okay?"

"Yes, I'm okay, Grandma. I'll call you back.

Click.

Naomi dialed Michael's mother.

"Oh my God. Thank heavens you called. Are you okay?" Ms. Winston said when she answered Naomi's call.

"Yes, I'm okay."

"I saw the bank was on the news and a robbery occurred and there was a big shootout and three of the perpetrators got away! Where's Michael? Is he okay? He hasn't been answering any of my phone calls."

Naomi couldn't fix her mouth to tell her the truth.

"Hello?"

"They shot him!" Naomi blurted it out in tears.

"Oh my God! No! Please don't tell me he's dead please. Where is my baby?"

Naomi didn't respond just loud sobs were all she could muffle out.

"Hello? Naomi? "What hospital is he at? Please Naomi. Tell me something."

Naomi hung up. She couldn't find any words to say. She broke down in tears. The water streamed from her eyelids and her wet sobs were muffled in a sea of anguish and despair. Naomi cried out for Michael's soul, but he couldn't hear her as he entered a new paradise. His life on earth was over and a new home awaited him. His spirit was now free.

The Aftermath

I can't believe he's gone, the day that he was killed we got into a big fight. I never got the chance to say I'm sorry."

Naomi sat in Michael's mother's living room, wrapped in the heavy silence that hung between her and the others gathered there. His family's grief was palpable, a weight pressing down on her chest. It still felt surreal without Michael sitting beside her. That very sofa had been where he had introduced her to his mother years ago, back when they were young, starry-eyed high school sweethearts, certain of forever. If Naomi had imagined losing him, it would never have been like this.

"You can't blame yourself for any of this. Nobody expects to come to work, and the place gets robbed, and someone gets shot and killed. I know it's hard, but you're going to get past this. Michael is in a better place now and no matter where you go you have an angel watching over you."

Michael's funeral had ended hours ago. Naomi had been forced to say her final goodbye, but she still couldn't make herself fully accept it. She looked into the eyes of the woman who had raised Michael, searching for the depth of her grief. What she found instead was remarkable strength.

"How can you be so strong when you just lost your son?" Naomi asked, her voice trembling.

"It's hard, but God gets me through. He's the one getting us all through it. I think you should start to come to church with me. I think you it will do you some good. At times like these, God is the only thing that can help you."

Naomi nodded silently. Ms. Winston was right. She needed the Lord now more than ever. She hadn't been to church since living with Big Mama, and the shame of neglecting her faith weighed heavily on her. She had never prayed consistently, only calling on God when she needed something. Now, she prayed for forgiveness and for the strength to carry on.

The following Sunday, Naomi sat in the pew with Ms. Winston. The church was packed, the air thick with the voices of people praising, crying, and praying, each one carrying their own burdens. Faces, most unfamiliar, offered her smiles and words of encouragement. Their shared humanity was a quiet balm. Naomi joined the congregation in their songs, her voice blending with theirs, and for the first time in weeks, a small light sparked in her chest.

The preacher's sermon lasted hours, but his words dug deep into Naomi's soul, reminding her that the Lord's word could guide her through grief.

"Ms. Winston, I'm glad you talked me into going to church with you these past Sundays. The word of God is what I've needed to hear. It's the only thing helping me stay strong."

"God's word is all you need for anything no matter what you're going through. There ain't a thing God's word can't get you past."

They sat around Mrs. Teresa's dining room table for Sunday dinner. Ms. Teresa, one of Ms. Winston's church sisters, looked at Naomi with compassion.

"You know child, I lost my son's father at a young age just like you." Mrs. Teresa said. "It was a very rough time in my life too. He was the love of my life. We were together since teenagers and at the time I couldn't imagine life without him. That is until he died, and I was left with no choice."

Teresa understood Naomi's pain. Her own heartbreak had shaped her into a resilient woman.

"What happened to your son's father?"

"He was shot and killed over a dice game on the streets."

"I'm so sorry to hear that."

"Girl, that was years ago, and it only hurts me today because my son had to grow up without a father. I've tried my best to raise him to be a good man and not to fall into the same life that his father did. I just wish his father was here to tell him. Did you have any children by that man of yours?"

"No ma'am."

"That's a good thing because that child would always be a reminder of the love you lost and it's hard trying to raise a child without his father."

"How did you get over the pain? I've never had my heart broke like this before. All the memories. I wish I could forget them because every time I think about the moments we shared; I get so upset."

Even as she spoke, Naomi fought to hold back the tears.

"The memories will always be there. If you try not to think about them you won't allow yourself to heal, Honey. One thing I know is that time heals all wounds. I can tell you're a strong young woman so I don't doubt that you will be just fine. When the grief hits, you have to pray. Don't ask the Lord to ease your pain, ask Him for strength because every storm we go through in life is to help us become stronger in Him."

"Ms. Teresa, you are so motivating. I really needed to hear that."

"Anytime you need to talk, Honey, I'm here. You just pick up your phone, give me a call and I will pray with you. I've been where you're at before and I know you will get through this. Lord knows, I wish I had somebody to pray with me in my hard times."

Naomi drew comfort from the positivity of these women, letting their encouragement wash over her.

Months passed. Every day without Michael brought a fresh wave of grief. Naomi, now jobless, spent hours applying for positions, trying to reclaim a sense of purpose and distract herself from the void left behind. She longed for her old busy life, for the routine that had kept her anchored and most of all, she longed for Michael.

Bills piled higher. The light company threatened to cut her electricity, rent was overdue. Naomi looked around her apartment at the shelves of purses and shoes, weighing what she could sell to stay afloat. She began dumping clothes from her closet into a heap, her motions frenzied. But then she froze.

Everything in the closet had belonged to Michael.

The clothes, the shoes, even his senior prom suit still hanging in the dry-cleaning bag. Each piece a living memory of him. Naomi sank to the floor, surrounded by the tangible remnants of her first love. Tears rolled freely, and the grief that had been simmering boiled over. She wept for the life she had lost, the future that would never come.

Buzz! Buzz! Buzz! Buzz!

Her phone vibrated against the floor. She ignored it, knowing the leasing office was calling about overdue rent. When the voicemail came, her heart sank.

"Good afternoon, Naomi, this is Natasha with the leasing office. I am calling to inform you that after today, you will have three consecutive balances on your account that have not been paid. Currently the balance is two thousand eight hundred fifty-nine dollars and thirty-four cents... you do have until the end of the business day tomorrow to pay your balance in full or we will file a judgment against you."

Naomi's world narrowed. Eviction. Three days. No money. No backup. Only one option remained: Big Mama's house.

Returning to her grandmother's crowded home was a shock. The noise, the chaos, the lack of privacy. It was overwhelming. Naomi shared her space with her sister Alexis, her sister's deadbeat baby daddy Daquan, and a gaggle of unruly children. She could barely move without bumping into someone.

Weeks passed. Naomi fought to reclaim her focus. Big Mama took the kids out for the day, giving Naomi a rare window of peace. She pulled out her laptop and finally began working on an essay when the phone rang.

"Hey girl. I thought you'd be at work right now."

"I called in," Tashi said, her voice low.

"What's wrong girl? You don't sound okay."

"Me and Kevin broke up."

"Let me guess, he cheated on you again? Girl, this is the third time which means it's the charm. You can't keep letting him do this to you."

"That's not all that happened."

"There's more to it?"

"Yeah, and it's bad."

"What the hell happened?"

"He got another bitch pregnant."

"Damn, that's foul. I hope you kicked his trifling ass to the curb for good this time."

"Yeah, I put him out, but I just can't believe he would go to the extent of getting somebody pregnant. Out of the three years we've been off and on, I've never been pregnant by him, and he knows how much I want a baby."

"Don't worry girl. I'm on my way. I'll be there in a little bit just hang tight, okay?"

Naomi packed her things, threw on an outfit, and stepped into the shower, blissfully unaware of the storm waiting on the other side of the house...

Roc twisted a fresh piece of chalk around the tip of his pool stick, the grit scraping against the leather like a warning. Quinn leaned over the pool table; eyes locked on the last target. He had pocketed nearly every ball in sight, leaving only the eight-ball standing between him and victory.

"Eight ball, corner pocket," Quinn called, lining up his shot with deadly precision.

The stick struck the cue ball clean, sending the eight-ball rolling right on target. It dropped with a satisfying clink into the corner pocket, sealing the final game.

"Once again, I'm the champ! You still haven't learned after all these years of me spanking that ass."

Roc slammed his stick down and shook his head, a mix of frustration and admiration. Quinn had the edge, always. It drove Roc insane.

"Kiss my ass. One day I'm going to beat your cocky ass, just watch."

"You will never beat me. Get that understood."

Quinn slapped fives with Terrance, who had been lounging on the couch, eyes following every movement like a hawk. Quinn pulled out his iPhone, thumbs flying.

Quinn: What's up baby girl? What you doing?

Almost instantly, Jayla replied.

Jayla: Nm bored, what about you?

Quinn grinned, leaning back into the plush leather chair.

Quinn: I could be doing you if you let me.

His fingers danced across the screen.

Jayla: I don't fuck with broke niggas, so I hope your pockets ain't hurting if you trying to hit this pussy.

Quinn: You ain't talking to the old me this a whole new man right here baby.

Jayla: "Mmmhmm we'll see, I hope you know how to work it. You talk a good game."

Quinn smirked, pocketing his phone. He and Jayla had been texting since the club. Rumors, reputations, street whispers, he had learned she played the game well, sponging ballers dry without a second thought. And Damon? Fat wasted opportunity, perfect for her to use. Quinn shook his head at the thought. It was almost funny.

Their digital flirtation had escalated. Nudes had been exchanged. Mutual promises of physical exploits lingered like smoke in the air.

"What's up with it, T? Are you trying to get this work next or what?" Quinn asked, setting his phone down to rack the balls for the next round.

"Man, things ain't been the same ever since L'z got locked up and Quik been gone," Terrance admitted, his voice heavy with frustration. "We can't hit any more spots. The cops are watching our every move, waiting for us to slip and make a mistake. Every other day I walk out the house, I see one of those muthafuckas parked out front. You know the streets are talking and those muthafuckas are getting hints leading them to us."

Quinn's eyes narrowed, the memory of their last botched robbery weighing on him.

"We need to continue to keep our noses clean. One slip up could send us right upstate with Lavere, you feel me?"

Months had passed since the chaos, but the sting was still fresh.

"I'm still trying to figure out how they caught on to us on that last mission. It's like they knew exactly where we were going to be, and they were waiting for us as soon as we came out the building."

"You think Lavere snitched and put them up to it? He was acting strange before he went in the joint."

"If he did, all of us would be locked up right now. All he would have to do is drop a dime on our names and where we stay, and the cops would rush all three of us."

"Yeah, you right. I know he's in there hurting though."

"How's his old man doing?" Roc asked, concern cutting through his usual bravado.

"Not good, he had been taking it hard. L'z is facing twenty years, fifteen with the possibility of parole if he takes a plea." Quinn's jaw tightened.

"I just wish we could talk to him and tell him to keep his head up, you know," Terrance said quietly.

"The cops are waiting for us to reach out so they can sting us too. Lavere wouldn't want us to do that. It's a miracle we even got away. I just wish we could have got away with more loot."

"At that point in time, freedom was more important," said Terrance. "If we would have stayed in there any longer, we wouldn't have even got a chance to get away with anything."

"Money has been slow for a minute now. We been living like regular civilians, only spending a couple hundred dollars a day."

"Most regular people don't even spend that in a day fam."

"Yeah, but we ain't regular, we ballers. We spend two hundred dollars on T-shirts. Without no licks to hit, our paper is going to dry up. Money goes fast when you ain't getting none."

"We gotta stay low key, the cops are watching."

"They can't book us. If they could, they would have already. We need to hit a lick on the strip club," Roc said, eyes gleaming. "There's nothing but a bunch of trick-ass ballers in there wasting money to see some dancers slide up and down a pole. That's a lot of loot if we clean that hoe out."

"Nah dude, you can't rob a club without shooting up the place. Then the spot is going to get shut down; then people don't have anywhere to go kick it and that draws attention. Plus, once you hit one spot you move on to the next, and then the next, and then the next one. Once you rob a place you can never go back to the same place because the next time, they'll be suspecting you. Robbing is all about the art of surprise, but you already know that."

Quinn's hand smacked the table, emphasizing his point.

"Then how about this, we can use the strippers to lure these trick-ass ballers to a hotel, then we come in and break their pockets."

"Breaking pockets is only going to get you pocket change, you feel me? I learned that will only get you so far. Eventually, you get caught up like we almost did. After the last bank we hit took us on a high-speed and led to Quik dying and Lavere getting locked up, I realized we had reached our limit."

"So, what do you suggest we do? We need to get money somehow."

"It's time to move into another lane. Real hustlers don't just drive in one lane, they take over the entire interstate. It's time for us to move on to different ventures and get legit so the feds will get off our asses. And since you mention a strip club, I always wanted to run a fancy night joint, and if we all put our money together, we'll have enough paper to do it."

"You know my cousin Randy that works as a bouncer for Club Live?"

"Yeah."

"Well, he said the club is close to being shut down. The owner wants to retire."

"Damn, really? Why haven't you said anything? I think that could be the opportunity we been waiting for."

"That club is easily worth over a million dollars. We're all going to need to chip in three hundred thousand dollars apiece. I don't have that much bread to invest," said Terrance.

"Maybe we can talk him into a lower number or get him to agree to a payment plan."

"First, we need Randy to let him know that we're interested. Call Randy and see if he can set us up a meeting with the owner."

Roc grabbed his phone and dialed. Three rings.

"What's up fam? I need you to let your boss know I have interest in acquiring his business. See if you can set up a meeting with him."

"You want to buy the club?"

"Yeah nigga, that's why I'm asking."

"Okay. I'll chat with him later today and let you know what he says."

"Make sure you come through for me on this. I really need it fam."

"Don't I always?"

"You right. I'll catch you later though."

"Fasho. All right. Peace."

Later that night, Roc's phone buzzed. He answered on the first ring.

"Yo, what you got for me?"

"I was able to pull some strings and convince the boss to meet with you next Sunday at three."

"Right on! Good looking out, Cuzzo. I owe you for this one."

"Just pass me one of them freaks you be smashing, then we can call it even."

"Hahaha, you know I can most definitely do that. I'll get at you later."

"All right, peace."

It Costs To Be A Boss

Quinn, Terrance, and Roc arrived at Club Live, dressed to impress wearing tailored suits with ties. They were ready to sit down and discuss a legitimate business venture like legitimate businessmen. They concluded that they were ready to make an offer of up to a half million dollars, then make payments for the remaining balance that was needed to take full ownership of the club.

"The boss is awaiting y'all in his office," said Randy escorting them into the club.

They were inside for the first time during daytime hours and the club looked so much different without people partying in it.

"Good afternoon gentlemen," said one of the club's hosts. "Follow me and I'll lead you to the boss."

Walking into the owner's office, it looked more like a conference room. Everything was plush and purple. *"The color of royalty,"* Quinn thought. The man who had to be the boss sat in a big leather chair, puffing a cigar. Quinn could instantly envision himself in that same spot. He had always wondered what the owner looked like because it was rare to ever see him. He called shots from his chair in the back of his office. His perm was bad but his clothes were Versace from head to toe. Rings made of gold and diamonds occupied every single finger on both of his hands. He reminded them of an old school pimp. After taking his time to finish enjoying his cigar, he spoke.

"Gentlemen, before we talk business allow me to introduce myself," he said in a thick southern accent. "Good afternoon, fellas. My name is Avery Waters and I've been running this nightclub for the past eighteen years. When I started this business, I was thirty-nine years old and all I had was a dollar and a dream. I grew up on the Eastside and was the first man in my family to graduate college. I worked for an insurance agency for fifteen years until I was tired of working for other folk and decided to go into business for myself. Let me give you a little history about the building you're sitting in."

"It started out as a two-stepping joint for couples that were thirty and older. Then we lowered our club to twenty-five and older. Now my club is open to anyone at the legal age of eighteen and older. The younger crowd brings the most business. Fridays are the best days for club attendance. We make more money on that day than all other days combined.

Those are the things that you need to know working in this business. You have to know the likes and dislikes of each age group of customers then tailor the business to give them the best time they've ever had. That's how you get them to keep coming back to party. Now I've gotten some offers from a few different people about acquiring this place. Some want to turn it into this, others that. I'd much rather keep it in the hands of my own people, you know. I'm looking to put my club in the hands of someone who will keep the tradition going. So, tell me why you want to take over my club and why should I choose to give it to you?"

"Well, Mr. Waters, I hope you excuse me when I say this, but we definitely don't want to turn it into some bullshit. I have plans to expand on all the hard work that you've put into this establishment. One of the first things, we plan to add is a dining experience for the guest along with a happy hour for the business professionals who want a place to mingle after work. Thinking long term, we would also establish this brand as a franchise and open new clubs in other cities. You also say the younger crowd is the most profitable, so who better than someone my age that knows exactly how to reach them?"

"What type of experience do you have in business management?"

"Honestly, I've never ran a business before, but I grew up in one of the roughest neighborhoods in town just like you Mr. Waters and I've always been one to create my own route and become my own boss just like you did for yourself. That's why I am able to sit across the table from you. I can assure that by putting your business in the hands of my team, it's in the safest place possible.

"I like you, Quinten. You remind me of myself when I was starting out. I can see that same hunger in your eyes. I'd much rather keep the money in my own community too. Problem is, the only people who have been able to reach my asking price are them rich white assholes."

"If you can meet my price, I'll be more than willing to pass you the torch."

"How much are you asking?"

"I want one point six million."

"The number is a little higher than we'd like. Can you go any lower?"

"I've already lowered it."

"My first asking price was two point three. I'm not willing to budge any more.

"Mr. Waters, we are willing to make a down payment of five hundred thousand dollars. If you allow us to make payments on the rest, we can put down fifty thousand a month to have it paid off in the next twenty-four months."

"Sorry Quinten, but I don't accept payment plans. I've had bad experience doing that type of business. It's either the full amount or there won't be any deal. Can you match my offer? If not, there's no reason for us to waste each other's time."

"Yes, we can match your offer. All I ask is that you give us some time to collect the funds."

"I'm a little pressed for time. I have one guy pressuring me to close in next week so if you can you bring your money by next Thursday, this place will be yours."

"No problem, we'll have it."

"You will?"

"You have my word."

"Well, if that's the case, I'll get the contract ready."

"Thank you very much. It's nice doing business with you, Mr. Waters. We will be back next week," Quinn said extending his hand. The two men shook then parted ways.

"Where are we going to get a million dollars by Thursday? That's in ten days." Roc questioned Quinn's decision to make such a gutsy deal once they were out of the club.

"Don't worry. I have a plan."

"This got to be good. What's your plan this time?"

"You remember that chick Jayla?"

"That pretty young thing you been trying forever to score with?

Yeah, I remember, but what does she have to do with this money we need to get?"

"We'll that's all about to change. She been hitting my line up every now and then, but lately she's been pressing me to hit that. I've been holding her off, waiting for the right time. The anticipation is killing her by now and I know it."

"And what does that have to do with this money we need to come up with?"

"You know her man is Damon, and I know he got a nice stash."

"Oh ok, now I see what you are saying. You think we should kidnap her?"

"Something like that."

Quinn, Terrance, and Roc pulled up to Club Live in sleek, tailored suits. Their ties were straight, shoes polished, and eyes locked on their goal: a legitimate business venture. For once, they were stepping into a room where money talked in dollars, not street licks. Their plan was to make an offer of half a million dollars and negotiate the remaining balance to take full ownership.

"The boss is awaiting y'all in his office," Randy said, escorting them into the club.

Inside, the club looked different without the usual chaos of weekend crowds and flashing lights. Daylight spilled across the polished floors, revealing the full scale of the venue.

"Good afternoon, gentlemen," said a host. "Follow me and I'll lead you to the boss."

The owner's office looked more like a high-end conference room with plush seating, deep purple walls, and a desk that screamed power. Sitting behind it was Avery Waters, puffing on a thick cigar. Quinn's eyes immediately sized him up, imagining himself in that chair one day.

Avery's perm was dated, but his Versace outfit and diamond rings gave him the aura of someone who'd always played to win. He leaned back in his chair and exhaled smoke like a king surveying his court.

"Gentlemen, before we talk business, allow me to introduce myself," he said in a slow southern drawl. "Good afternoon. I'm Avery Waters, and I've been running this nightclub for the past eighteen years. When I started, I was thirty-nine and had a dollar and a dream. I worked fifteen years in insurance before deciding I wanted to control my own destiny."

He gestured around the room.

"This building started as a two-stepping joint for folks thirty and older. Then we brought it down to twenty-five-plus, now anyone eighteen and older can come. The younger crowd brings the most business. Fridays are prime. More profits than all other days. You need to understand your customers to run a club successfully. That's the essence of the business."

Quinn nodded, mentally filing every detail.

"I've had offers from a few people," Avery continued, "but I want this club in the hands of someone who will respect its tradition. Tell me why you want to take over my club and why I should choose you."

Quinn leaned forward.

"Mr. Waters, we don't want to turn this into something it's not. We plan to expand on your work by add a dining experience, a happy hour for professionals, and long-term possibly franchise the brand. The younger crowd? That's our peers. We know how to connect with them."

Avery raised an eyebrow.

"And your experience in business management?"

"I've never run a traditional business," Quinn admitted. "But I grew up in tough neighborhoods, just like you. I've always carved my own path, built my own empire. I know what it takes to make something work, and I can assure you your club would be in the safest hands."

Avery studied him, nodding.

"I like you, Quinten. You remind me of myself starting out. Only problem? My asking price is high is one point six million. I've already lowered it from two point three."

Quinn and his team exchanged glances.

"We can put down five hundred thousand now," Quinn said, "and make monthly payments of fifty thousand to settle the rest in two years."

Avery shook his head. "No payment plans. Full amount, or nothing. Can you match that?"

Quinn didn't flinch. "We'll get it to you by next Thursday. You have my word."

Avery smirked, extending his hand. "Then we have a deal."

Outside, Roc shook his head. "A million dollars by Thursday? That's ten days. What were you thinking?"

Quinn smirked. "I have a plan."

Roc's eyes narrowed. "This better be good. What's your move?"

"You remember Jayla?"

"That pretty young thing you've been trying forever to score with? Yeah... what about her?"

"She's been messaging me, pushing hard. And her man, Damon? He's got a stash. Big stash. We're about to tap into that."

Roc's jaw dropped. "You're talking about… kidnapping?"

"Something like that," Quinn said, his grin sharpening.

Later, Quinn parked across from Damon's mansion. The house looked straight off an MTV Cribs special, skyline views, sprawling driveway, manicured gardens. He checked his pockets: handcuffs, duct tape, pistol. He was ready.

When Jayla greeted him at the door, wrapped in a luxurious robe, Quinn smiled. "Time to make this work," he murmured, following her through the mansion as she guided him to an empty wing, just as planned.

Inside, they walked past art-lined halls and massive bedrooms until they reached the master suite. Quinn's mind raced, not with desire this time, but with strategy. Every step, every move, was about positioning. The money they needed to save the club wasn't going to appear magically, it was going to take precision, timing, and nerves of steel.

Jayla, unaware of the full plan, smiled at him. Quinn's eyes scanned the room, mentally running through contingencies. This was it, the move that could turn him from street-level hustler to legitimate nightclub owner.

And he wasn't going to fail.

"You know I've been mesmerized by you since the first time I saw you," Quinn began to drop game, feeling kind of cocky that he would soon conquer a woman that he had failed to get before.

Jayla loosened the knot holding her gown together, letting it fall to the floor. Red lace lingerie by Victoria Secret hugged her body, matching the red lipstick she wore. She had freshly manicured French tip nails and toes. Quinn licked his lips wondering if she tasted as sweet as she looked. He could see why Damon had her as his main chick. From head to toe, she had the face and body of a goddess. Her body was slim but curvy with oversized boobs.

"Come here," she said desiring the affection of a man.

Quinn slowly walked up to her and grabbed her chin giving her a slow passionate tonguing. Jayla reached for his crotch feeling the bulge in his jeans.

"Chill baby, we got a little time, don't we?" Quinn gently swept away her hand. "How about I give you a nice massage?" Quinn wanted Jayla to be as relaxed as possible before he got into what was in store. "You have any body oil?"

Jayla went into the master bath and came out with some massaging oil then she lay on top of the rose pedals and onto her stomach. Quinn's hands were strong but gentle the way he rubbed her body down. Once Jayla was completely covered in the body oil, she felt extremely relaxed. She watched Quinn undress down to his boxers, looking hypnotized by the sight of his body. Quinn did five hundred sit ups and pushups a day, so he was very toned. In no time, Quinn and Jayla were both tonguing each other while she rubbed and squeezed on the bulge in his boxers. He sucked on her neck and massaged her plump booty.

"I've been wanting to sex you for a long time, so I hope you don't disappoint me. First, I need to see what you got to offer."

"Why don't you see for yourself?"

Jayla unsnapped her bra, and her boobs plopped out like two melons. Quinn didn't budge. He pulled his boxers down and his junk flung out and saluted her like a lieutenant to his sergeant. Jayla's eyes got big when she saw the package.

"I must say, I'm impressed, but do you know how to use it?"

Jayla squatted to the floor and kissed the shaft of Quinn's rod.

"You have a big ass dick."

She pushed Quinn all the way down her throat until his entire length was in her mouth. She was savoring the taste of him while she sucked. For Quinn, the feeling was nothing short of bliss. He thoroughly enjoyed the fellatio until Jayla cut off his pleasure.

"Where's my money?" Jayla asked firmly. She was back up on her feet with her hand out.

"Damn baby, I'm not going to stiff you."

"Yeah, uh huh, this ain't no free fuck."

Quinn reached inside his jeans and pulled out a wad of cash. It was all crispy hundreds. Jayla's mouth began to water as she flipped her fingers through the bills. She was definitely going to put him near the top of the list of tricks she kept on speed dial. Jayla put the money in her drawer.

"Now back to where we left off," Jayla said before she returned to her knees and spit shined him until he was ready to return the favor.

Quinn usually didn't give head on the first night, but he was going to go all out and show Jayla just what she'd been missing. Quinn laid Jayla down on the bed pulling her booty to the edge of the mattress then threw her legs over his shoulders. He kissed down her thighs and everywhere around her hole purposely avoiding it. Once he had teased her enough, he gently licked her clit from top to bottom. Using his entire mouth, he licked her clean, leaving no spot untouched. Her body shivered with pleasure as an orgasm rose and she released on his tongue.

"Oooh shit! Damn!" Jayla's continuous slurs let Quinn know he was doing the trick.

Quinn placed his lips around her clit then slurped her in and out of his mouth. Jayla loved a man who could clean his plate.

"Yessss! Suck on my pussy just like that!"

Jayla's hands gripped the sheets. Her back arched she lifted her body trying to maintain control; she creamed all over Quinn's lips. Her legs were wobbly, and she clamped her knees together too overwhelmed by the sensation. Quinn had Jayla exactly where he wanted her.

Next, he slid upward licking around her belly button up to her thick nipples sucking them like those sweet chocolate Hershey kisses that they resembled. He continued to migrate upward sucking on her neck then earlobe playfully biting as he positioned himself on the entrance of her vagina. Quinn brushed against her outer lips in an up and down motion then eased inside until his full length was in.

"Ugh!" Jayla exclaimed gasping for air.

The sex was so good it made her lose her breath. Quinn felt an orgasm coming just a minute into stroking. *"Damn this bitch got some good pussy!"* It was ten times better than he expected it. He fought to keep himself from getting hypnotized by Jayla's box, having to stop in the middle of his penetration.

"Fuck this pussy like a man, hold that nut and make me cum!" she challenged him.

"Let's switch positions," Quinn said. He was trying his best to prolong his climax.

Jayla got off the bed and bent over grabbing both of her ankles. Quinn slid back inside her and while gripping the sides of Jayla's hips as he thrusted. It was easier for him to control himself from that position, but he was still struggling not to release.

"Fuck me deep and hard!" Jayla screamed out. "Deeper! Harder!" The more she kept demanding the more effort Quinn put forth. He had to be touching uncharted places.

After Jayla's orgasm came, she tapped out stopping Quinn from causing severe damage to her guts. They moved onto the floor, and she rode him in reverse cowgirl. It was the fourth position they had switched to. Unlike Damon, Quinn was fit and had the stamina to keep up with her.

"I got something I want to do," Quinn said stopping to pull out the cuffs in his jean pocket.

"I knew you were nasty," Jayla said when her eyes landed on the handcuffs.

Quinn placed one on each of her wrist then he connected the cuffs through the bars of the headboard. Without the ability to fight back, Jayla had to take the pounding that he was about to put on her.

"Oh shit...Fuck this pussy...*Ooooh*!" she screamed as an uncontrollable orgasm overtook her body.

She began to shake and squirm. Quinn was beating it up with all his might. Jayla felt so good that Quinn couldn't hold back any longer. He released everything he was holding back. He jerked and twitched while releasing. Once Quinn came down from the high, he eased out the pistol he had secretly hidden underneath the pillows and pressed it against the side of Jayla's temple.

"Just be still or I'll kill you."

"Jayla was instantly covered with fear for her life."

"Okay, don't kill me. You can have that money back."

"Sorry baby girl. I really like you so don't take this personal."

Quinn went to his jacket and grabbed the large roll of duct tape, ski mask and other pair of handcuffs that were in his pockets.

"What the hell are you doing? Are you crazy? Take these cuffs off me!" Jayla snapped.

"Nah, I can't do that," Quinn said calmly

"Nigga, you better un-cuff me! My man will be home soon, you better leave before he catches you in his house. If you don't, I promise you won't make it out of here."

"I'm not worried about your punk ass man. I got something hot for his ass."

Quinn took the duct tape and closed Jayla's mouth off then took the other cuffs and locked her legs, so she had no way of moving.

She was still talking but he didn't understand a damn thing she was saying. She was probably pleading and begging him not to kill her. He still hadn't made his mind up on whether he was going to let her live. Quinn got dressed and made himself comfortable. He knew any minute; her man would be home, and he was going to be in for a rude awakening. For now, he just waited. Quinn heard keys jingling then a lock turning.

Click.

There was the creaking sound of the front door opening. A couple of seconds later, the same door slammed shut.

"Jayla!" Damon shouted but she didn't answer.

Each step that Damon took climbing his steps sounded like an earthquake.

127

Thump! Thump! Thump! Thump! Thump! Thump! Thump! Thump! Thump!

When Damon opened the bedroom door, he was stopped cold in his tracks.

"Don't try anything stupid." Quinn said pointing the gun at Jayla's temple.

Jayla was butt naked and the smell of sex was still in the air. Quinn knew Damon felt hurt realizing she had been cheating behind his back.

"Shoot that bitch!" Damon said out of anger then reached for his pistol.

Pow!

Quinn quickly focused his aim at Damon, realizing Jayla didn't mean as much to him as he thought.

"Aargh!" Damon grunted.

Quinn had sent a bullet slicing through Damon's shoulder.

"Who are you? Take that mask off!"

Damon wanted to know who the man was so just in case he lived, he could kill him.

"Call Brooklyn and tell him you need him to loan you one million cash. If you say anything other than that it's curtains for your ass."

"What?"

"Nigga, do you want to die tonight? If so, then don't do what I said."

Damon pulled out his cell and made the call. He could barely move his shoulder due to the bullet lodged inside of it. His entire arm was bloody.

"Brooklyn, I need to talk to you. I need to borrow one million. Just bring it now. I'll explain it all when you get here."

"Good job, now say your last prayers before you die." Quinn had plans for Brooklyn, but Damon, he would handle himself.

"What is this about? Is it money you want?" Damon couldn't believe he was being held at gunpoint in his own home.

"You damn right. Now where's the safe at. Lead me to it now."

Quinn figured Damon had a stash in his crib that he could add to the million that Brooklyn was on the way with.

"If you cooperate, I will let you live," Quinn lied.

Damon began walking as slow as a turtle leading Quinn down his stairs towards the part of the house where he kept his stash.

"You stalling, hurry up!"

"Don't shoot me. I promise nobody will come after you if you just take the money and leave."

"I know nobody's going to come after me, you don't even know who I am."

Damon took Quinn to a hidden room inside the walls on the lowest level of his house. It was small and contained nothing but a safe. It was a stash spot you wouldn't find unless you knew where it was. Damon took his sweet time unlocking the safe. He fumbled with the combination acting as if he forgot. Damon was trying to buy himself some time.

"I'm running out of patience. You got less than ten seconds to get the safe open or I'll kill you." Quinn coked the pistol ready to end his life. Finally, Damon made the safe knob click indicating it was unlocked.

"Look at me," Quinn said then removed his ski mask. He wanted his face to be the last thing Damon saw before he died. "Remember me?"

Damon was shocked. He was from the streets, so he always remembered faces. It was the same little nigga he should have murked and made an example of by leaving his dead body in the middle of Glenn Park. He underestimated the little nigga. It's always the nigga you don't expect that comes to kill.

"The tables always turn," Quinn said. This time Quinn was on the other side of the gun.

POW!

He sent Damon to his meeting with the devil. He remembered Jayla was upstairs handcuffed to the bedpost. He still hadn't made up his mind whether he would kill her too.

"This better be important," Brooklyn said aloud to himself as he exited his car and began walking toward the front door of Damon's house that overlooked the downtown skyline.

Roc was lurking in the bushes that filled the yard watching Brooklyn and he was completely oblivious. The frown on Brooklyn's face let Roc know he was upset that he had gotten up in the middle of the night. Brooklyn was carrying a gym bag that contained the million dollars. It was a hefty sum of money, but not enough to have him sweating it. Quinn knew a man like Brooklyn could come up with that easily.

Ding! Dong!

"Look, don't shoot me," Brooklyn said when he realized two unknown men with assault rifles were standing next to him. "I'm getting too old for this gangster shit," he said next.

"Get in the car and drive back to your house right now," Roc instructed.

"My wife and kids are back at the home. What do y'all need? Is it money? I have a million dollars cash right here." Brooklyn held up the bag full of money.

"I don't want your money," Roc lied. "Just do what I say."

Brooklyn got back in the car left with no choice but to cooperate.

"Your family won't get hurt as long as you do what we say. Now drive this muthafucka before you end up dead," Brooklyn didn't utter another word as he drove back home.

"I know where you live. It's a straight shot so don't try to take any detours."

When Brooklyn reached the driveway of his house, he hesitated to go inside.

"What you waiting for?!"

"Please man, my daughters are in their room sleeping."

"They'll never know we were even here, now move."

Brooklyn walked through his house with guns pointed at his head.

"Take us to the safe," Roc instructed. Brooklyn led them right to his room where his safe was located.

"Baby? What did Damon want?"

"Nothing honey."

"What are you doing in the dark? She kept hearing him fiddling around as if he were looking for something.

Brooklyn didn't respond unable to think of a lie. His wife turned on the nightlight and held her hands over her mouth to conceal the screams that would have awakened her daughters.

"Don't move," Terrance said focusing his weapon on her. He was watching her every move as Brooklyn led Roc to his closet keyed in the code to his safe then opened it up.

"This is only about twenty stacks,'" Roc said disappointed at the sight of two large money stacks. His pistol smacked the back of Brooklyn's head.

"Ahh!"

"I know that you got more than that. Show us the real money or your family dies!"

'I'm sorry man, I'll do whatever you want just don't touch my girls."

"Well, you better find some more money and do it fast."

Brooklyn went back to the bedroom and pulled up the carpet of the floor near the bed revealing a jackpot of money and so many bricks of cocaine that Roc couldn't even count how many there was. *This has to be at least ten million dollars in cash and drugs,* he thought. "We just hit the Jackpot. Now go get us a suitcase and clear all that shit out."

Roc followed Brooklyn back to the closet where Brooklyn grabbed his largest suitcase then he went to his bedroom and dropped to the floor. He was on his hands and knees scooping up all the money and bricks he had until it was all in the suitcase.

"Good job. I promise your daughters will live but I can't make the same promise for you."

Pow! Roc sent a single shot into Brooklyn's skull.

He and Terrance walked out the room and out the house with a suitcase full of money and dope while Brooklyn's wife was left screaming and crying over the body of her dead husband.

Ring…Ring…Ring!

Quinn answered his iPhone.

"It's done and we got a lot of loot," Roc said. "So, what you wanna do about ol' girl. I know you felt bad about killing her. Is she still alive?"

"No, she won't be an issue."

"Good. We on the way to your spot. Meet us there."

Quinn popped the trunk of his car and looked at Jayla's lifeless body wrapped in sheets. He lifted the body out the trunk and carried it to the edge of the downtown bridge. He couldn't leave her dead body in the house with his DNA still inside her. He tossed her over the bridge and watched her dive feet first into the Missouri river.

"You had the chance to be with a real one, but you chose that clown instead."

Three Weeks Later...

Jamir knelt next to the tombstone of his brother Brooklyn. It had been three weeks since the night his brother had been robbed and killed. He now had to step up for his nieces and his sister-in-law. Without his brother around, the streets were already moving slow and everybody's pockets were hurting.

Jamir took a big gulp of his forty-ounce wrapped in a brown paper bag. He poured out the rest of the liquor over his brother's grave.

"The twins miss you; Mom and Pops miss you. Your wife really misses you. Everybody man. We're not the same without you." Jamir did his best to hold back his tears. "This can't be real, I never thought I would have to visit you like this, but you always said the game runs deep and now I know what you mean. I promise I'm going to kill whoever did this to you bro."

Jamir stood to his feet and walked to back to his Jeep. He was stressed to the max. He had to find a new connect because the plug wasn't rocking with him. Nobody had the relationship with Hugo except Brooklyn. Without him, nobody in the Midwest Connection's organization could cop weight. Jamir grabbed his cell and gave a call to Chris to see if word had come back on who'd smoked his family. So far, the streets were quiet, but he knew it wouldn't be long before they started talking.

"Yo!" Chris spoke picking up on the other line

"You got word on those suckers yet?"

"Nah, I still haven't heard anything, but I got my ear glued to the streets. I'm to going get some answers."

"What's taking so got-damn long, huh nigga? I put you on assignment weeks ago!"

"The streets haven't been saying that much, nobody knows for sure who did it."

"You better get to making them muthafuckas talk! I don't care if you have to ride through every neighborhood, walk up to every nigga on the streets and beat it out of them! Get me some answers now!"

"I can't wait to body me a nigga," Jamir said angrily after he hung up the phone.

Until somebody told him who had killed his brother he didn't want to talk. He was about to go on a man hunt and when he tracked down Brooklyn's killer, he was going to kill him.

The Game Runs Deep

Quinn overlooked the large crowd of people that stood outside the building of his new restaurant The Parlor Room. All his employees, a few local news broadcasters, and the city's hottest Hip Hop & R&B station, Blazing 103 were in attendance for the grand opening of the new restaurant located right next door to Club Live.

"Okay everybody, listen up!" Quinn projected his smooth voice over the crowd of employees and guests who were eager to try out the new spot. "Profits are high as you can tell by the size of your bonus checks."

"Wooo!" All the employees cheered in gratitude.

"All right, calm down," Quinn said. "We are about to make even more revenue plus establish this business as more than just a club, but the ultimate socializing experience. When my partners and I took over the ownership of Club Live, I had a vision of adding an open late restaurant to our business. I wanted to give our guest a place to eat drink and have a great time so they wouldn't have a reason to go anywhere else. Most of the contractors that I reached out to didn't support this project. So, I'd like to thank Supreme Realtors for believing in my vision and making this possible. Also, I'd like to thank my partner, Devante Richards and Terrance Smith along with all the guest who come to Club Live night after night making it the most popular nightclub in our city. Today, we have officially added an open late restaurant next to our club and now it's open to the public. This is just the beginning. Now we are going to start our countdown."

Terrance held the red ribbon between the shears of the giant scissors. "Five! Four! Three! Two! One!" As Terrance cut the ribbon, everyone cheered.

"The Parlor Room is now officially open!" Quinn yelled out over the crowd.

It had been nearly three weeks, and Naomi hadn't done much besides sit inside the house sulking. Tashi was starting to get irritated by her friend's prolonged stay and the constant cloud of negativity she brought with her. Naomi spent most of her days sprawled on Tashi's couch.

"You are starting to cramp my style," Tashi said as she walked into the living room.

Naomi didn't move, eyes glued to a reality television show. The drama on the screen made her own life feel even duller. Tashi stood there, arms crossed, waiting for

Naomi to react, but she just lay there, seemingly trying to ignore her presence.

"Oh no. I'm not about to do this with you today." Tashi pressed the power button on the side of the TV, turning it off. Then she walked over to the window and threw open the curtains, letting sunlight pour into the living room.

"All right, now get your ass up," Tashi said, trying to pull Naomi off the sofa.

"No, Tashi! Stop!" Naomi protested, refusing to move.

"Girl, get up. It's a beautiful day outside, and I'm not letting you sit in here moping another day. You need to fix yourself up and get out of the house."

"I'm not in the mood, Tashi. Just let me chill."

"So, are you just going to let yourself go? I can't take care of you forever. Eventually, you're going to have to get up."

"I'm broke! I don't have anything to my name, and Michael's gone! He's gone, Tashi!" Naomi's voice cracked as tears threatened to fall.

"Look, girl, I'm sorry, but it's time to stop feeling sorry for yourself. The negativity isn't helping. I've never seen you like this before. You look awful." Naomi shot Tashi a sharp look.

"You know what your problem is? You need to get back to loving yourself. That's the only way you'll find your happiness, even in the middle of the storm. I know exactly what you need to get your groove back. Today's a spa day for us. I've got passes for a full body massage and a facial. I was going with Kevin, but that's over now. You're my new spa partner. After the spa, we'll get our hair and nails done. Trust me, by the time we're finished, you'll feel like a new woman."

Naomi showered and dressed in her grey sweatsuit and white Nike Air Maxes, packing an extra outfit for after the spa. Tashi drove them to the spa, where two young masseuses worked on them with skillful hands. Both women emerged glowing, relaxed, and refreshed.

After changing into dresses and heels, they stopped at Starbucks for frappes before heading to the nail salon. Tashi chose orange nails to match her turquoise sundress, while Naomi opted for French tips with a cute design. Next, they made their way to the beauty salon where their friendship had begun, sharing the same beautician, Cynthia.

"Girl, I haven't seen you in a long time," Cynthia said when Naomi walked through the door.

"How long before I can get a chair?" Tashi asked.

"I can get both of y'all in about ten minutes, after I finish this client under the dryer. Go sit at my booth," Cynthia said.

Naomi walked over to Marco, who had an open chair.

"Hey Marco, can you hook me up?" Naomi asked.

"Sure, honey girl, please take a seat!" Marco said flamboyantly.

Cynthia raised an eyebrow. Naomi never let anyone else touch her hair, but today was different. Marco specialized in short cuts, and Naomi had something new in mind.

"Girl, I am not about to let you cut all this perfectly good hair!" Marco exclaimed.

By now, both Cynthia and Marco were standing over Naomi, running their hands through her thick hair that hung all the way down to her waist.

"Girl, you are blessed. Most women would kill for this," Cynthia said, shaking her head in disbelief.

"It'll grow back," Naomi replied calmly.

"I think we should pray," Marco joked. "Lord forgive this child, for she knows not what she does!" Everyone laughed except Naomi.

"Just cut the damn hair!" Naomi said in frustration.

"Que Lastima!" Marco said, shaking his head. He positioned the scissors and snip! The first chunk of hair fell to the floor, and Naomi felt an immediate sense of relief. With each section that dropped, the weight of her past, the drama at Big Momma's house, the bank robbery, Michael's death all lifted from her shoulders.

"Girl, this cut is going to be the bomb! Just wait until I put this color on," Marco said excitedly.

After coloring, washing, blow-drying, and flat ironing, Naomi's hair was perfect. Marco snapped photos for his hair book while Naomi beamed at her reflection. The short bob accentuated her cheekbones, and the bright red color made her light brown complexion glow.

"That cut is fire!" Tashi exclaimed.

"Thank you, girl. And you look good too," Naomi said, feeling confident.

"We just some bad bitches!"

"Ayyyeee!" they shouted, cracking up.

"My plan worked better than I expected," Tashi said, smiling. Naomi was a brand-new woman, her confidence restored.

"Girl, I'm starving. Let's get some grub. I know the perfect spot," Tashi said.

"Do not take me nowhere nasty."

"You know Club Live, right?"

"Yes. Everybody goes there."

"That's my spot. It's right next door. After eating, we can hit it up."

"I'm not going to a club with you! You don't know how to act."

"Bitch, you're boring! Club's under new management, and the restaurant next door is bomb. Plus, you look cute. You might as well go be seen."

They arrived at The Parlor Room. Naomi was impressed by the upscale vibe, the live band playing "Before I Let Go," and the happy-hour crowd. Men checked them out, but no one approached until a lanky man named Malcolm finally had the courage.

"How you ladies doing?" he asked, trying to look confident.

Tashi and Naomi exchanged looks, silently agreeing to ignore him. He leaned in close to Tashi.

"I know you can see yourself coming home with me," he said, flashing car keys.

"Am I supposed to be impressed? Boy, get your funky ass out of my face," Tashi snapped.

Malcolm got aggressive, tipping Tashi's glass of water onto her dress. Tashi retaliated with punches, and Malcolm grabbed her neck. Naomi sprayed him with mace, and before he could swing at her, a powerful man lifted him and delivered a serious beatdown before he was tossed out by restaurant staff. The whole restaurant watched, some recording the incident.

"My apologies, ladies," said the man, now calm and collected. Quinn had arrived just in time to intervene.

"I can assure you, this matter is taken care of," Quinn said smoothly.

Tashi and Naomi were grateful. Quinn introduced himself formally.

"Quinten Walters," he said, extending his hand to Tashi.

"It's nice to meet you, Quinten," she said flirtatiously.

"And to whom do I owe this pleasure?" he asked Naomi with mesmerized eyes.

"Naomi," she said, flatly.

"It's a pleasure to meet you," Quinn said, placing a gentle kiss on her forehand. Naomi felt a tingle and quickly pulled away.

"You two beautiful ladies should come by my club later. I'll have V.I.P. passes waiting, plus drinks on the house," he added before walking away confidently.

"He's definitely the owner," Tashi said, impressed.

"Yeah, he's cool," Naomi admitted.

The band restarted, the restaurant returned to normal, and the ladies enjoyed drinks on the house. Later, they headed next door to Club Live, VIP access in hand, spending the night drinking, dancing, and laughing.

The next morning, Naomi woke with a hangover but a clear memory of the man she had met. Quinn had left an impression she couldn't shake.

After some medicine to ease her hangover, Naomi refocused on her studies. Despite all the stress and hardship, she maintained a perfect 4.0 GPA. She was ready to hustle, find a new job, and her own place. She missed Michael, but she prided herself on being strong. It was time to move forward.

Ever since Quinn laid eyes on Naomi, he couldn't get her out of his mind. She was flawless, every inch a vision of perfection. From the moment he saw her, he wanted her on his arm. She looked familiar but he couldn't put his finger on it. Her name was all he knew, but it was enough. He had reach in his city; no one was out of touch. Within days, he would have one of his resources pull her entire background.

The next day, Quinn utilized his network, calling people who could provide intel on his new interest. A striking, light-brown diva with short, bright-red hair and the body of a goddess wasn't easy to miss. Yet, a week passed, and none of his contacts could locate a Naomi matching the description. Quinn suspected she was new in town. The city was like a small town so if she had been around long, someone would know her.

He regretted not getting her number at the restaurant. Women like Naomi always had men fighting for her attention. He had to make his move count. Quinn could only hope they would cross paths again.

"They're outside," Terrance said, watching the cameras from the club office.

Tank and Slime were at the back door, each carrying large duffle bags. Roc headed down to the entrance, where his cousin Randy stood guard.

"What's up, Roc?" Tank asked.

"What up, youngsters?" Roc replied.

"C'mon, dude. You're only two years older. Quit with that old-man energy."

"I'm still older, so respect your elder, young boy. Randy, make sure they're clean. Y'all know the procedure."

"Okay, hands up," Randy said, patting the young men down to check for weapons. "All clear."

"Can we come up now?" Slime asked.

"Yeah, y'all good."

They followed Roc upstairs to the office.

"What's the deal, young bloods?" Quinn asked.

"Not you too," Tank said, shaking his head.

"What can we do for y'all?" Quinn inquired, already knowing the answer.

"We need to place an order."

"How much?"

"Three kilos apiece."

"That'll run you a hundred twenty stacks."

"Not a problem," Tank said, placing a duffle bag of crisp cash on the table.

Quinn counted it, then Terrance pulled six kilos from the closet. The operation was smooth. Roc, Terrance, and Quinn coordinated the middleman work for trusted dealers. They didn't touch the streets or handle the cooking—clean and fast profits. Club money was steady, but drug money was fast and lucrative. Within months, Quinn was a millionaire, even closing on a ten-thousand-square-foot home in Madison Hills. The plan was to push the product for a year, then expand— opening clubs out of town and turning Club Live into a franchise. The American Dream was his for the taking.

The losses he'd endured like his father and one of his best friends had been painful, but Quinn believed he deserved this. He had fought too hard and survived too much to settle for anything less.

Across the street, Jamir and Chris watched Tank and Slime emerge from the club, duffle bags in hand. Since Damon and Brooklyn's demise, the Midwest Connection had crumbled. Their crew had lost access to the plug, leaving the streets dry. Suddenly, Tank and Slime had risen, their icy jewels and twin Audi coupes marking them as new shot callers.

"It's definitely going down with these niggas inside that club," Jamir said. "Inside those bags is money or dope."

"The owners are this clique called The Mafia. They used to do bank robberies until one of their homies got stung. They got out of the heist game and are running the club now," Chris added.

"Whatever it is, it's about to end. We're going to pop all of 'em—and anyone rolling with 'em," Jamir said, loading his semi-automatic. Revenge for his brother's death burned in his veins.

Meanwhile, Tank checked his phone. Jamesha's text flashed across the screen: *Come dick me down, daddy.* He smirked. Even though she belonged to another man, Tank had a weakness for taking what wasn't his.

"All right, my dude. Be careful with that sneaky bitch," Slime warned, knowing Jamir was a loose cannon.

Tank jumped into his Audi, speeding off to meet Jamesha. Slime popped the trunk of an old Toyota and loaded the two duffle bags inside, trying to remain inconspicuous.

A car across the street flashed its lights, engine revving. Slime tightened his grip on his pistol.

The car barreled toward him, high beams blinding his vision. He fired wildly, but the vehicle swerved past, unleashing a hail of bullets that pierced his body multiple times. Blood pooled around him as his body collapsed onto the asphalt.

The unknown car sped through the dark alley behind Club Live, disappearing into the night.

Knock! Knock! Knock!
Teresa heard three loud knocks at her door. Next, her doorbell was being rung repeatedly.

"Just a minute!" Teresa shouted as she made her way from the kitchen to the living room to answer her front door.

Ding! Dong! Ding! Dong! Ding! Dong! Ding! Dong! Knock! Knock! Knock! Knock! Knock! Knock!

They were pounding on her door like they were trying to break the thing down.

"I said just a minute, doggon- it!" Lord have mercy! That don't make no damn sense!" she shouted as she flung open her front door ready to curse somebody out. She didn't care who it was. When she looked out onto her porch it was empty.

"Them bad tail kids need a good old-fashioned whipping," she said referring to the kids who lived next door.

Their bad asses were always causing trouble and meddling in somebody's yard. It was obvious their parents weren't disciplining them the way they just ran around the neighborhood being mischievous. *"These young girls nowadays push out more babies than they can take care of.* Teresa thought to herself. *They let their children do whatever they want then wonder why they don't know how to mind nobody."* Teresa shut her door and walked back to her kitchen.

Knock! Knock! Knock! Knock! Knock! Knock!

Teresa hurried back to her front door ready to catch those kids before they ran away, but three unfamiliar men were standing on her porch when she cracked open her front door.

"How can I help y'all?"

"Police." Chris stated holding out his gold badge so she could see it. Teresa instantly spotted that it was a fake.

"Do you have a warrant?" Teresa asked.

"Look lady, open the door we need to ask you some questions."

"Sorry, but I can't help you," she said attempting to close her door but the three men kicked it open breaking the chain and causing the door to swing back and strike Teresa on the side of her forehead. She placed her hands on the part of her face where she had been struck. The three men barged into her house, one holding a gun.

"Get the hell out my house!" Teresa yelled at the intruders who had just kicked her door in. One was large and looked rugged. He was one of the roughest looking men she'd ever seen.

"Mmmm, it smells good in here," said Jamir who was holding a gun. He had Chris and his little homie Joc with him.

Teresa remembered her sweet potato pie that was in the oven. She had cooked a complete Sunday dinner with fried chicken, macaroni, yams, mashed potatoes, meatloaf, and corn pudding. She was waiting for her church sisters, to arrive for the dinner that she had prepared.

"What's that you cooking?" Joc asked.

"I'm calling the cops!" Teresa said rushing toward the kitchen to the telephone.

Before she could make it through her dining room, one of the men had pulled her by her ponytail causing her to fall backward into his chest. It was the one with

147

the gun. His hand was gripped firmly around her throat now. His grip got tighter and tighter until he was cutting off all oxygen from entering her lungs. She started feeling dizzy and desperately tried to gasp for any ounce of oxygen she could possibly inhale. After just one minute of being choked out, Teresa felt her lungs giving out and her body drifting into unconsciousness. *"Lord Jesus help me!"* She silently pleaded as she fought with every bit of strength, she had left to break free from the man but he was much stronger than her.

She squirmed like a worm throwing her body weight around causing him to briefly lose his grip around her throat. She clamped her teeth into his arm and bit into his skin ferociously.

"Got damn!" Jamir shouted. He was rubbing his arm that was leaking blood from being bitten.

Again, Teresa tried to dash to the kitchen, but the speed of a forty-three-year-old woman was no match for the young man. The big ugly one quickly blocked her path. He slapped her then grabbed her by the neck. You a fine little old bitch Chris said blowing scorching hot breath into her ear. He was choking the life out of her.

She felt his hard penis against her buttocks, and he was licking around her ear lobe then began biting while grinding his hard penis against her. Teresa felt nauseated and her stomach formed into knots. She threw up in her mouth, but it went right back down. She used her elbow to send a blow to his groin causing him to buckle to his knees. Joc grabbed her and threw her onto the ground. The three men began stomping and kicking her repeatedly. Her body anguished as they crushed her feeble limbs. She blacked out on the verge of complete unconsciousness. The gunman man stood over her as he pointed his gun at her.

"You're dead bitch, and your bastard son is next!" Joc said.

Teresa thought about her only son. He was her entire world. *God, I forbid anything ever happen to my baby. Protect him Lord please.*

Pow! Pow! Pow!

Jamir fired three shots into her frame.

Cold As Ice

Quinn turned down the block where he grew up in his brand-new black Mercedes Benz G-Wagon. His mind was elsewhere, thinking about his mother's future. The house his grandfather had passed down would soon be just a memory. She was moving somewhere far away, somewhere bigger, better.

Quinn had just received the keys to his new home in Madison Hills, a mansion where she could live free of the hood's chaos. This had been his dream since he was a kid—to give his mother a life free from struggle. On top of that, he had a legitimate business she could be proud of. After years of sacrifice and hardship, it was finally over. She would never have to work again. He imagined handing her the keys to the Benz, watching her drive to her new home, free from worry and danger.

But lately, danger had been closer than he liked. His little homie, Slime, had just been murdered, and the guilt gnawed at him. More than that, the killer was still out there, and Quinn's paranoia grew by the day.

"What the hell happened here?" He pulled the G-Wagon to a stop in front of the house he knew so well.

Yellow tape blocked the front porch. Cop cars filled the driveway, red and blue lights flashing and painting the block in chaos. Something was wrong. Quinn's hand went to his hip, brushing the gun tucked between his Versace boxers and Hudson jeans. He tucked it into the glove compartment, stepped out in his Giuseppe sneakers, and scanned the scene. Half the neighborhood had gathered across the street, whispering and staring.

"Quinten!" Sister Robinson's voice broke through the chaos. She ran toward him, tears streaming down her face.

"They shot her!" she cried, grabbing his shoulders and shaking him. "They kicked down the door and shot her in her own house!"

Quinn froze. "Wait... they shot who?" His voice was sharp, urgent.

She couldn't answer fast enough before his mind raced to the worst. He bolted toward the porch, stomach twisting with dread. A dozen officers turned, blocking his way.

"This is a crime scene. You need to leave," a young cop said firmly.

"This is my mama's house! What happened?!" Quinn barked, ignoring the officer.

"Sir, this premise is under investigation. Detectives can assist you..."

"I don't care about no detectives! This is my mama's house! Where is she? Tell me what happened?!"

His phone rang. Roc. Quinn snatched it up.

"Hello?"

"Bro, where are you at?" Roc asked.

"I'm at my mom's. Cops everywhere. They won't let me in. I'm trying to figure out what happened."

"They haven't told you?"

"No. What's going on? What happened to my mom?" Quinn's heart pounded like a drum in his chest.

"She was rushed to Renaissance Hospital. I was riding down the block and seen the yellow tape. Neighbors outside said ambulance rushed your moms out her house. I just left. I'm driving to the hospital now."

"Did they tell you what happened?"

"Man, just get over there." Roc hung up before Quinn could protest.

Quinn tore back to the Benz and sped toward the hospital, nausea clawing at his throat. Sister Robinson had said she'd been shot, but he prayed the God his mother believed in was real—that she was still alive. A sharp pain in his chest whispered otherwise. He ran every red light, racing against time and fear.

At the emergency entrance, he skidded to a stop, ignoring tow trucks or tickets. Roc and Terrance pulled up behind him. Quinn barreled through the hospital doors, pushing toward the check-in desk, where an indifferent aide was scrolling her phone.

"I need to know what room Teresa West is in!" Quinn snapped, voice rough.

"I'll call you back," she said, annoyed. Quinn could see the irritation in her eyes.

"Can you hurry up!"

"Sir, calm down before I call security."

"Fuck security! My mother just got shot!"

"Ms. West is in intensive care, third floor. There's a waiting room for family—"

Quinn didn't wait. He bolted to the elevator, hitting the up button, his heart hammering in his chest.

On the third floor, two large doors led to the waiting room. As Quinn entered, Aunt Joanne barreled toward him.

"You did this to her!" she screamed, spittle landing on his chin. "If it wasn't for you, none of this would've happened! Because of your reckless actions, thugs kicked down my sister's door and shot her in cold blood! Now she has to suffer!"

She slapped him, then swung again. Quinn dodged, Terrance stepping in to separate them.

"Look, he doesn't need this right now! His mom just got shot! We need to keep it together and pray she pulls through," Terrance said, breathless.

Quinn sank into a chair, head in his hands. It all felt unreal, like a nightmare he couldn't wake from.

♦ ♦ ♦

"We have a black woman in her forties with two gunshots to the appendix and one to the spine."

Cindy handed Stephens her cell phone with a photograph of the injured victim who was lying in a pool of blood with three gunshot wounds. "A friend of hers walked in to find her like this."

"Looks like whoever tried to dust this lady was in rage," Detective Stephens said, frowning at the severe bruises to the victim's face.

"Yeah, but why, who would this forty-three-year-old woman have that kind of beef with?"

"I bet its gang related. She's obviously somebody's mother or even grandmother. These young gangsters are ruthless. If you have beef, they're going to hunt you down and if they can't kill you, your closest relatives they'll pay a visit. It's a cold game. Do we have a murder weapon?" Detective Stephens inquired.

"We do not have one. Whoever committed this act collected the shell casings prior to fleeing the scene."

"What about fingerprints?"

"None, we scanned the entire house and found only matches to the victim."

"Are there any other tenants occupying the house?"

"The victim lives alone and whoever killed her definitely took advantage of that."

"Hey, Whitmore!" Detective Stephens waved over the newly hired young detective.

"Detective, how can I be of help?"

"You can start by getting into contact with forensics. I need a full inspection on the entire place for any fingerprints or DNA evidence. Cindy, I need you to get me info on any relatives of the victim or close acquaintances. If the victim does not survive, I'm sure there's someone close this woman who's going to have her blood on their hands."

Meanwhile at Renaissance Hospital, about forty-five minutes had passed. Quinn looked up to see Tank,

Terrance, Roc, and Vanilla, his Aunt Joanne and her family and his mother's church sisters and even Pastor Jonathan had showed up. Tension inside the hospital room was thick. Everyone sat quietly waiting for the results of the surgery. No one said a word as they waited to hear good news. Pastor Jonathan gathered everyone in a circle to say a prayer. It was the first genuine prayer Quinn said in a long time.

Two hours had passed, and everyone was getting restless and anxious. Quinn's stomach was in knots. He needed to hear his mother's sweet voice, to touch her and tell her he loved her. All he wanted to do was lift her up, but in the process, he had let her down. After two hours that felt like an eternity, the doctor who held the life of his mother in his hands slowly walked into the waiting room. Everyone stood up almost all at the same time.

"Who may I speak to about the patient?" the doctor asked.

Quinn jumped in the doctor's face. "Me, I'm her son. I'm the closest person to her."

"I regret that we were unsuccessful in our attempts to revive the patient."

"So, what are you saying?"

"The patient did not survive the surgery, and she has passed away."

Quinn's heart dropped to his feet at that very moment.

"What? No! You have to do something else man! You can't let her go! You can't do that!"

"I'm sorry, but we did everything thing we could to try to save the patient."

"Arrrrgh…" The vomit that Quinn was trying to suppress was forced out.

"Are you okay, dawg?" Terrance said trying to hold Quinn up because he was struggling to keep his composure.

At that very moment, Quinn felt like he passed out even though he was conscious. He couldn't hear or see anything. There was sharp pain in his chest like a dagger stabbing through his heart. It was the worst pain that he'd ever felt.

Love In The Midst Of Tragedy

The church smelled faintly of lilies and candle wax. Quinn hadn't stepped inside one in nearly three years, and today he wished more than anything he didn't have to. But this was his mother. Teresa.

The sanctuary was full of neighbors, churchgoers, people who had known her forever. Some glanced at Quinn with thinly veiled judgment. He could feel their stares crawling over him, as if they could see the serpents of his sins winding across his skin.

He didn't care. Not about their looks. Not about the pastor, Jesus, the Virgin Mary, or any of the other holy names painted on stained glass. If there was a God, how could He let a woman who prayed every night, who lived her life by the book, die like that?

Quinn's brothers slid into the front row with him. Terrance leaned close.

"I'm sorry for your loss, family. I can't even imagine how you feel right now."

Quinn nodded once. Without them, he wasn't sure he could've walked in here at all.

The casket was closed—his decision. Nobody needed to see her as she had been when she died.

Pastor Jonathan stepped up to the altar, waiting for the last coughs and whispers to fade before beginning his sermon. Naomi and Ms. Winston slipped quietly into the back. Naomi's chest tightened when she saw the memorial photo of Sister Teresa. She still couldn't believe the woman who'd been so kind to her was gone.

The pastor's voice filled the room.
"Good morning, family and friends…" He read from Second Corinthians, his words rolling through the church like a tide. Verses about judgment, about choices, about the lake of fire. About salvation.

Quinn stared straight ahead; jaw locked. He wasn't here for sermons.

"The Lord's word says in verse ten, "For we must all appear before the judgment seat of Christ, so that each of us may receive what is due us for the things done while in the body, whether good or bad." So, we should know that Sister Teresa was called home to be with the Lord and we know that by the type of life that she led exactly where she will be in the afterlife.

"My brothers and sisters, if any of you are non-believers, I strongly suggest you take heed to what I have to say today. For all my non-believers there will be consequences to pay for your actions here on earth. There will be a judgment day and Christ will either say, "job well done my faithful servant," or he'll say,

158

"I never knew you." You must choose your actions wisely because the type of life you choose to live here on earth will determine where you go in the afterlife. See, God gave us all free will, the choice between good and evil, dark and light, life and death. His word says therefore choose life!..."

Most of the church began to shout praises, but Quinn had heard enough. He wasn't feeling it and tuned out the rest of the sermon until the pastor began to conclude his righteous rant.

"At this time, we'd like to invite to the alter anyone who would like to come pay their respects and speak on behalf of the deceased."

From the back, Naomi rose. God's voice was urging her to speak. Quinn's breath caught. *It's her.* The girl he couldn't find but looked high and low for. *What is she doing here?* Out of all places where he could run into her, he would have never expected it. Several people had gotten up to speak on behalf of Sister Teresa. Most of the people who spoke, praised her for being a saint.

When Naomi reached the podium, she hesitated, then spoke.
"I may not have known Ms. Teresa as long as most of you..." Her voice trembled but held steady. "...but for the short amount of time I was able to spend with her she touched me very deeply. I was dealing with the loss of a close loved one when Ms. Teresa and I met, and she was there to comfort me in those hard times."

Naomi vaguely spoke of dinners, check-in calls, prayers, and kindness. Of how Teresa had lifted her in her own time of grief.

At the cemetery, the air was cooler, the sky washed in gray. The final prayer was said. Red roses lay across the polished wood of the casket. Quinn stayed behind as everyone drifted away, murmuring to his mother's grave about everything he never got to say.

Roc stepped up, offering a joint. "This won't take away the pain, but it'll ease your mind, fam."

Quinn shook his head. "I just need time to myself right now."

"Okay, but we will be checking up on you." Roc and Terrance hugged Quinn then left him alone to deal with his grief.

When his friends finally left, Naomi lingered in the distance, watching. She walked up quietly.

"Who was she to you?"

"She was my mother."

"I'm so sorry for your loss."

She was one of the few who'd spoken to him without judgment. She didn't know the rumors—how people said the men who killed Teresa had been looking for Quinn. She didn't know he half believed it himself.

"I hate this had to be the place where we'd cross paths again," he said.

"I remember a woman told me there's a reason why things happen, even bad things. Ms. Teresa was a very sweet lady. She was one of the people who was there for me when I recently lost a close loved one. I will be praying for you and your family."

"Thank you for coming to pay your respect. I appreciate that."

"No need to thank me, you just take care of yourself. Maybe I'll see you around."

Before Naomi could completely turn away to leave, Quinn caught her by the wrist. Instantly she felt the electricity between them when they touched.

"It was a pleasure see you again, Naomi." Quinn kissed the backside of her hand again sending a chill up and through her arm. He smiled at her warmly and she couldn't help but to blush.

"Oh yeah, Quinten, right?" she said as if she didn't remember his name, but the truth was she remembered him clearly and was attracted to him the first time they'd met.

That same attraction was still there even at a gloomy moment in time, and it was different not like when she'd met Michael, this attraction was much stronger.

"I don't think it's good for you to be alone," she said surprising herself that she was being so straight forward. "I mean, if you don't have anyone to talk to, I wouldn't mind keeping you company."

"I'd like that. You can come to my place. We can talk and have a drink," Quinn said still holding onto her hand.

He was in need of having someone around to comfort him, but the love of his homies was too rough. He needed a soothing voice to speak to him.

"Where do you live?" Naomi asked as Quinn walked her back to her Honda. He was still holding her hand.

"Madison Hills."

"Isn't that like a gated community?"

"No, there aren't any gates or guards at the front entrance, but it is kind of a private community. Just follow me over there."

Quinn opened Naomi's driver door and then closed it after she got it in.

Quinn got into to his Mercedes G-Wagon and pressed a button to start the engine. The houses grew larger, grander. When they reached his, her eyes widened at a brick estate at the end of a cul-de-sac, complete with a fountain in the circular drive. It was like something out of another world.

Naomi stepped through the front door, her eyes scanning the room. "This is a nice place, but do you ever clean up?" she asked, taking in the clutter.

"Sorry, I just haven't gotten around to it lately," Quinn admitted.

Dirty dishes cluttered the counters, dust clung to the floors, and the faint odor of garbage lingered in the air.

"It's okay. I'll help you out, but first, where can I sit my coat and purse?"

"I'll take that from you," Quinn said, relieving her of the coat and hanging it neatly in the coat closet.

"So how about you pull that trash and I'll help you handle the rest."

Naomi made her way into the kitchen, found a stash of cleaning supplies under the sink, and rolled up the sleeves of her blouse. She began scrubbing the dishes while Quinn rinsed them beside her. From there, they moved through the house sweeping, vacuuming, dusting the ceiling fans, and wiping down windows.

An hour later, the place looked transformed. Naomi even unearthed a few forgotten candles, lit them, and let the warm, sweet fragrance drift through the rooms. When they were done, they collapsed together onto the living room sofa, catching their breath.

"You are better than when the cleaning service comes, plus it smells wonderful. I mean really, thank you for cleaning, it's immaculate in here."

"I'm a little beat, it's not like this place is small, but if you have to hire a cleaning service, that means you're definitely in the need of a woman in your life."

"Maybe one day that could change?"

Naomi felt her cheeks warm. "So, tell me why you're single. You're young, successful, and good looking— I'm sure you have a lady in your life or should I say multiple ladies."

"So, you think I'm handsome?"

"Just answer the question," she said, blushing again.

"See, I made you do it twice."

"Do what?"

"Smile."

"Are you going to answer my question, or is this one of your player moves to avoid that?"

"Okay, well the truth is I actually don't have any women in my life. I just haven't found that special one, as they say. Now what about you? Do you have a man?"

"No."

"Why not? A woman as fine as you, I know brothas are trying to get at you left and right."

"After my last relationship ended, I haven't been in the right space to even think about being with another man."

"What caused things to end?" Quinn tried to keep his tone gentle. He didn't want to pry, but curiosity tugged at him.

Naomi's gaze dropped. "My boyfriend passed away and I've just been taking things slowly. It's a process, but I'm getting through day by day."

"Damn, really? I mean, I'm really sorry to hear that. How did your man die?"

"I don't want to talk about that," she said softly, fighting to keep her emotions in check.

"If you ever want to talk, I'm here."

A silence fell over them—heavy, awkward, and difficult to break.

"I just want to help you how your mother helped me. That's the least I can do."

"You still haven't told me how you know my mother."

"She was like a mentor for me. I met her at the church. My boyfriend's mother is a member there. When he passed, we spent so much time together helping each other mourn. We spent so much time at the church, I'm surprised we never met each other there."

"I hardly ever go to church. Even as a kid, I'd think of every excuse to stay home, so eventually my mom stopped making me go."

"Ms. Teresa used to invite me over to her house for Sunday dinner sometimes. She did mention she had a son, now that I think about it. How come you never came over?"

"Anything that has to do with church and God is something I'm just not into. I prefer not to be around a bunch of people when they're preaching that gospel stuff. My mother tried to push it on me, but it just didn't make any sense to me."

"So, you don't believe in God?"

Quinn hesitated, choosing his words carefully. "I just find it hard to believe there's a God with all the bad going on in this world. My mother was an avid believer in God, and the way she died... I just don't know if I can believe in a God that would allow something like that to happen to her."

"She was a very nice woman, but God's working is unexplainable. You must trust him even when things are bad. He doesn't want someone who only believes in him when things are going well. That means you don't really love him. That's one of the things God has been teaching me."

"So, you're one of those church girls who go to church every week, virgin until marriage, huh?"

"No, I'm going to be honest. I'm a sinner just like anyone else, but I do believe in the Lord and that he is the highest power."

"I don't know God, and I don't know if there is a heaven or hell. All I know about is right now, and that's how I've always lived my life."

"Maybe one day that can change. Life is deeper than what's happening in the here and now, Quentin. Your body will die one day just like your mother's, but whether your spirit lives forever will depend on you. This life is a test to see if you really want to live or die, so choose life."

Her words lingered in Quinn's mind. *Choose life.* That was exactly what the preacher had said earlier. For a flicker of a moment, he wondered if they might all be right—his mother, the preacher, and Naomi. But just as quickly, he pushed the thought away. He had already chosen his path, and it wasn't one that led to church pews.

"It does make me feel good that my mother had a positive impact on your life."

"She was such a strong believer."

Naomi could see his thoughts turning behind his eyes. She wanted to help him find the faith he'd lost, but she knew now wasn't the time to press.

"So, how did you get into the club and restaurant business?" Naomi asked, easing the mood.

"Well, I started about a year ago. My partners and I put our money together and purchased the club from the previous owner. I wanted that club so bad. Now, I honestly don't even want to think about it."

"I get it."

"So, what are you into?"

"Right now, I'm a full-time student."

"That's cool. What are you majoring in?"

"Accounting."

"That's interesting. What made you want to pursue that field?"

"The money, really. I need a career, not just a job. Plus, I have finance experience."

"That makes sense. So how many years of school do you have left?"

"Three more years and all my hard work will finally pay off."

"College was never for me. After high school, I needed money and didn't have time to wait years for a degree."

"Looks like you knew what you were doing."

"Anybody can do what I did. You just have to have the mindset that you're going to be your own boss. Then you make a plan to do what it takes to make it happen."

Naomi studied him for a moment. His confidence wasn't just talk—he carried himself like a man who had never doubted a decision in his life.

"Do you mind if I play some music for us?" Quinn offered.

"Sure, that would be nice."

He crossed the room to the stereo and queued up Jill Scott's Do You Remember.

"This is my jam; I absolutely love her! She is my favorite artist."

"Mine too."

Naomi's lips curved into a smile. They were racking up more things in common.

"I have a few bottles of wine in my cellar. What kind would you like, white or red?" Quinn asked.

"What do you mean a few bottles? That thing is stocked like a liquor store. Anyway, I would prefer a Merlot if you have that."

"I definitely do. That is my favorite."

"I guess that's another thing we have in common."

Quinn returned a moment later with a tray, two wine glasses, a decanter, a vintage bottle, and a wine key. He poured, set the bottle on the table, and leaned back in his seat.

"What are your hobbies?" he asked.

"I read a lot."

"That's cool. I like to dabble in a book sometimes."

"I love it. It opens your mind to new perspectives and outlooks you may have never considered. Plus, I consider the art of storytelling the greatest art of all. Isn't that why we're all here, to tell our own unique stories? No matter who you are, woman or man, old or young, everyone has one to tell the world."

"I couldn't agree with you more. Can I be honest with you, Naomi?"

"Yes, I want you to," she replied, caught off guard by his tone.

"When I first saw you in my restaurant, I was captivated by you. I even looked around everywhere, hoping I'd see you again."

Naomi's pulse quickened. She wanted to tell him she'd felt the same spark, that something about him had stayed in her thoughts. The way he looked at her now made her feel like he could see every thought she wasn't saying.

"I was attracted to you too," Naomi admitted.

Quinn's gaze held hers. She could feel her breathing change, heat curling in her belly.

"I want to kiss your lips," Quinn said.

He leaned in slowly, stopping just short until she closed the distance herself. Their lips met, slow, deep, and unhurried. Naomi felt herself melt into the warmth of him.

"It's getting late. I should go," she murmured, realizing how quickly she'd let her guard down.

"You don't have to go."

"I can't stay the night with you, Quinten. I mean, we just met."

"I apologize for coming on too strong but trust me when I say I don't want anything from you. I just want to keep enjoying your company."

"I need a shower. Plus, I don't have any night clothes or even a toothbrush."

"Don't worry. I have a spare toothbrush, and I can wash your clothes. You can shower and put on a pair of my shorts and one of my T-shirts, I don't mind. I'll get you some towels so you can shower in my bathroom. When you're done, you can sleep in my bed. I'll sleep here on the sofa."

"Really, you don't have—"

Before she could finish, Quinn stood. "Follow me."

It was more command than request, but Naomi didn't argue. His quiet authority was oddly magnetic.

Upstairs, he handed her a stack of towels and a new toothbrush. "My shorts and shirts are in my dresser. Help yourself to whatever pairs you want," he said before leaving her alone.

Naomi shut the door behind her, undressed, and stepped into the shower. Four jets of hot water cascaded from every angle, washing away the sweat from their cleaning marathon earlier. Steam clouded the glass until she wiped it clear with a hand towel and froze.

Through the glass, a shadow moved.

For a moment, she imagined Quinn standing there, naked, watching her. In her mind, his body was sculpted, his gaze hungry. She pictured herself opening the shower door, inviting him in, feeling his hands and lips, the slow press of him inside her until her body arched in sweet surrender.

The fantasy was so vivid she almost laughed at herself. *Pull it together, Naomi.* She shut off the water, wrapped a towel around herself, and brushed her teeth.

In Quinn's dresser, she found a plain white T-shirt and, instead of oversized shorts, a pair of his boxers, tying them at the side for a snug fit. His bed was large, soft, and smelled faintly of his cologne.

A soft knock came at the door.

"Come in."

"Are you doing okay?" Quinn asked.

"Yes, I'm good."

"I have your clothes being washed right now."

"Okay, thank you."

"No problem."

"Good night, Ms. Naomi."

"Good night, Quinten."

Nearly three weeks passed, and Naomi and Quinn were living like a couple. Naomi took the time alone while Quinn was working to prepare for her next semester which was just a few days away. She was beginning to feel like a housewife, aside from the fact that she had no children. She spent most of the day cooking, cleaning, reading, watching soaps and chatting over the phone with Tashi. Tashi asked every day if they'd had sex yet, but the answer was no.

Quinn purposely avoided intimacy which made Naomi sometimes wonder if he was into her. He assured her that he has was. If he wasn't, he definitely would not have allowed her into his space in the way she was currently occupying it.

A few times they had shared a passionate kiss that she felt would lead to something, but Quinn always put a stop to it. His reason was that he didn't feel it was the right time and he wanted Naomi to know that he wanted more than just sex with her.

It was the first time a man had shown her that he was more interested in her mentally than physically. The bad part was it only made Naomi yearn for him even more. It had been a while, and her womanly desires were growing while the sexual tension was becoming too strong.

One cozy evening Naomi and Quinn cuddled up on the couch. As she nestled in his arms, her hands were on his chest. He consistently smelled good, his scent one of the things she liked most about him. Quinn stroked Naomi's hair playfully his fingers running through her short hair. He massaged her temples with his fingertips.

"That feels great." She looked up at Quinn her hazel eyes sparkling.

"You're so beautiful," Quinn admitted, looking into them

"Don't do that."

Naomi couldn't handle when he looked at her in that way. Quinn licked his lips and then bit his bottom lip and Naomi felt a tingle. He pulled her up to his eye level their faces so close enough to feel each other breathing. Quinn gripped her chin; Naomi closed her eyes. She liked how he took charge. Their lips touched, Naomi and Quinn were momentarily lost in time. The light moisture of Quinn's lips heightened the sensation.

He made love to Naomi's mouth. Their passionate tonguing felt so great that neither one of them could control their lustful craving. Naomi could feel Quinn throbbing against her pelvic area. There was so much heat between their bodies that their clothes were summoned off.

Quinn descended into Naomi's Ocean like a submarine. Like a warship, he submerged himself to the depths of her abyss. *"Sheesh its, so big. He's hitting my spot,"* Naomi thought.

Naomi was extra tight since she hadn't been opened in several months. Quinn took it easy but could barely control himself. Naomi opened her legs wider, Quinn wanted more. Her pussy pulled him in like a suction cup. Quinn stretched her walls with his strokes. It was the sweetest pain Naomi had ever felt. He switched up his rhythm, slow and gentle then hard and fast, giving her variety until she found the perfect pace.

"Oh yes! Right there!" she screamed.

An earthquake surged inside her. It was her best orgasm ever, a few minutes later it was more intense. Her body trembled; she gripped the cushion of the leather.

"You feel so good," Quinn whispered in her ear. "Whose pussy is this?".

"It's yours," she responded without protest. His whispers in her ear while he rocked in and out were activating a faucet that flowed down her thighs. *It's happening again.* Naomi thought.

Naomi felt Quinn's muscles tighten as she wrapped her arms and legs around his back. She knew what that meant. He was about to feel the same pleasure that he'd given her.

"Cum for me again. I want to feel you," Quinn spoke into her ear. His command was instantly granted.

Naomi climaxed for twenty seconds then it lingered. Her walls were sore from his size. Quinn pulled back from inside her using all his might to do it. He spread his seed all over. The sticky warmth dripping on Naomi's skin, she gently stroked his wood until the last drop oozed out.

"That was so amazing," Naomi said while looking up at Quinn who had sweat above his brow.

He wiped his forehead then lifted her body, carrying her in his arms then up the stairs to his master bedroom. Inside the bathroom is where he sat her down in the Jacuzzi tub. Quinn turned on the water and pressed his jets, causing bubbles to flow through. He walked out of the bathroom, leaving her alone in the small pool of rising hot water.

Once the tub was almost completely full, Naomi turned the hot and cold knobs to the off position. Sitting back, she relaxed her body. Her kitty felt sore, but immensely satisfied. Quinn re-entered the bathroom with a bottle of wine and two stemware to pour them both a drink.

"Was it good to you?" Naomi questioned.

Quinn had not spoken a word since their finish. He seemed as if he were deep in thought.

"That was amazing."

"You're so quiet."

"I'm just thinking."

"What's on your mind?"

"You are."

Naomi didn't say anything else and neither did Quinn. He just held her as she laid between his legs. The combination of the great sex, a relaxing bath, and champagne had them both tired. Quinn crawled into bed and nestled behind Naomi placing a kiss on the back of her neck. She smiled at his sweet and affection. Within minutes of sinking into the mattress sleep hormones were triggered and they both knocked out cold.

Quinn stood over her as Naomi opened her eyes.

"Were you watching me sleep?" she asked, rubbing her eyelids.

"I was."

"That's creepy."

"How? I'm admiring a beautiful woman, lying in my bed. How are you feeling this morning?"

"I feel great. The D you gave me put me in a coma. Last night was amazing, the way you made my body feel."

Quinn grinned coyly.

"Get dressed; I have plans for us today."

Naomi was learning that Quinn was quite assertive and thought ahead. It was sexy to her. She took a quick shower and put on an easy outfit that she'd packed. Quinn took her out for brunch at one of his favorite spots. As a full-time college student, it wasn't often that Naomi got to eat at fine restaurants.

"I have a surprise for you," Quinn said as they were walking out, bellies full.

"What is it?"

"If I told you, it wouldn't be a surprise now, would it?"

"Ugh you suck," Naomi faked a pout poking her lips outward.

"You won't be looking like that when you see what I have planned, just wait. And just to make sure you don't cheat; you have to wear this over your eyes." Quinn took a blindfold from his pocket and positioned it over Naomi's eyes.

"Where are you taking me?"

"Do you trust me?"

"I do."

It was true. Even though Naomi hadn't known Quinn long, she felt safe in his presence. Quinn drove them for about forty minutes.

"Are we there yet?" Naomi questioned feeling restless.

They'd been driving long enough that she could be halfway out of town somewhere. Several minutes later, she could feel Quinn was slowing his Mercedes to a much lower speed and then the car stopped for several seconds. Quinn made a phone call to someone.

"I'm here."

Naomi heard the sound of something loud but could not make out what it was, then the SUV pulled off slowly. A minute later, they stopped again. Naomi heard very loud noises on the outside of the SUV.

"Okay. We're here. You can finally look now."

Naomi removed her blindfold, and she was staring at a jet ready to take off.

"Where are we going?" she asked baffled. She didn't have any luggage and was completely unprepared for a trip.

"Don't worry, we're not going far."

"Where's not far?"

"Los Angeles. I'll have you back in town by the weekend."

"But why?" What's the point?"

"Okay. I will tell you this, as much as I love seeing you in my T-shirts; I have some things in mind that I'd much rather see you in."

"So, you're taking me on a private jet across the country just to take me shopping?"

"Is that too much?" Quinn asked seriously.

"Yeah. I've never had anyone surprise me like this."

"You've never met a man like me baby."

Quinn got out of the G-Wagon then went over to the passenger door and opened it for Naomi.

"Will you take this flight with me?" he asked, extending his hand.

"Yes."

Naomi was lost for words. Quinn's surprise was over the top. Completely in shock, she boarded a private jet for the first time. It was spacious and comfy. They had two pilots and a personal flight attendant. After leaving the LAX private airport, they arrived in the world-famous Beverly Hills shopping district better known as Rodeo drive.

"You look gorgeous." Quinn complemented as Naomi walked out the dressing room in a black Fendi dress and heels in front of a full body mirror.

"I must admit, I definitely agree," said the sales associate.

"How much is this dress?" Naomi asked

"It's seven hundred and fifty dollars," the sales associate stated.

"It doesn't matter the price. She'll take it and whatever else she likes."

Quinn cashed out in the Fendi store but that wasn't the only store he dropped dough in.

They explored, St. Laurent, Dolce & Gabbana, Tom Ford, Neiman Marcus, and Fendi just to name a few. Very few stores were left untouched. Naomi had so many bags that they were both struggling to carry them on top of fitting them in their car. Quinn had spent over twenty thousand dollars and didn't even break a sweat about it.

"Okay, so you remember that I said I had a surprise for you?" Quinn asked once they were back in their car and heading to the Waldorf Astoria hotel where they would be spending the night.

"I thought this was your surprise." Naomi couldn't imagine what other tricks Quinn had up his sleeve.

"I promise it's not anything outlandish. It's just that we have this big event we have going on at the club and I want you to be my date for tomorrow night. I'm sure you'll have no problem picking out an outfit since you have so many new items."

"Are you kidding? Having so many options, is the difficult part."

"So, will you go with me?"

"Of course! I'd love to."

"Great!" Quinn said with a big smile like he was super excited.

The next morning, the private jet shot them back home. Naomi had an entirely new closet. Most of her old clothes would be discarded now that she owned so many high-end materials. After setting up her clothes, she had only covered a piece of the space in the closet. Quinn's master bedroom had a second walk-in closet that he hadn't even touched. It now belonged to her since she had basically moved in. She was moving fast with a man she'd just officially met a few weeks ago. It wasn't like her to ever get involved quickly but Quinn had her falling for him hard.

Nonetheless, their new companionship was helping them both heal the pain of their losses. Naomi pulled out the Fendi dress and a pair of red bottoms. She slipped

DEON WRIGHT

on the dress and heels, then grabbed the clutch she would be using for the night.

Cynthia had touched up her mane and Tashi hooked up her makeup once she'd gotten back in town. Naomi was flawless. Quinn watched in amazement as Naomi walked down his stairwell. He'd never seen a woman wear short bright hair so well and in an upscale dress, Naomi was extremely classy but still sexy.

"You look stunning," Quinn said before placing a kiss on Naomi's cheek. Quinn couldn't wait to enter his club with her on his arm.

"You're pretty dapper yourself."

"Thanks," he bit his bottom lip then tugged at the sides of his blazer.

Quinn walked her out to his Mercedes and then opened Naomi's door. He drove them to the front of his nightclub parking right outside the front of the building. After pulling the passenger door, he extended his hand to help Naomi out. Quinn led Naomi past a crowd of people waiting to get inside. They walked right through the front door, past the metal detectors and the bouncers patting down everyone who entered the building.

Everyone in the club was dressed in their best for a special black-tie affair. It was a great impression for their potential investor that Club Live was a classy and upscale place.

"Who is this?" Vanilla asked when Quinn entered the club with a pretty young thing clinging to his arm.

"This is my lovely lady, Naomi. Naomi, this is Vanilla."

179

"It's nice to meet you, Naomi. You've done well, she's beautiful, Quinn. He even introduced you as his lady, that's a first. You must be someone special," Vanilla said giving Naomi a wink.

Quinn began to introduce Naomi to everyone including Roc, Terrance and a few of his employees. Shortly thereafter, Mr. Rosenberg was escorted up to VIP by the club host.

"Good evening, Mr. Rosenberg." Quinn said extending his hand to the investor.

"Hello, Quinten. It's nice to finally meet you."

"Please sit down and join us." Quinn poured Mr. Rosenberg a glass of his favorite wine.

"This is a nice turn out you have tonight."

"Let's let the men tend to their business, we need to have our own little chat." Vanilla whispered to Naomi.

"So, how did you and Quinn meet?" Vanilla probed while they walked.

"I met him in the restaurant next door."

"And how long has Quinn been hiding you?"

Naomi laughed. "We actually just started seeing each other."

"Uh huh. Are you and Quinn fucking?"

Naomi was appalled that Vanilla would straight up ask her that. She didn't feel comfortable exposing her intimate business.

"Hey, I see some friends of mine, can you excuse me for a second?" Naomi had just found the perfect excuse to avoid Vanilla's question.

"Yeah, go ahead." Vanilla smirked knowing the answer to her question.

DEON WRIGHT

She stopped a table where Tashi and Cynthia were sitting.

"Hey girl!" Naomi said, approaching the women.

"Girl, look at you!" said Tashi

Naomi stepped back a little so they could check her out from head to toe.

"Are those Christian Louboutins? This man must have you wide open because I've never seen you glowing so much."

"Girl you are a mess."

"I'm just calling it how I see it. I can see wedding bells and little rug rats in the near future."

"Hold on, we haven't gotten that far yet."

"Why not? He obviously he has the means to take care of you."

"Girl, I am focused on school. Right now, that is my main priority."

"Are you going to introduce us to the man who's been taking up all of my friend's time?"

Quinn and Roc had put their finesse on Mr. Rosenberg now Quinn was ready to lure him in and secure the deal.

"I'm sure you noticed that we are very busy, in fact we are the most prominent night club in this city. Our clientele is growing which is why we are looking to expand. We have seen much success because we stand by one simple principle. That is, "Know Your Guest." We get intimate with them in a way that most other nightclubs don't. If there's a certain cocktail, we know one of our most consistent guests prefers, we offer it to them on arrival. We let that guest know we remember.

181

It's all about building good relationships. With that being said, I've also been thinking ahead to the future and want to expand to other major cities. I believe we can achieve the same level of success or greater no matter where we go. Our first target would be Atlanta. It's a city known for its nightlife."

"Mr. Walters, how did you get your start?" Mr. Rosenberg questioned cutting him off.

"Well, Mr. Rosenberg, to make a long story short, my partners I had a vision to own this nightclub and through all of our mutual efforts, we were able to make that happen."

"I've done some background research on you and there's no trail leading to where you are. It's as if you just came about out of nowhere. It leaves a guy like me with a lot of suspicions about the integrity of how you built your empire. So, Mr. Walters, what I really want to know is what exactly you did before this."

"Boss, I'm sorry to interrupt your meeting but there's and emergency downstairs." One of the club's hosts had and urgent expression as he walked into the club office.

"I'm in the middle of an important discussion it will have to wait until later."

"Sorry boss, but it can't wait."

"What is it?"

The host could hear the agitation in Quinn's voice. "Someone just drove by and shot up the place. There are three people who got injured downstairs and we already called the cops and paramedics. They're on their way."

"I guess this wasn't a good time for our meeting. I'm going to excuse myself so you can tend to your issue," Mr. Rosenberg said nervously.

"I assure you that things like this don't happen often. In fact, this is the first time we've had an incident like this occur," Quinn tried to assure him.

"I'm sure it is but if things like this are happening at all, it makes me question do you really have it together? I'll need some time to think over my decision to invest. Good night, Gentleman."

Quinn needed to find Naomi and make sure she was okay. It was going to be a late night, and he needed to make sure she got home. He walked out of his office to see the club clearing out. He spotted Naomi and Vanilla both sitting at the table where Naomi and her friends were sitting.

"Hey babe, take my key and drop Vanilla off and then go back home. I'll be back there in a few hours. D and I have to handle this ordeal."

"I understand. Promise I'll see you tonight?"

"Of course." Quinn kissed Naomi.

"Excuse me sir, If I recall correctly, you are the owner of this here night club?" Quinn turned around to face the man who had tapped him on the shoulder.

"Yes, I'm the owner."

"My name is Detective Stephens. I questioned you about the shooting that happened in your back lot a few weeks ago."

"You don't have to remind me; I remember who you are."

"Well, it seems like you have a bit of an issue with shootings at your club. I have a few questions I'd like to ask you pertaining to what happened tonight."

"What do you want to know?"

"Do you know what transpired here at your club this evening, was there any type of altercation?"

"No sir. I have no idea what happened. One of my workers who was downstairs at the time informed me that several shots had been fired from the outside of the building."

"Does your club check all of your guest for weapons before entering into the building?"

"Of course we check everyone who comes through our doors."

"We may have to issue a search warrant and conduct an audit of your business to ensure you aren't involved in anything illegal. There's a drug war going on and this club has been involved in two shootings."

"A drug war? My club doesn't have anything to do with that."

"So, you wouldn't happen to know why your mother got shot and killed."

"Don't ever speak on my mother muthafucka."

"It doesn't take much for the real you to come out I see. I know this fancy little night club is a cover up for what you really do. You can't fool me with your expensive suit and shiny dress shoes."

"As far as you know I'm a legitimate businessman, you can't prove anything otherwise."

"Bullshit, you're a seasoned bank robber. You're right I can't prove it yet, but your day is coming."

"Whatever day you say is coming for me, it sure as hell ain't today. Now if you'll excuse me, I'd like to go tend to my club."

"Sure, go ahead and check on your little club but I'm going to let you off with one last warning. You may want to tighten up your security maybe even outside the club or you won't have much of a club to tend to. I mean who wants to go to party at a gun range. My team is going to search the premises for any evidence and question some of your guest about what happened. We won't be long. Hopefully we can find out any clues as to who's causing all this recent violence."

"Yeah, hopefully you can find out who it is detective, in the meantime feel free to look around all you want."

The last of the customers had stumbled out of Club Live, leaving the place eerily quiet. Quinn and Roc pulled the doors shut, twisting the locks. What was supposed to be a big night for business had fallen flat.

Since Quinn had given Naomi his car key, he needed Roc to give him a ride home. He was already thinking about her and ready to see her, missing her more than he wanted to admit.

That's when a black limo rolled to the curb, slow and deliberate.

Before they could process it, three men in trench coats spilled out, moving fast. Their guns were already drawn, chambers cocked, barrels aimed before Quinn and Roc could even clear their own.

The back window of the limo lowered just enough for a voice to boom out.

"You two in the car now!"

The men yanked them toward the opposite door, shoving them inside.

A heavy-set white man lounged in the seat opposite them. His suit screamed expensive; his expression screamed arrogance. Quinn had never seen him before, but the way he carried himself told him all he needed. This man had money and power, and he knew it.

"Do you know who I am?" the man demanded.

"Should I know you?" Quinn shot back; eyes locked on him.

"Well, if you didn't know who I was before, you will become very familiar with me soon. I'm the boss! Johnny Hugo! I run these streets! I have controlled the flow of dope in this city for many years. My guy's Brooklyn and Damon that used to work for me; we did good business together for a long time. So, when I found out that they were both dead, I knew it had to be a real bad ass that took them out."

"You think I killed them?" Quinn asked evenly.

"I know you killed them, took their supply, and have been selling my dope out of your fancy little nightclub."

"People say a lot of things in the streets. That doesn't make them true now, do they?"

Hugo smirked at Quinn's nerve. "You're right about that, Quinten. But I hear everything, and when it comes down to finding out the truth, I get to the bottom of it."

Beside Quinn, Roc stiffened remembering the dope that had gone missing the night he killed Brooklyn.

"Now you and I have a problem," Hugo went on. "The dope I fronted them has come up missing. I'm not making any money, and if I don't start to make some soon, things won't be pretty for you, to say the least. I like this whole idea of the nightclub. It keeps these junkies getting high and keeps the cops away. It's a good cover for our business.

You're going to be my new distributor. You're going to keep selling my dope out your club, bring me sixty percent. You got that! I'll start off by giving you twenty kilos to handle before upgrading you to fifty. But first, you bring me two million dollars next Friday to settle the debt you've caused me. This is not an offer, it's an order. You don't want to screw with me. I can make everything you ever knew disappear if you don't comply with my demands. And one other thing... I know who killed your mama."

Quinn's jaw locked so tight his teeth ached. The mention of his mother's death was like striking a match near gasoline.

"This guy Jamir, he's Brooklyn's little brother. However, I never liked that prick, nothing like his brother. I did good business with those guys you killed, but I know in these streets, no one lasts forever. He's upset you killed his family. Center Heights, his crew hangs out there. That's all you need to know. You will want to handle those types of issues, or your problems will continue, and you will be the one dead next."

"I can handle my beef, don't you worry about that," Quinn said, staring Hugo dead in the eye.

"We will see."

The limo slowed, pulling up right where they'd been taken outside Club Live. Quinn realized the driver had just been circling the block the whole time.

"I'll be paying you another visit soon, so remember what I just said. You two are free to go."

Revenge

Including Slime, a few of the Mafia's major members were dead. Quinn pushed his Benz through his new neighborhood thinking heavily about the murders. They were all Quinn's homies. They ran with his crew and repped The Mafia making them apart of the family.

Their deaths now left the blocks they were supposed to be running in chaos as street soldiers fought for power. Jamir was sending the Mafia the message that he wanted war and by killing their main associates, he wanted to let them know that their beef was personal. For that reason, Quinn had been forced onto the front line of the war.

Jamir had one major flaw; he was too noisy. Jamir was walking around the streets like he didn't have a price tag on his head. He had announced his beef with The Mafia and was taunting them for the losses they had taken. Quinn had stopped his supply of drugs from flowing into the streets leaving most of his workers with no reason to come outside. He felt it was needed to prevent anyone else on his team from dying.

While tracking Jamir's whereabouts, Quinn was trying to keep his own location discrete. He hardly showed his face at the club and moved all his drugs to a safe house. He was waiting for the right time to personally put an end to Jamir's existence. However, until he could vouch that Jamir and the rest of his team was eliminated from being a threat, Quinn would have to continue moving cautiously.

Quinn also needed to make sure Naomi was safe until things cooled down. It was a side of his life that he wasn't ready to introduce her to. Purposely, he kept her away. Enemies out to harm him would take out anyone he was close to, so Quinn paid a watchman to discreetly trail her every move.

Unlike women he'd dealt with, Naomi wasn't insecure. She gave him space to handle his business but his free time with her had become pretty much nonexistent. He was being stretched thin from running a club, a restaurant, and playing chess in a street war.

Quinn set aside some time for a nice date by making a reservation for a nice dinner along with tickets to a comedy show afterward. He wanted to make sure Naomi knew that spending time with her was important to him no matter how busy he was.

Shortly after pulling up to his home, Quinn walked into his room late in the night. He took his clothes off and he was ready to wrap his arms around Naomi and enjoy some much-needed sleep. Quinn eased into bed and snuggled behind his lady. While he was half asleep,

Quinn felt Naomi's hands stroking his member. He was up, but his body wasn't. It had been about two weeks since they'd had sex and he wasn't avoiding it purposely; he just had been too busy.

"We don't have to if you don't want to," Naomi said.

"I'm sorry, Babe. I'm just really tired. We can wake up and have morning sex," Quinn offered, knowing that was the time when her urges were the strongest.

"I need it. I've been waiting two weeks now, and I need to cum."

"Daddy's going to stroke it for you real good, I promise," Quinn assured her.

Quinn had spoken those words just a few seconds before drifting off. He was sound asleep and lightly snoring in less than two minutes. Naomi turned over and kissed her king on the cheek.

In the morning, Quinn fulfilled his promised and they had mind blowing sex. Afterward Quinn had gotten a text from Tank to meet up later. Tank had been using Jamesha to track Jamir's whereabouts and it was time to put in some work.

"This nigga crossed game. I see he want a war and won't just lay down since the top dogs got taken out. Thinking he's next in line to fill that spot but he just punk in the way. Anybody left on the enemy's side gon' have to lay down or get put down."

After finishing his sentence, Quinn took a long puff on the spliff sitting between his fingers then he passed it to his little homie Tank. Tank and Quinn were sitting outside of the apartments where Jamesha lived, tucked discreetly inside a black Lincoln. Terrance was the driver while Quinn sat shotgun and Tank sat in the backseat behind Terrance.

Jamesha was Jamir's woman. Little did Jamir know; Tank was penetrating his woman whenever Jamir wasn't around. After making Jamesha cum a few times, she began to tell him Jamir's business. She bashed him for being a drunk who got abusive when too much alcohol was in his system. She was tired of him putting his hands on her and Tank convinced her that he would handle Jamir. He was playing his role well; being the one to console her when she was at odds with her man. Jamesha didn't know that Tank had much bigger fish to fry with Jamir.

"She just hit my line," Tank said reading Jamesha's text message.

"Can you come over? He's tripping again, I just threatened to call 911 so he is about to leave."

It's about that time. She should be getting ready to put his ass out any minute."

"About damn time. We have been waiting outside for nearly six damn hours." Terrance said feeling anxious.

Jamir came strolling out of the apartment building drunk and stumbling to his Jeep. It was early into the morning, just a little after three a.m. Jamir hopped in and took about five minutes to start up and pull off. He was too wasted to notice the black Lincoln with three men seated inside, watching his every move. Terrance followed Jamir out of the complex. Half a mile down the street, he caught a red light that would soon be the cause of his fatal fate.

"Y'all better clap this muthafucka. Don't be faking, you feel me?" Quinn said to let his homies know their time to prove themselves had come.

"Man, you don't have to tell me shit," Tank said.

Terrance eased the Lincoln up beside the Jeep. Jamir didn't even look over as the windows of the Lincoln lowered and a semi-automatic erupted from back window on the driver's side of the Lincoln. The Jeep's windows shattered. Jamir never saw it coming as one bullet struck his arm. Tank and Quinn ran over to the Jeep and pulled Jamir out the driver's seat and into the street. After several stomps and kicks to the face, Jamir was knocked out cold. They carried his body to the Lincoln and tossed him in the trunk. The light turned green, and the Lincoln fled from the scene.

Quinn and Naomi's relationship had accelerated so fast, Naomi barely realized how much time had passed until she stopped to count the months. Tashi finally had her own space, and Naomi was happily settled in with a man who seemed to have everything handled. School was going flawlessly. She had just wrapped her second year of college with her perfect 4.0 still intact.

Quinn was nothing like Michael. And though she still missed Michael in her quiet moments, she had to admit that sometimes guiltily that his death had been a blessing in disguise. Quinn was her blessing. If Michael had never died, would their paths have ever crossed? She doubted it.

Quinn refused to let her work, insisting she focus on her studies. He handled every bill and spoiled her relentlessly. She stayed draped in designer heels and luxury handbags from fur coats in the winter to thousand-dollar shades in the summer.

One afternoon he'd surprised her with matching Cartier watches; other times she'd find neat stacks of cash slipped into her purse. And beyond his deep pockets, there was the fact that he was fine as hell. His smooth chocolate skin, a smile so white it could blind, and an athletic build could tempt even the most faithful woman. Naomi knew other women would kill to be in her position.

The only flaw in the picture-perfect arrangement was how much he worked. Lately, his nights ran longer, his time at home shorter. The hours reminded her uncomfortably of when Michael used to party all night with Jacob, but she pushed the thought aside. This was different. Quinn was working. She told herself the pros still outweighed the cons.

Still, she missed him.

She thought back to the day she'd officially moved in. The same day they'd made things official and how excited she'd been for the life they'd start together. Tonight was supposed to feel like that again. Quinn had planned for them to see an R&B concert, and Naomi was determined to look so good he wouldn't be able to keep his hands off her. Their sex life had been quiet for weeks, and she was craving him.

She went all out: nails and toes freshly polished in deep red, hair touched up by Cynthia, the perfect dress paired with the perfect bag and heels. A swipe of red lipstick, a light foundation, fluttering lashes. She looked in the mirror and blew herself a kiss. At 7:34 p.m., she checked the clock. The show started at eight, and with a twenty-minute drive, Quinn was already running behind.

She poured herself a glass of wine to pass the time.

Five glasses and two hours later, the night was ruined. All her effort had been for nothing. Naomi stared at herself in the mirror, hair laid, makeup flawless, a vision gone to waste. With a bitter sigh, she washed her face, unwrapped the curls, tied her hair in a silk bonnet, slipped into silk pajamas, and removed her jewelry.

When she glanced at the clock again, it was 1:48 a.m. and Quinn still wasn't home.

She called his phone. Voicemail.

"Of course you're not going to answer," she muttered to herself.

Her mind started working against her. Where was he at nearly two in the morning when the club closed at one? In her past, that answer had been simple, he was with another woman. She hated herself for even thinking it about Quinn, but he hadn't been the same man lately. Distant. Preoccupied. And now, blowing her off without a word.

The doubt settled in her stomach like a stone.

Jamir's muffled yelling was starting to annoy Quinn. He had left Jamir locked inside the trunk for three long days. Unable to move his body, yelling for help was Jamir's only option before he died of thirst and starvation.

"Somebody open this!" Jamir couldn't even remember what happened besides the fact that he was drunk and left Jamesha's house after she had threatened to dial 911. "Somebody please let me out of here!"

"Pop it," Quinn said to Tank who released the lever and the back hood propped upward. When Jamir saw their faces, he was fearful. He knew whatever they were going to do to him would be pure misery.

"Help! Somebody help me now!" Jamir screamed to the top of his lungs hoping someone would hear him but there was no one around that could help. His fate was inescapable.

"Sit him down." Quinn said.

Jamir was placed in a chair that was sitting next to the Lincoln.

"My mom was the most loving good-hearted person anyone would have ever known. When your brother died, he had it coming. He chose this life and I understand you wanting revenge, but real men don't come after the innocent. They handle it with the man that offended them. But you don't know that because you're a fake ass nigga. That's the difference between us." Quinn leaned down and spoke directly in Jamir's ear. "Since you don't know how to shut up, I'm going to do something for that too."

"Hold his mouth open." Quinn instructed Roc and Tank.

Roc and Tank slid on heavy duty gloves and forced Jamir's mouth wide. Quinn went to the wooden table and grabbed the jumper cables and plyers. Quinn attached the end of the positive clip to Jamir's tongue.

With his pliers he latched onto Jamir's two front teeth. Quinn yanked with force ripping the teeth from their sockets. Blood overflowed from Jamir's mouth. Jamir's pain was excruciating. His screams were so disturbing that no ears should ever be allowed to hear those sounds. With each tooth that Quinn yanked, blood squirted out Jamir's gums.

"Tank, you want to do the honors?" Quinn said after he had yanked out an entire row of teeth.

Quinn looked over at his young bull who was itching to get a piece of Jamir for revenge over the death of Slime. Their dynamic duo had been broken and now Tank's heart was cold as ice. Tank started the Lincoln's engine then he walked back over to where Jamir was seated.

"The Midwest Connection is over." Tank then spit in Jamir's face to show the ultimate disrespect. "Rest in piss muthafucka."

Tank attached the negative clip to the battery post under the Lincoln's hood. Sparks whisked against Jamir's tongue. Tank sat back in the driver's seat revving the engine. More sparks ignited and Jamir's tongue was sizzled. His eyes bulging and his burnt tongue hung out his mouth as he slumped over like a dead fish.

Quinn picked up his iPhone remembering he had made plans with Naomi earlier. It was early in the a.m. and he had completely lost track of the time. He had several text messages and missed calls.

"Damn!" Quinn said to himself thinking about the explanation he was going to come up with for standing Naomi up.

Quinn walked into his house through the double doors of his four-car garage. Naomi was dressed in her pajamas and sitting in the kitchen at the island bar top, drinking a glass of wine.

"I haven't seen you in over twenty-four hours so tell me what's up because tonight you said you wouldn't be working late?"

"I was working because something came up at the club, then I lost track of the time. I'm sorry, I promise I'll make it up to you."

"You've been so full of promises lately, why are you acting so different suddenly. Are you seeing somebody else?"

"I told you I was at the club."

"This early in the morning? Your club closed hours ago."

"Look, I'm tired I don't have time for this."

Quinn hated lying to Naomi, but beef was heavy in the streets, and he couldn't talk to her about that side of his life. He would reveal his dark secrets to her one day when the time was right. He believed in his heart Naomi would accept him for who he was, but he wasn't ready.

Quinn attempted to move past Naomi toward the bedroom, but he was halted when she stepped directly in the way of his path.

"You don't have time because you don't want to keep it real with me. We've been honest with each other this far I don't see why that should stop now. I mean really, what's up. I thought we were better than that Q."

"Okay, I'll be real with you. Every day I'm out working. Every day I'm bringing home the money that keeps a roof over our heads, food on the table, those Chanel bags on your arm, and red bottoms on your feet."

"I never asked you for anything, so don't make this about what you do for me. I'm not like those hoes you're used to. I don't want anything from you, okay!"

Quinn grabbed Naomi by the chin then kissed her deeply. He circled her tongue with his then tugged her bottom lip before pulling away. Quinn looked into Naomi's eyes and bit his bottom lip.

Ugh he must know that turns me on. Naomi thought to herself. Naomi was quiet because her voice was caught in her throat so she couldn't speak. Whenever Quinn kissed her like that, she always lost control. She hated that he had her so open.

"You're so gorgeous," Quinn said before kissing her again.

Quinn felt bad after hearing Naomi's little rant. He worked his ass off to be able to live a lavish lifestyle, but he knew Naomi wasn't like most women. She would be with him even if he didn't have it. He had hardly sexed lately and figured she needed it to relieve some of her attitude. He cuffed her hips pulling her close then he kissed the center of her neck.

"Ahhhh!" Naomi exclaimed when Quinn slid his tongue downward between her cleavage.

With one hand he yanked at Naomi's pajama shorts, and they fell to her feet. He took his middle and index fingers then inserted them between her panties. With two fingers he gently circled around her clit. Naomi was already soaked. Quinn's middle finger spread her opening, and he glided between moving in and out tickling her clit with his index finger.

Naomi grinded slowly as Quinn tongue kissed her and fingered her at the same time. Her insides began to quake the more he toyed with her g-spot. The rush began to flow through her pelvic area, and she creamed on his hand. Quinn released his finger then lightly tapped Naomi on the ass. He moved past her on his way to the bedroom. Moments later, Naomi heard the shower water turn on upstairs.

Quinn stood in the shower letting the warm water from the shower head rain on his head. The water was relaxing after a long day. Flashes of dead bodies he'd just caught popped into Quinn's mind. He closed his eyes shook his head then splashed water in his face to shake away the horrific images.

His eyes opened to blood raining all over his body. He quickly turned the knob to the showerhead off. His heart rate was rapid, and his breaths were shallow. He spent a good ten minutes taking deep breaths until he was back calm. When he was finished, he threw his towel around his waist.

After he flicked off the bathroom lights, he opened the double doors that lead into the bedroom. The colder air being locked outside the bathroom gave him a slight chill. Naomi had the lights dimmed. Lavender incense sticks were burning on the dresser, giving the room a sweet-smelling aroma.

Naomi was naked on top of the bedspread. She was lying on her back with her knees bent upward and legs spread apart. Her body was slim-thick, toned and a smooth light brown. She was peering over at Quinn, wrapped in nothing but a towel. His chiseled physique alone was enough to get her extremely turned on. Quinn yanked his towel off and his genitals flung out. Naomi's toes curled at the thought of him being inside her.

Quinn went down on her and his strong hands gripped her breast as he sucked the inside of her thighs. He teased and continued to suck the inside of her thighs until he left his marks. His teasing had Naomi so wet that her juices began to drip down. His tongue made its way up to her belly button where he licked in a circular motion. Naomi groaned at the pleasure of Quinn's continued teasing. Naomi never knew that part of her body could feel so good until she met Quinn. She was amazed at his sexual prowess.

"Mmmm…" Quinn hummed as he savored the sweetness of Naomi's juices.

Her legs trembled uncontrollably, and she moaned so loud that her voice became hoarse. He sucked slightly harder, and she was climbing up the walls realizing her pleasure was getting too intense to handle. His tongue put a put a spell over her body that caused Naomi to vibrate every time he licked. He would take his tongue away as soon as she was about to orgasm swiftly preventing her from reaching her point of no return. He did this about four times until she had too much anticipation built up for it to be held back. Naomi shuddered wildly as Quinn stopped and watched her tremble.

Quinn came up from between her legs and kissed her. She could taste the sweetness of her nectar on his lips. Naomi jumped up off the bed then got down on her knees. She wanted to feel him inside her mouth. She opened wide so he could put him where she wanted. Her jaws were slightly sore she was ready to feel Quinn inside her, so she got up then pushed him down onto the bed and mounted him cowgirl style. She rode him like a champ until her legs gave out. Quinn rolled Naomi onto her side and grinded. Naomi could feel him touching depths that no one had ever touched before.

"C'mon let's shower," Quinn said pulling Naomi up and into the master bathroom.

Inside he washed her body while she washed his.

"I'm sorry I wasn't here tonight."

"It's okay. I know you had to work. I just want us to spend more time."

"Baby, there's nothing I would rather do than spend time with you. That's why I planned us something special to make up for my absence lately. I booked us a trip to Miami along with a private yacht to the Bahamas."

"Are you freaking serious? Yay! We're going to have a lot of fun on vacation." Naomi began messaging soap all over Quinn's flaccid penis."

"We most definitely are. Now stop before I bend you over in this shower."

"What if that's what I want you to do?"

Naomi's words were like magic the way they instantly summoned Quinn to an erection. His hands grazed her softly while caressing her shoulders, back, waist and thighs while his lips placed kisses all over her neck. He gently rubbed her clit. The sensation of his hands along with the warm shower water was driving her crazy.

"Put it in me," Naomi said feeling possessed.

Quinn pressed her body against the shower wall and lifted one of her thighs and went back to work.

"Let's get to bed before the sun comes up," Quinn said peering at the sky through the small bathroom window. It was almost sunrise, and he had been up for nearly twenty-four hours. Fatigue set in his body, and he needed sleep.

Straight Outta Hell

S tephens, my office. Now."
Lieutenant Jacobs didn't raise his voice
often, but when he did, the weight of
command filled the room. Stephens stepped inside and
closed the door. Sitting across from Jacobs were the
district attorney and a federal prosecutor, their faces
carved in stone.

On the board behind them were photographs of
several men. Faces that Stephens knew all too well.

Jacobs stood, tapping the first photo. "This
investigation has been open far too long. We now have
federal support to bring down the men behind the
Community City Bank robbery, along with a string of
murders tied to it. We have strong reason to believe the
owner of Club Live, Quinten Walters" his finger
lingered on the picture, "and his associates Devante
Richards and Terrance Smith are moving heavy
amounts of cocaine through the club."

He shifted to another row of photos. "One year ago,
Damon Young, one of this city's most notorious

dealers, and Brooklyn Fernandez of the Midwest Connection were both found dead in their homes. Shortly after, several of their key associates turned up dead too. We believe this crew who call themselves *The Mafia* wiped out the competition and took their place. Unlike the old guard, they're clever. They're using legitimate businesses to wash their money."

Jacobs pointed at another face. "You put away Lavere Collins, one of their former members. The feds want him back undercover. Pennington—" he nodded at the federal prosecutor "is assigning him directly to this case. He'll work with you."

The prosecutor leaned forward, voice firm. "We're done waiting for these men to slip up. Walters and his crew have been untouchable for too long. Between the robberies, the bodies, and the dope flooding this city, they've left a trail of blood. This time, we're bringing them down for good."

The silence in the room felt like the calm before a storm. Stephens knew what it meant: the hunt was on, and this time failure wasn't an option.

Inside a cramped private prison room, Lavere sat shackled, chains weighing on his wrists and ankles. Fifteen years or maybe more before parole just hung over his head like a death sentence. The thought of waking up every day to the stench of steel toilets and stone-hard bunks hollowed him out. Prison was hell on earth. The place was humiliating, violent, and relentless. It stripped men of dignity, forced them to fight for survival, for respect, for their very manhood. He hated it. He couldn't get used to it, no matter how long he stayed.

What stung worse was the fact that Quinn, Terrance, and Roc were free while he rotted. He'd wanted to take the deal once, to snitch his way out. Now, looking around this box of concrete and bars, he regretted not following through.

The door creaked open. Lavere straightened, expecting his lawyer. Instead, Detective Stephens swaggered in, with a man in a tailored suit behind him wearing expensive cufflinks gleaming, polished shoes clicking on the floor. Lavere's mood soured instantly.

"What does this dirty bastard want now?"

"Where's my lawyer! Guard!" he snapped.

"Shhhh," Stephens hushed him, closing the door. "What's the matter, Lavere? Not happy to see me? C'mon, man. I thought we were friends. At least I did, until you betrayed my trust. But that's okay. I'm here to give you a chance to make it up to me."

"Fuck you," Lavere shot back.

"Oh, those are strong words, Mr. Collins."

"I'm not interested in being your puppet anymore. Y'all can leave me alone so I can meet with my lawyer."

The two men ignored him, sitting across the table like they owned the room.

"There is no lawyer coming to see you, Mr. Collins," said the man in the suit, voice crisp and professional. "I arranged this meeting myself. My name is Alfred

Pennington, United States Federal Prosecutor. I'd like to make you an offer, the best one you'll get."

He leaned forward.

"We need another wiretap. Another video. This time, you bring the evidence back. No disappearing tapes. Your crew runs several businesses now, but their nightclub? That's their jewel. We know it's funded with dirty money. We want them for every crime they've committed. To get them, we need you."

Lavere's eyes narrowed.

"So, what's in this for me? You want me to bring down my crew, but what do I get in return?"

"We can cut your time in half. Better yet, time served for the two years you've already done, and five years of probation. Right now, you're facing fifteen years. That's your twenties and thirties gone. I can change that. But only if you work with us. The deal won't last long. May not even last until tomorrow. Are you in or out?"

Lavere leaned back, weighing the offer. Two years in hell had been enough. Cold mattresses, flavorless food, and living like an animal just wasn't life.

"There's really not much to think about, Lavere," Pennington pressed.

"Okay. I'm in," Lavere said finally. "But you better keep your end of the deal."

"I'm a man of my word, Mr. Collins. I knew you'd be smart enough to accept. You're sharper than your friends. They'll die behind bars. You? You've got a shot at a second life."

Lavere frowned. "What exactly do you want me to tell them? If they see me out, they'll know something's up."

"Oh, don't worry. Records will show your appeal was granted. Just don't let us down. We're counting on you."

Stephens smirked as he stood. "We'll be in touch."

A few weeks later...

"Collins! You've been released," the prison guard's voice ordered Lavere's attention, and he stood to face the bars of his cell.

"Keep your head up in here," Lavere said as he shook hands with his cellmate and said his final farewell.

"I'm on my way out. This ain't nothing but an iron vacation anyway," his cellmate responded ready for the next time he would see freedom.

The guard opened the cell gate then led Lavere down the hall of the precinct to the small departure room.

"Someone will be with you shortly," the prison guard stated then left Lavere alone in the small room.

There was only a chair, toilet bowl, and gated window in the tiny room. Lavere waited for about twenty minutes and the window was unlocked and raised.

"Are you Lavere Collins?" asked an older white lady who appeared in the window. "I need you to sign these release forms and verify all of the items on the checklist and sign at the bottom."

Lavere silently thanked God for answering his prayers as he signed the release papers. The lady gave him a plastic bag with the clothes and shoes he had worn the night he was taken in.

"You can change in here. Leave your jumpsuit and sandals in the chair."

She closed the gated window to give him privacy. Lavere changed into his normal clothes and felt so much better being out of his jail suit. He felt like a human being again, not some zoo animal that needed to be caged and confined. After a few minutes the door to the small room was opened. Lavere walked out the tiny room and followed another guard down a narrow hallway to a large glass door where the guard swiped his badge against a black pad. A moment later the lock clicked and the pad flashed the color green signifying access to enter.

"Go through," is all the guard said.

Lavere walked through the door and right past a set of metal detectors. Visitors were being searched to make sure no contraband entered into the prison. On the other side of the metal detectors was freedom. The gates of hell had finally opened. Lavere couldn't believe it. He almost thought that he would never see the outside of prison walls again.

He smirked at the guard standing next to the gate switch as he strutted in the direction of freedom. The guard didn't even acknowledge him or look his way. He wasn't even going to make any effort to stop him from leaving. That's when it really sunk in; he was a free man again. He hadn't had that feeling in years. Now that he was back on the streets, he was here to stay. There was a navy blue, Crown Victoria parked along the sidewalk outside the prison. Standing next to the vehicle was Detective Stephens and his partner.

"Lavere! It's good to see you buddy!"

"Shit, not these Muthafuckas already," Lavere said to himself.

"Get in. We need to talk," said Detective Stephens.

"I've said everything I needed to say to y'all, we don't need to talk about nothing."

"Unless you want your release from prison to be very short lived. I suggest you get your black ass in the car! Before you get too comfortable; remember you have work to do."

"Yeah okay," Lavere ducked inside the cop car with Stephens and his partner Cindy.

"How does it feel to breathe this free air again?" Detective Stephens asked with sarcasm.

"It was good until I had to see you."

"We're watching you buddy," Cindy said in a serious tone. "One wrong move and your play time is up."

"You heard the woman," Stephens chimed in. "We need you get us Quinn. We need evidence and you are going to get us what we need, and you have to testify for us, that's a part of the deal. You uphold your end, and you get parole and are a free man. If, however, you don't comply with our agreement, your going back to the hell hole you just came out of. I personally will make sure you never see the light of day for the rest of your natural black life. Now your friend, Quinten Walters runs this fancy nightclub. He also has a house in Madison Hills. I want you to go pay him a visit."

Detective Stephens handed Lavere a piece of paper with two addresses written on it. The first address had Club Live written next to it and written next to the other address was Home.

"Now that you're out, you have work to do. Don't waste any time. We're giving you six months to get this done. These are wiretap cameras equipped with audio recording. Wear these at all times when interacting with the suspects." Cindy handed Lavere the undercover audio and surveillance device.

"Now beat it loser!"

Stephens stopped at the nearest street corner where Lavere got out and walked down the sidewalk. He planned on catching a cab after finding an ATM to withdraw the few dollars he had on his prison prepaid card. The small amount of money he had in commissary was all he had to his name.

Lavere had a couple of tricks up his sleeve now that he was fresh out. He sat crouched outside the house where Quinn now resided. It was the third day he had cased his home to figure out his times of leaving and arrival. The art of studying your target was a skill he had learned from Quinn. Lavere needed to make his move, and he knew timing was imperative.

Quinn's crib was a brick mansion with a circular driveway and large fountain in the middle. Lavere was hidden in the bushes of the front lawn. A super sexy young lady walked out the front door with Quinn. She was one of the finest women Lavere had ever seen. Short red hair made her appeal exotic. Lavere watched her hips in her sundress. He got rock hard as his eyes roamed her body. He noticed that Quinn didn't stop to lock the door when they walked out. They walked to a car parked in the driveway and Quinn opened the driver's door for her to get in. After she rolled down the driver's window, Lavere watched as she and Quinn shared a kiss. It was the perfect moment for him to creep inside the front door.

It had been a long tiring week and Quinn was happy to be at home with time to sit back and relax. He had been so busy running his operation and protecting his empire, he hardly had time to relax with his woman. She was currently on her way to attend class, so he had some time to himself. After seeing Naomi off, he walked into his foyer and flicked the lights on and then it dawned on him that he hadn't turned them off before he walked out the house. Instantly, he heard a semi-automatic being cocked. He tried to rush toward the location of his piece, but he was halted when he felt the barrel of a pistol touching the back of his skull.

"Freeze, Nigga," a voice whispered to him.

Quinn slowly raised his arms with his fingers spread.

"Now give me one good reason why I shouldn't blow your damn head off!" said the man behind the gun.

"Just chill man it's not worth it," Quinn said in a soothing tone.

"Don't tell me what to do!"

Lavere shoved his gun further into Quinn's scalp. Quinn's jaw tightened but he kept his anger in check. Slowly he rotated his body to face the man. His eyes widened with amazement once he laid eyes on a familiar face.

"Lavere?"

"It ain't Santa Claus, Nigga."

"But when did you get out? And how?"

"My appeal. The case was dropped due to acts of misconduct by the law and if you'd taken time to check up on me, you would've known I was coming home. Never mind all that. I'm the one who needs answers, not you. So, this is what you been up to. I must say, I'm proud of you. You always said you would move out the hood and you did. This is a lovely home by the way."

"How did you find my house?"

"Bitch, didn't I say I'm the only one asking questions."

"What do you want L'z?"

"Don't L'z me nigga. What I want to know is why haven't I heard from you in two years?"

"I got no phone calls, no mail, and for damn sure, no commissary."

"Calm down, Fam." Quinn said noticing Lavere's anger rising. If he wasn't the homie, he would have been broken Lavere's neck.

"Calm down? Is that all you can tell me to do is calm down? No, I can't calm down. All the work I put in for you? I helped pay for this house. And if it wasn't for me taking the fall for that robbery, your ass would have been locked up too!"

"L'z, I had to stay away from you! We couldn't let the cops see us contacting you. Who do you think was giving you commissary? Your grandpa? Nah, I was the one giving him money to support you. When you got taken, we had to lay low, or they would have thrown our asses right in there with you. We had to do it for ourselves because we thought that's what you would want us to do. Remember the plan we made? It was your idea. It just went south. They had a chopper hovering over us, so it was your plan to split up. I can't thank you enough for staying solid and not giving us up to the cops. I could never repay for that, but I'll do whatever I can. I'm still your brother just like I was then. Nothing has changed. Just put the gun down so we can talk."

"I want what's mine." Lavere demanded. "I want in on whatever you got."

"Don't worry, I'm going to look out for you. You should know that."

Lavere stared at Quinn with his gun still pointed at his forehead. Tears filled his eyes as he thought about Quik's death. It had been haunting him every night for two years. Lavere let his weapon drop to the floor and then he hugged Quinn again for the first time in two years.

Quinn poured Lavere a shot of Hennessy. "Throw that shot back." He chanted. The two men now were seated at Quinn's Island bar with a bottle of XO placed between them.

Lavere took the shot, and the alcohol burned his esophagus. He cleared his throat slightly.

"It's been a while since I've drank."

"Takes you back, don't it?"

"Yeah, it does."

"How did you get out again?" Quinn probed happy to see his friend but confused about his release.

"My appeal was granted due to acts of misconduct by law enforcement. I won an appeal."

"I'll be damned, that's great."

After a couple hours of talking with Lavere, Quinn heard the garage doors opening meaning his baby was home. Moments later, Naomi came into the house.

"Baby, I have someone I want you to meet. This is a good friend of mine, Lavere, but we call him L'z."

"Nice to meet you, Lavere." Naomi said politely. She couldn't remember Quinn ever mentioning the man's name.

Seeing Naomi earlier from a distance did her no justice. Now that Lavere was close to her, she looked even better. She was absolutely stunning. Her hazel eyes full lips and light brown skin tone blended perfectly. Lavere felt another erection starting to grow. After two years in the joint, his penis had a mind of its own.

"Why don't you stay for dinner, Lavere?" Naomi offered to be polite.

Lavere and Quinn talked while Naomi prepared dinner. Most of their conversation was spent reminiscing about their childhood.

"This food is delicious," Lavere said after cleaning his plate. It was one of the best meals he'd ever had. "What's the name of this dish you made?" He asked inquisitively.

"It's called paella. It's a Spanish cuisine."

"I haven't had a meal like this in a long time. You eat this good every night, Que?"

"I must admit, I am spoiled. I'm a very lucky man." Quinn said right before placing a kiss on Naomi's lips.

"That you are, but I guess I'm kind of lucky too," Naomi blushed.

"I'll take you to the club tomorrow L'z. T and Roc will be there."

"How's T?"

"He's cool, just helping run the businesses and trying smash every honey in the town, trying to keep up with Roc."

"None of us will ever be able to keep up with him. Same old Roc I see. Is he still messing with Vanilla?"

"Hell yeah, they've been off and on. Those two are meant for each other."

A little while later Lavere looked up and it was late into the night. Quinn and he had been talking for several hours. Quinn offered for Lavere to stay the night, but he declined since all his belongings were at the hole in the wall motel where he was now residing.

"I'll pick you up tomorrow and take you to the club. Roc and T are going to flip when they find out your free. I missed you fam, it's good to have you back."

"I missed you too, Dawg." Lavere and Quinn dapped each other up then embraced again before Lavere left out the front door.

The next day at Club Live Roc rushed Lavere as soon as he saw him.

"L'z! My nigga, what's up?" Roc yelled as soon as Lavere walked into Club Live. Quinn had already spread the news of Lavere's return.

"When you get out, Fam?" asked Terrance.

"I'm fresh out."

"I thought you had like ten more years."

"They granted my appeal and dropped the charges due to acts of misconduct on the prosecutors and law enforcement end."

"Damn, I can't believe it," Roc said.

"It's good to have you home," Terrance said.

"I'm glad to be home. This feels like old times."

"All we're missing is my boy, Quik," Quinn said.

"You ain't lying," Roc said. "I wish he could be here to see all this."

"He's looking down on us right now smiling," Terrance said.

"No doubt. We have to catch you up with everything," Roc said to Lavere.

"I'm hurting right now since y'all spent my cut to take over Club Live and open that fancy restaurant next door."

"As you can see, it was money well spent but don't worry, that's pocket change now. We got you. First, we got to get you out these played out clothes and into some fly drip. Ayo Randy!" Roc yelled over to his cousin stationed by the club entrance. "I need you to go tell valet to bring my car back around front. We got somewhere to go."

Many of the people they affiliated with claimed The Mafia, but they were the originals. With all but one of them together again, it felt like the beginning. They stood outside the front entrance as the valet pulled Roc's Audi up to the front of the club.

"Damn, that's how we doing it now?" Lavere was impressed when he saw how Roc was rolling.

"This is just one of the toys I play with," Roc boasted.

They all hopped in the SUV and drove to the downtown Palazzo shopping district.

"Where have you been laying your head at since you been out?" Roc inquired.

"You know I been back in the hood with my old man," Lavere lied.

"He still stay in the Jungle?"

"Hell yeah. Ain't nothing changed."

"I remember that block. We plotted all of them licks on that street."

"Ayo, y'all remember the time Lavere's Firebird damn near broke down outside that Jewelry & Loan shop we hit?"

"Aw yeah. That was funny. I was shitting bricks when that happened." T laughed

"I thought it was over. Then that old clunker finally started." Quinn said.

"But nah, you remember what Quinn said though?" Roc was laughing as he reminisced. It was only a few years ago but it seemed like it had been longer because much had happened since then.

"I said why did you turn that junker off?" Quinn said.

"I remember it all like it was yesterday." Lavere stated. He had been locked up with nothing to do but reminisce, so it was clear in his mind. "Y'all big time now. I remember when we were running in banks, now y'all got businesses. I must say, I'm proud of y'all niggas. What I really want to know is, how did y'all do it?"

Lavere's wiretap had been recording since he walked into the club. He was getting the information he needed to be used as evidence.

"Roc, give him the scoop," Quinn said.

"Look Bro, before we took over this club, we got the money from a lick we did. Remember Damon and Brooklyn?" Roc looked back at Lavere through his rearview mirror.

"Hell yeah, they were big time before somebody took them out. Some goons ran up in both of their cribs left them both stiff and took all the paper they had. I heard about it in prison."

"We the goons who did that and we got more than just money. We got bricks of that yayo and we turned that into another profit. Well, there's this crazy muthafucka named Hugo, he's the kingpin who Damon and Brooklyn used to work for. Somehow, word got back to him that we were the ones with his product. Now he has us taking over where they left off but instead of pushing it out on the street, we rinse the money with club and restaurant dollars, that's why the cops can't touch with us."

"No wonder y'all getting so much paper. I know the club is bringing in dough, but not that much. I want in on this operation."

"We will get to that later. First, let's get you fresh. You can't be out here looking like you fresh off lockdown."

They all arrived at the palazzo mall and balled out. Lavere had enough clothes to wear a new outfit each day for over a month. His homies put new Jordans on his feet, plus several other pairs of the freshest footwear in stores.

Later that night, Lavere walked back into Club Live and noticed the decor was completely different. It had a more upscale appeal, but it was packed with a large crowd just like it was years ago. Judging by the quantity of people in attendance, it was still the place to be on a Friday night.

Roc, Terrance, and Quinn went all out and threw Lavere a welcome back party. Upstairs in VIP was where the real party was. VIP was completely closed off with a large velvet curtain preventing anyone from being able to see inside the section. At the bottom of the stairs that led up to the area, bouncers prevented partygoers from entering. Lavere was occupied with getting a private lap dance from a sexy little stripper.

Thanks to Quinn, he had a pocket full of money and didn't have to throw a single dollar. The stripper was paid for in full. Lavere smacked both of her booty cheeks as she twerked them in his face. He loved the view of her juicy ass bouncing, but he needed more than just a tease. It had been two long years without sliding up in something warm and wet.

"How much for more than just a dance?" he asked while peeling six hundred-dollar bills off the big bankroll that was in his pocket.

Quinn had hooked him up with a hefty lump sum of cash so unlike most dudes fresh out the joint, Lavere wasn't hurting for a thing.

"I can do a lot more for that," Brandi said before snatching up the Benjamin's.

"Well show me what you can do baby."

Brandi had a caramel complexion and had cheeks so fat that they had to be implants. Her boobs were excessively large too. She was too damn thick but the doctor who did her surgery did a good job and Lavere was sure it cost a pretty penny. In less than five minutes, she had sucked his soul out. Lavere knew she was a certified freak when she swallowed everything he had been holding back for two years.

Roc and Terrance came thru just as Lavere was pulling up his pants. Roc was grinning knowing exactly what just went down. Brandi had a disappointed look. She had gotten her hopes up and was not ready to finish yet.

"Why don't you take my number just in case you want to hook up later?" she offered.

"Fasho, Shorty," Lavere said interested in linking up with her later. "What's your number?"

Lavere pulled out the brand-new smart phone that he could hardly even work. It was significantly more advanced than the phones the world was using before he got locked up.

"Sorry, I don't know how to operate this damn device," he admitted.

"Let me help you with that," she said, finding his contact log then entering her information into it.

Lavere was going to call her no doubt. There was a lot more he planned to do to her later.

"Come downstairs, Bro. We got a surprise for you Fam," Roc said.

He led Lavere from VIP over to the DJ's booth. The bartender brought over a tray with four glasses of champagne. Roc got the DJ to cut the music.

"Sorry to interrupt y'all groove!" Roc said grabbing the DJ's mic. "I have a very important announcement to make. My boy L'z just came home! The punk police locked him up on some bogus charges, but he beat that case, and now we're stronger than ever! Everybody hold your drinks up in the air right now! It don't matter what your sipping! We got some Moet over here but to each his own. Anyway, I want to toast to new beginnings. L'z, now that you're home, this is only the beginning baby. Everybody say, Welcome back L'z!"

"Welcome Back L'z!" everybody cheered. The crew's glasses of champagne clanked against one another, and they each downed the entire glass.

"I got one more surprise for you and everybody else to see. Everybody, make your way out to the front entrance!" The entire crowd rushed to the front of the building to see the big surprise.

"You really went all out for this welcome back party, Baby." Naomi and Quinn were parked in the back lot of Club Live.

"I had to. L'z and I are like brothers. We grew up together. When were young, we were wild as hell, and we got into a lot of trouble. It caught up to Lavere before the rest of us. That's when I realized we needed to change and do something positive which is what led us to taking over the club."

"You're loyal. He's lucky to have a friend like you."

"Nah, he spent years in prison while I was able to turn my life around and still be a free man. I'm the lucky one."

With Lavere's return, Quinn began to reveal some of his past to Naomi. She was receptive of the few things he shared with her. "I'm especially lucky to have this beautiful woman in my life."

"Is that right?"

"Of course." Quinn kissed Naomi while his hands were gently petting the kitty between her thighs.

Ring! Ring!

Quinn's phone rang. He answered even though he didn't want to. He wanted to sex Naomi's fine ass inside the brand-new Porsche they were sitting in.

"Hello?"

"Pull it around," said Terrance.

Lavere's jaw dropped when he spotted Quinn driving down the block in a brand-new, drop-top Porsche with a bright red bow on its hood.

"Yeah, baby. I told you, we got you!" Roc said. "This is a welcome home gift for being a loyal friend."

"I love you, Bro," Quinn said, getting out of the car.

"I love you too, My Nigga."

Lavere and Quinn embraced.

"Go ahead and hop in."

The car was the epitome of luxury. The lights on the dashboard glowed in the dark and Lavere felt like he was in a spaceship.

"Before you take off, I got something else for you," Quinn pulled out an envelope and handed it to Lavere. When he opened it, there was a key inside.

"What's this?"

"It's the key to your new spot. The address is inside the envelope too."

Lavere looked inside the envelope again and sure enough, there was a piece of paper with the address written on it.

Lavere's new crib was official. His homies had hooked him up with a fully furnished penthouse suite located on the top floor True Light Luxury Condos located in the Power and Light District. Lavere sat in his new bedroom smoking a fat spliff. He was butt naked with Brandi sprawled out on the bed next to him. After two years without pleasure, he had an enormous sexual appetite. The pounding he had just put on her would leave her walking funny for the next couple of days.

Lavere knew all his fun was about to be short lived because his reality was that he needed to set up a plan to take the Mafia down. He was grateful for all the love they had shown upon his return home however, all that was small compared to what he had done for them. Lavere didn't feel any remorse for what he was about to do. He knew if it were any one of them were in his shoes what they'd do.

When he got locked up, they were still on the come up. Now they had made it big and didn't even bother to check in on him once the entire time he had been in prison. Now that he was out, Lavere played like everything was sweet but deep down he was still angry. He was just waiting for the right time to reveal it.

Karma Is A Bitch

After being out of prison for a couple months, Lavere's envy of Roc, Quinn, and Terrance had grown deep. He was jealous of how well they had been living while he was on lockdown. The cold nights behind bars turned his heart cold.

Lavere had been wearing a wire whenever he was around Roc, Terrance or Quinn. He had so many conversations with them admitting to several different crimes they'd committed. His next step? Get physical evidence and that would seal the deal. After that, he planned to take over Club Live. And with Quinn out of the way, he would be the new boss.

Roc, Lavere, Quinn, and Terrance were all seated around the round table of the club's office discussing their ideas on how to grow the business. Lavere's wiretap was recording every detail of their conversation.

"We need to find a new investor to help us expand because due to that shooting, we lost our last investor and now we have bigger problems. The cops have us under a microscope and are waiting to hit us with a drug investigation and an audit that will shut our operation down." Quinn stated.

"Well, I have good news, Roc stated. I have another investor who wants to meet this Friday. His name is Joshua Nickels, and he owns shares in several successful business' chains."

"This Friday's not going to work. Can you reschedule? I already have my vacation plans set plus you and Terrance are supposed to do the drop with Hugo."

"This investor is a busy man; I had a hard time getting him to agree to this Friday. At first, he told me he was busy, then yesterday he called and said Friday night had freed up on his schedule."

"I'll handle the drop myself," said Terrance. "You just enjoy your vacation, so Naomi doesn't kick your ass."

"Roc, you sure you can handle this investor on your own?" Quinn questioned.

"Of course, Fam. I have the perfect pitch as to why he should invest in this club, everything I learned from you. He'll be writing that check before the night is over after I'm done with his ass.

"I'll make the drop with Terrance so he can have some back up," Lavere offered.

"I can handle this alone, you just got out the joint, you need to be laying low."

"Nigga, I can handle myself plus you're going to need some backup for just in case purposes, nah-mean? Quinn, you got a piece I can borrow?"

"Yeah, no doubt. I keep a ratchet."

"My man."

Quinn unlocked the drawer behind his desk and handed Lavere his spare Glock.

"Take care of that," Quinn said.

Nigga, I'm the one who gave you your first piece when I took from my old man's stash. I know you not forgetting that."

"Oh, I remember well. Now, if y'all will excuse me, I have to get home and start packing for my vacation." Quinn said raising up from the table.

Naomi and Quinn exited their private aircraft, gathered their luggage then got in a limousine that Quinn had ordered to transport them over to the luxury rental car agency where the Maserati he reserved was being held. After getting everything squared away with the rental car agency, they loaded their luggage from the limousine into the Maserati and then proceeded to the Ritz Carlton of BAL Harbor hotel. Outside of the hotel building, there were palm trees everywhere. The scenery vividly green and tropical. A warm humid breeze and felt good against their skin.

Inside the lobby, white marble and crystal chandeliers occupied the floor and ceiling.

Exquisite paintings graced every wall along with fine sculptures scattered throughout the walls seated inside architectural glass. Front desk attendants greeted them with glasses of champagne while bellmen gathered their luggage. Once Quinn collected the room keys they proceeded to their hotel suite. The rest of the hotel was just as marvelous as the lobby.

There was a lounge room with plush lazy boys and giant televisions. There was a full workout room, swimming pools indoor and outside, a hot tub, sauna, several restaurants and gift shops. Their room was located on the top floor with a great view overlooking the hotel's private beach. The suite had a full living room, kitchen, dining area, and California King Bed. The bathroom contained a Jacuzzi, double head shower, and a walk-in closet to place all their belongings.

Because she was so anxious to see their destination, the three-hour flight had taken a slight toll on Naomi. She needed rest. Quinn decided to hit the gym for blowing off some steam while Naomi slept. After a good one-hour workout, he was relaxed. He entered their hotel suite to find Naomi up and dressed in her bikini.

"Let's go to the beach, Baby," Naomi said slipping into her see-through cover up.

"We can do whatever you want. This is our time," Quinn said then kissed her cheek. In reality, Quinn had a whole itinerary of activities planned for them.

White sand sank beneath their feet as Naomi and Quinn walked along the ocean shore of the private beach. Quinn had purchased a picnic basket and sandwiches for them to enjoy for lunch. After carrying the contents for a while, his hunger began to set in. They found a nice spot to sit and eat. A pack of hungry seagulls surrounded them while they ate. Quinn would get up to shoo them and every time he sat back down, they would come back. Hours later, they were back in the suite fitting into their best going out attire.

Naomi and Quinn hit the most popular nightclub on Ocean Drive. Quinn had dreams of owning a club of the same stature. Even though he was the king in the Midwest, it didn't compare to being the king of Miami. The celebrity presence was major and there were three A list names in the building. Quinn was beginning to feel like LeBron James. He needed to move his talents to South Beach.

A lot of eyes were on Naomi and Quinn as they walked around the club and even mingled with some of the other partygoers. Quinn was sure most people were trying to figure out exactly whom they were. Their faces were new to town but the look and smell of money that lingered on them let people know they belonged with the elite.

The next morning, Quinn woke up not remembering too much from the night besides the fact that he had more than enough to drink. One minute, Naomi was grinding against his wood while his hands roamed every part of her body. Next, they were being spontaneous and sneaking back in the private beach where they sexed in the sand. Quinn was too drunk to pull out and he ended up ejaculating inside of Naomi. After that, he did not remember how they made it back to their hotel that night.

Quinn decided to spend their second day on vacation recovering from the wild festivities they had on South Beach. Naomi and Quinn ate breakfast at their hotel before going over to the port of Miami. Quinn had chartered a private yacht for the next three days. Hot Florida sun rays tanned Naomi's skin as she lay out on their yacht's deck, Cartier shades protecting her eyes. After a good thirty minutes of sunbathing, the sun had baked Naomi's skin to a beautiful golden brown. The slightly darker complexion against Naomi's bright red hair gave her an exotic appeal.

For several miles there was nothing but the Atlantic Ocean surrounding their small ship. It took just a couple of hours for their yacht to land on the shores of Nassau. After reaching the island, Quinn had reserved tickets for them to explore nearly every excursion the island had to offer. Their most memorable would be their time spent skydiving. It was the first time Naomi had faced her fear of heights.

After taking a helicopter thousands of miles into the air, Naomi began to fear the altitude she was being taken to. Then the copilot instructed them it was time to take that leap of faith, literally.

"No, Quinn I can't!" Naomi looked down from the open doors of the helicopter and the ground was so far down that she could barely see it."

"You can do it baby. I promise everything is going to be just fine." Quinn tried to assure her.

"What if the rope breaks then were dead, nope I don't trust it. I can't believe I let you talk me into this."

Skydiving had been something Quinn wanted to do forever. It had taken two days of begging to convince Naomi.

"Babe, it's completely secure."

Naomi touched the straps around her body to confirm her parachute was intact.

"This is crazy, black people don't do this type of stuff, Q."

"Sometimes us black people need to step outside the box and live a little. This will be a liberating experience. I promise you; you're going to feel great after you do it."

"Baby, I'm so scared." Naomi was feeling like she was going to shit on herself.

"Just hold onto to me tightly and close your eyes if you can't look but I promise you'll want to see the view."

Naomi held tightly to Quinn from behind as he leapt like Tarzan into the open sky. The sound of their bodies cutting through the wind drowned out their screams. Naomi kept her eyes open, and she was overlooking the entire island. It was a bird's eye view of the land and ocean. It was the most beautiful sight she'd ever seen. A rush of blood surged throughout Naomi's veins and her stomach sank like a roller coaster going downhill.

She couldn't believe something that seemed so scary could be so much fun. When her feet touched the ground again it felt weird. In such a short amount of time she had gotten more comfortable being in the sky like she belonged there. Extreme heights had always been a fear for Naomi.

With Quinn, she was able to let go of that fear and felt as if she could accomplish anything. Quinn was so safe, assuring and Naomi had so much trust in him. With Quinn by her side, an empty space Naomi never knew was there had been filled ever since the day he entered her life.

Three long and adventurous days passed, and their yacht lodged back in the port of Miami where the couple would enjoy two more days vacationing before heading back home. Naomi and Quinn explored the major landmarks and museums of the city. Quinn was amazed with the fact that there was so much to do and realized he didn't plan a long enough trip to experience everything he had wanted.

After going back to their hotel and taking a quick shower, the couple dressed into casual attire and then hopped into the Maserati and drove across the street to the BAL Harbor shopping district. Naomi spent hours browsing through the merchandise of each designer. Since she'd been with Quinn, shopping had become Naomi's new favorite hobby. If she hadn't gotten tired of walking and carrying so many bags, she would have shopped the whole day away.

Quinn didn't mind spending because as much as Naomi loved to shop, Quinn loved to spoil. On their way out the mall Naomi couldn't resist her temptation to step inside one of the mall's jewelry shops. Naomi spotted a beautiful diamond baguette necklace with white and canary yellow stones. One of the attendants noticed her eyeing the necklace.

"You've got good taste," said the middle-aged man who looked like he was of Middle Eastern descent.

"Can I see that one?"

"Of course, ma'am," he said then placed it around her neck. "That looks beautiful on her," he said grinning at Quinn.

"Yes, it does." Quinn admired how the diamonds complimented the beauty of his woman. He was in awe of how her beauty was more astounding than the flawless stones that graced her soft brown toned flesh.

"If you love that then I definitely know you'll love this," said the jeweler.

He walked behind the counter and opened another glass filled with jewelry. He came back with a matching white and yellow diamond bracelet. Naomi gasped at both pieces together.

"This is prefect baby," she said to Quinn.

"You don't have to take it off if you don't want," laughed the jeweler.

"Well, it looks like we have some business to do," Quinn said to the jeweler then motioned for him to meet at the checkout counter.

Quinn pulled out his wallet and handed the jeweler a black American Express card. He paid nearly thirty thousand dollars for her bracelet and necklace.

"Thank you for your business," the salesman said escorting them out of the jewelry store.

"Babe, I am so in love with my new pieces," Naomi was smiling from ear to ear.

"I have a big surprise for you back at the hotel."

"Babe you are too much. I don't need any more surprises."

"It don't matter, I already have it planned."

Naomi began to wonder what planet her man had come from. The fact that he always planned ahead and never lacked surprises was so sweet and romantic. He was the type of man a woman dreamed of.

Quinn could feel Naomi's glare as he drove the Maserati down Ocean Drive.

"I love you, Daddy," Naomi said staring at Quinn while his eyes were focused on the road.

"You better love me," Quinn joked without looking over.

"You know I do," Naomi said then grabbed his right hand that was resting on the gear.

Quinn's left hand was firmly gripping the steering wheel. Naomi placed his fingers between her legs. Warmth and sticky moisture coated her lips. Naomi lifted her dress revealing nothing but brown legs and the pot of gold sitting between them. She began to purr as Quinn gently massaged her kitty. Quinn eased his middle finger inside of his woman and explored her insides. She was now breathing heavy with her eyes facing the sky through the moon roof.

Quinn listened to Naomi's arousing moans as he maneuvered through traffic with his left hand and in and out of her pit with his right hand. As he sped up, the rhythm of his penetration so did her breathing until she momentarily lost air then loudly gasped to catch her breath. They arrived back at the hotel ready to finish where they'd left off.

"I'm going to go request some more towels to our suite. You go and get yourself ready for when I get up there."

"Yes Daddy" Naomi said before trailing off.

Quinn needed to make a call and check on his business before he diverted his full attention back to Naomi. He pulled out his iPhone and called Terrance.

"Hello?" Terrance said, picking up Quinn's call.

"Did y'all handle the business?" Quinn inquired.

"Yeah, we're good, Dawg. We are on our way to make the drop right now."

Terrence hung up his call with Quinn and pulled across from an abandoned warehouse in the old downtown. It was a discrete hideout, the perfect place to make an illegal drug deal without any unwanted attention. Terrence flashed his lights twice to signal his arrival. After a few moments, the warehouse door was lifted for them to enter inside.

"All right, let's go," Terrence said to Lavere.

"Yes Sir," Lavere said with sarcasm.

"Follow my lead; I'll do all the talking. You just back me up if needed."

Lavere nodded and followed Terrance into the shop. The lights inside the building were very dim to keep anyone outside from seeing what was inside. Two of Hugo's men were standing by the entrance as a guard.

"No weapons beyond this point," one of the men instructed.

Lavere and Terrance each handed him their piece then got the pat down to ensure they weren't holding. Lavere and Terrance walked past him as he pulled down the door then flicked on the bright lights. Hugo and two more of his men stood across from Lavere and Terrance.

The two groups of men stared at each other waiting for either one to make a move.

"Let's do this," said Terrence.

"Who is this guy?" asked Hugo, looking at Lavere with a scowl.

"Can we just get to business?" Terrance said trying to smooth over the situation.

"Who is this guy?"

"He's cool. I trust him."

"Well, I don't. Get that prick out of here."

"Yo who you talking to bruh?" Lavere wasn't keen on taking disrespect.

"I said he's good he's a good friend of mine." Terrance tried to ensure Hugo.

"Don't ever bring a new face to do business with me! For all I know he could be a narc! I was expecting Quinn and your other guy, Rocky or whatever his name is."

"Look, I'm Quinn today muthafucka; you got a problem with that?" Lavere was getting annoyed with the man talking about him indirectly.

"Shut up Nigga!" Terrance barked. Lavere was about to get on his nerves.

"What you say to me?" Hugo responded to Lavere

"You heard me, muthafucka."

"Shoot that son of a bitch!" Hugo ordered his men.

"Look, you've done this multiple times with me. You going to hand over the stuff or what?" Terrance pleaded with Hugo.

"If you trust him then you better make sure you can vouch for him. As soon he fucks something up, you're both dead. You got that."

"You know I got it. Do you have the dope?" Terrance countered.

"You got my money?"

Terrence showed the money in his duffle bag. One of Hugo's men unzipped a black duffle bag revealing several kilos then both men sat down their bags and walked clockwise until the exchange had been made.

"Let's go," said Terrance. He and Lavere exited the shop and got back inside Terrence's Range Rover.

"Open it up and make sure it's all there," Lavere said.

"Nah, we good. We got what we needed."

"You can never be too sure."

"All right. I guess you're right about that," Terrance said as he grabbed the duffle full of drugs out the back seat then unzipped it. Lavere watched as Hugo's limo drove down the street then turned off the block.

"I thought I told you to shut your damn mouth and let me do all the talking?" Terrance said as he counted the bricks.

"I'm not your kid. I can handle myself and I damn sure don't need you to speak for me."

"Look Dawg, you better start watching your mouth. Sometimes you have to bite your tongue, what you pulled back there could have got you killed."

"You must have forgotten who helped get us started."

"This ain't back then, you been gone for over a couple years and think you going to come back and tell me how to handle an exchange?"

"You damn right because I spent a couple years in prison taking the fall so yo' ass could walk free."

"You did two years because you were the only one who got caught."

"I got caught to save yo' ass."

"At least you didn't run your mouth when the pigs got a hold of your ass. That is the only time I can say you ever kept your mouth shut."

Lavere's tongue got caught in his throat. Terrance's words ate at the corpse of his honor and integrity, a part of him that had died the day he chose to be an informant.

Terrance zipped up the bag full of bricks then looked Lavere square in the eye. He had a killer instinct and could sense Lavere's uneasiness. Lavere clutched the Glock on his waistline.

"How do you think I got out of prison?"

"What? You snitchin'?" Terrance questioned. His ears couldn't believe what they'd just heard.

Lavere removed the Glock from his waistline.

"What you going to do with that? You going to shoot me you fucking rat?"

Lavere squeezed the trigger and fired two shots into Terrance's torso then one more to his head. Blood splattered across the inside of the windshield and driver's window. The impact of the shots caused Terrance's head to bang against the driver's window then instantly his chin fell to his chest. Lavere grabbed the duffle bag full of drugs out of Terrance's lap hopped out the vehicle, then pulled his hoodie over his head. He looked around to make sure there were no witnesses watching then calmly walked away from the scene of the murder.

Naomi opened hotel suite's doors overwhelmed by what she saw. A heavy trail of rose petals was made into a pathway lit by several candles on each side of the trail. It led to the large balcony overlooking the ocean and wrapping around the length of the suite. A well-dressed butler stood in the doorway.

"Good evening, I will be serving you tonight. May I escort you to your candlelight dinner, Ma'am?"

"Yes. Certainly," Naomi responded.

The table was set with a silk white tablecloth and lightly covered with rose petals. An oversized candle sat in the center inside of a clear vase. Next to the vase, a bottle of Moët was seated in a bucket of ice. The butler pulled out Naomi's chair and she took a seat. A few seconds later, Quinn entered onto the balcony taking a seat across from Naomi. The butler proceeded to give a detailed description of the menu. Naomi and Quinn ordered the same meal.

"I'll be right back with your courses," the butler stated before stepping out.

"This is so beautiful. I've never had a man do anything close to this for me. I'm so glad we could spend some much needed time together just you and me.

It's what I've been missing about us lately," Naomi spoke to Quinn while they both locked eyes.

"With everything that's been going on, I felt this was a vacation you and I both needed. But I don't want to even think about anything back home. While we're here, I want to make the best of our time here in paradise. I could wake up to this every day and still never get used to it."

Quinn looked out over to the ocean that glistened from the stars shining over it. The ocean's waves roared as they repeatedly washed up onto the beach shore. The sound of the ocean is so peaceful, when I listen to it all my anger releases and I feel at ease."

"You and I both could get used to this. I've had the time of my life since we arrived. This entire trip has been amazing."

"A woman like you deserves this all the time. You're special unlike any other woman I've met. I've never loved any woman the way I love you." Quinn grabbed Naomi's hand, and she felt a tingle in her center.

"It never fails," Naomi said.

"What never fails?"

"Every time you touch me, I feel weak and want you to have control over my body. It's like its instinctive and I can't resist you. No man has ever made me feel that way before."

The butler returned pushing a cart carrying a large, covered tray. He lifted the top revealing two large dishes with Wagyu steak, lobster, mashed potatoes and asparagus. They began to devour the meals, savoring flavors as if it were their last supper.

"Oh my God, this is so good," Naomi said.

She never imagined that she would be enjoying a candlelight dinner overlooking the Atlantic Ocean under a star-studded sky with the man of her dreams. Quinn was making her life nothing short of amazing and she was beginning to believe in fairytales.

"Did you enjoy the meal?" Quinn asked once they had finished stuffing their faces.

"Of course. It was one the most delicious meals I've ever had."

"You can have some desert too if you'd like?"

"It depends on what kind of desert you're talking."

Nasty and lustful thoughts roamed Naomi's mind. Quinn looked at Naomi with a smirk then arose to help Naomi out of her seat.

"Since you say that I think I have something you'll enjoy even more than dinner."

Quinn's words made water stir in Naomi's center.

"I want you to have all of me."

Naomi was ready to let Quinn have his way with her. Quinn led her into the steam room of their suite. They undressed then settled into the warm air. The steam began to moisten their skin causing their bodies to stick. Naomi caressed Quinn's strong arms while his hands firmly gripped her backside. For several minutes they kissed passionately, their tongues dancing together, performing a rhythmic tango.

After leaving Terrance stiff in the front seat of his Range Rover, Lavere caught a cab back to Club Live. Lavere entered the building searching for Roc in the crowd. He spotted Roc chatting with the investor. Without being noticed, he made his way to the back of the building and into the club's office. Lavere planted the murder weapon he'd just used to off T back inside the drawer of Quinn's desk. Next, he made his way back out with the duffle trying his best to continue to remain unnoticed.

"Why is he carrying drugs through the front door, and where is Terrance?" Roc thought to himself as he watched Lavere walking swiftly out the club with a duffle in his hands. He was just about to finish up with the investor and planned to find out more as soon as he finished.

When Lavere got outside, he approached the young valet attendant.

"Terrance needs to see you in the office now. I'll look after the front for you."

"Okay thanks," The valet attendant responded.

The valet attendant handed Lavere the key to the valet booth then went inside the club. Lavere searched through the keys hanging inside the booth and found Roc's key then proceeded to the valet parking lot. When he spotted Roc's Audi Truck, he hit the unlock button to pop the trunk. He tossed the duffle in the back and locked the vehicle then went back to the valet booth where he placed the key back in its previous spot.

"Where are you going? You're supposed be watching the booth." Roc said spotting his young valet attendant walking toward his office.

"Lavere is watching the front for me. He said Terrance needed to talk to me. He's in the back, right?"

"I don't know, let's go find out." They headed back to the office and Terrance was nowhere to be found. "He's not here, get back down to your booth. I'll have him come get you if he needs you."

"Terrance wasn't in the office," the young valet attendant said to Lavere once he got back to his work spot.

"What? I just talked to him. I'll find him for you. Don't worry about it."

Lavere hurried back to the side of the building and got into his Porsche. He unlocked his cell then speed dialed Detective Stephens.

Roc pulled out his cell to call Terrance. After two tries, each time he reached the voicemail. He walked out to the front of the club where Lavere was supposed to be, but he was gone.

"Where'd Lavere go?" Roc asked the young valet attendant.

"He just left around back."

Roc went around back to the valet parking lot to see Lavere pulling off. He called Lavere's phone and was sent straight to voicemail, so he decided to call Terrance again. Roc let the phone ring until it went to voicemail. *"Why isn't anybody answering the damn phone?"*

Roc was confused then he got overwhelmed with a bad feeling of uneasiness. His gut was telling him that something was wrong, it was a feeling that he never ignored so he decided to trust it. He went to valet to grab the key to his Audi. He sent Randy a text to watch over the club while he made a run.

Roc drove over to Terrance's condo figuring he needed to see Terrance face to face to get some answers to what had gone wrong during the drop. When he arrived at the condo, the Range Rover Terrance had driven wasn't present so instantly he knew Terrance wasn't home. Roc shot back to the club and when he arrived, he thanked himself for trusting his instincts, they never failed him. He was watching the whole thing while he sat parked across the street in his Audi.

There was a large crowd of people, angry that their groove had been cut short by the law. The club was surrounded with cops who'd closed off the entire building. Being escorted out the front doors were several of his staff members with handcuffs around their wrists. It was a raid, and he knew the cops would tear down the entire building looking for evidence.

Roc ran through his house after racing home. On the way there he had made almost a hundred phone calls between Lavere, Terrance and Quinn. Every phone was going to voicemail. Next move was packing his most valued personal items. He unlocked his oversized safe to clear out all its contents, his jewels, his favorite gun, and most importantly, his stash. Only half of it was stashed in his house. The rest of it in a safe spot that he would get to later. That was all he needed. Everything else in the house could be replaced. He was about to go on the run, so he was going to have to lay low then get out of town without being noticed.

Rushing down to the garage, he tossed his bags into his Escalade. Out of his five cars, he could count on one hand how often he drove it. It was his best option since no one really saw him in it. Within seconds, he was pulling out of his driveway and racing out of his neighborhood. Just as he merged onto the interstate, he saw cop cars getting off the exit coming from the opposite direction. He knew they were headed to his home. He called Tank and his phone rang but he didn't pick up.

"Nobody's answering their gotdamn phone!" His mind frantic.

He called right back and Tank picked up after a couple of rings. Roc heard loud moaning on the other line.

"I fuck you better than your ex, huh? Say it!"

"You fuck me better... Better than my ex, Baby!"

"Yeah, that's right!"

"Hello! Hello! Hello!" Roc hung up the line and called right back.

"What's up, Man?"

"Are you fucking right now?"

"Yeah, so what." Tank was slamming Jamesha from behind.

"The cops just raided the club, and I saw them on my way to my crib as I was leaving. You need to meet me at the safe spot now! And make sure you don't get followed!"

Roc made what seemed like a hundred more calls to Terrance, Lavere, and Quinn. There was no answer from anyone.

◆ ◆ ◆

"Damn, you feel so damn good."

Naomi was on all fours with a fistful of hair being gripped tightly in Quinn's hand. He spanked her demanding her to say his name.

"Tell me, who's Daddy baby?"

"You Daddy!" Naomi screamed loving the pleasure he was giving her.

Quinn stroked and smacked her cheeks then released his seed inside her with no care. He was still rock hard, and he wasn't finished just yet. Naomi turned around and lay on her back then opened her legs so Quinn could enter her missionary. They were a perfect match for each other. Naomi's body was slim and curvy while Quinn's was lean and toned.

Naomi rubbed her fingers across his abs, through his pubic hair, then down to his pleasure pipe. She massaged it around the hole of her center while Quinn gently kissed from her neck down to her breast. Naomi's dark nipples were erect, and Quinn evenly sucked each nipple while easing inside of her. Naomi's insides had already begun to tighten, and she groaned as her man's girth opened her back up.

"Yes! Please Daddy!"

Naomi gripped Quinn's muscular physique and squeezed tightly as his body rubbed against hers. His

246

manhood throbbed in and out of her brushing against the side walls causing them to strongly contract with every stroke. Quinn tried his best to fill every inch of space in her canal. Quinn felt so big. It hurt her to take it all, but the pleasure was worth it. Her walls being stretched to capacity, but she didn't care.

"Please beat it up, Daddy!"

Quinn incessantly poked her A spot making her orgasm intensely. Naomi had cum a few times and her waves were becoming more frequent and intense. Quinn's breathing increased heavily as he unleashed a more powerful inner beast. His erection became as hard as steel as he penetrated her. His body began to wobble, and he could feel his orgasm building.

Naomi thought about how good he had to be feeling inside her making her cum again. Her contractions made Quinn curl his toes, and his body grew numb with pleasure as a blissful overtaking caused him to cling to her tightly. For a brief moment, they both lost their breath then let out gratifying moans as their bodies floated in ecstasy. Quinn let his seed swim inside Naomi's warm ocean while holding her body tightly as she trembled. Neither one of them made an effort to move after it was over; Quinn stayed inside her as they laid clung to each other by moist and sticky flesh.

Quinn awoke from his deep sleep to see daylight peering through the curtains of the window of his suite. He looked over at Naomi nestled underneath his arm. She was sound asleep looking so peaceful. He smiled and gently kissed her cheek. This vacation had given him a chance to relax and get away from all the stress and chaos back home. He was getting the best sleep he ever had these past few days.

This was the type of life he yearned to have, one with peace, quiet and waking up to his beautiful woman by his side for the rest of his life. Just the two of them living quietly and comfortably was all he needed to be happy. Quinn was ready to settle down and begin a family with Naomi. He loved her and there wasn't a doubt in his mind that she was the woman he wanted to be with forever. He could picture the beautiful kids they would produce, and she would be a wonderful mother to their offspring.

After being away with Naomi, Quinn yearned to stay away even more but since he had taken over the town's most popping nightclub and restaurant, his life had become more boisterous. However, night after night of packed crowds that kept profits coming in was now allowing him to expand the business into a franchise. He had plans to open up a Club and Restaurant next door in every major city. The idea was genius because each business fed off the other.

Even with the club and restaurant making him lots of money, Quinn was still living dirty. His drug operation was the true reason for his new lavish lifestyle. He could stop selling and give up his connect but the money was too good and easy.

"Would Hugo even let me out the game? If so, I would have a large debt to pay," He wondered.

Quinn promised himself that he would get out. He had to do it for peace of mind. He was tired of keeping secrets from his woman too.

"I will do it for one more year, then I'm out for good. Once my club and restaurant empire expands, I won't need to sell dope." He tried to convince himself.

Once he started getting money, there had been nonstop problems. Each day since the loss of his mother, he cried. He did it alone and by himself. It reminded him why he had to leave the bullshit behind plus Naomi was showing him that a cautious lifestyle was what he needed. He was tired of looking over his shoulder. More importantly he was tired of death. He couldn't take anymore losses.

Quinn reached over and called room service to order breakfast. After he placed the order, he grabbed his phone from the hotel nightstand. He was only going to check up on business but wasn't ready to entertain anything that had to do with work, so he decided to leave his cell phone off until he was back home. He trusted that his brothers had everything under control plus his baby deserved to spend time with him without any distractions.

Knock...Knock...Knock!

Quinn got out of bed and went to answer the room door. He opened the door and was greeted by a young blonde butler.

"Good morning, Sir. I have a Belgian waffle combo and steak omelet."

"Yes, one moment please."

Quinn went over to the side of the California king and grabbed his wallet from out of the jeans he had worn last night. Quinn gave the butler a fifty-dollar tip before sending her on her way. He opened the door to the suite balcony then sat down and enjoyed breakfast. Thanks to a drug dealer he'd met on Ocean Avenue, Quinn was able to buy some good smoke so after he ate, he rolled a joint. Quinn walked to the edge of the balcony while inhaling the weed smoke.

Looking out over the beach, he enjoyed the great scenery and sounds of the ocean waves. He wished he could pause the moment he was having and save it for later. To be able to wake up to something so beautiful was extraordinary to him. When he was living in a two-bedroom dump with his mother he imagined what it felt like to be in a place like this. Now it had become his reality. *"We came a long way from the hood mama. I miss you so much."* A tear rolled down his cheek.

Naomi pushed up against Quinn's back and caressed his shoulders. "Look who's up. Good morning," Quinn said quickly wiping his face while still looking over the balcony.

"You know every time you put it on me, I sleep like a baby."

"Are you ready to catch our flight tonight?"

"No, I want to stay here," Naomi said slightly pouting.

"Me either, Babe. But let's make the most of this time. I'm going to get us back out here soon maybe for good."

After a long private flight, Quinn and Naomi landed back in their hometown. Their trip had been the perfect getaway, but Quinn had to get back to business. He was tempted to go by the club and check up on things, but his body was jet lag, and he really wanted to lay in the bed and hold his woman. *"I'll go check up on things later."* Quinn still hadn't turned on his phone. He didn't want to get a call or text that reminded him of anything at the club, the restaurant or his drug operation.

Naomi and Quinn walked thru their home leaving their luggage at the door. They were way too tired to unpack. They undressed and made their way to the bed.

A few hours later Quinn was awakened by a noisy commotion coming from outside of his home. He jumped up and walked to his bedroom window that overlooked the front of his house. Peering through the blinds, he saw a cascade of red and blue lights. Numerous police officers were surrounding the premises of his home. He was confused as to what was going on.

"Babe, get up," he said to Naomi. "Hurry up and get dressed. There are cops everywhere."

"Huh?"

Naomi was still halfway sleep. Before she could get out of the bed, the cops had already kicked in the door. She managed to get her clothes on just before they stormed into the bedroom. Quinn was placed in cuffs and escorted outside. Naomi followed the officers out the front door of the mansion. The officers were reading Quinn his Miranda Rights as they pushed him into the squad car.

"Baby, what's going on?" Naomi asked in confusion.

"Wait for me to call you," Quinn instructed. "Until then, I need you to contact my lawyer. He will get me out."

Before the door of the squad car shut, he gave her a serious look and nodded his head from side to side. Naomi knew exactly what that meant but he said it anyway just to be clear.

"If they ask you anything, don't answer any questions."

What's Done In The Dark...

Walters! You can come out now. You get three phone calls," The county holding cell was opened by a guard and Quinn walked out to the phone to call his attorney. He'd been trapped for the past twenty-four hours.

"Hello? This is Attorney Patrick Perkins."

"Patrick, I'm in jail. I need you to get me out this joint."

"Yes, I know. I got news of your arrest from Naomi. Right now, you're being held without bond. You're going to have to wait until your court date until I can request bail from the judge."

"When is that?"

"You're scheduled to go before a judge in two months."

"That's not for a long time!"

"I know but these types of cases take time. Just sit tight until then. Have your girlfriend drop off your payment. I'll be working on getting you out of jail by next week."

"Have you gotten any information on what I'm being charged with? I need to know what I'm up against."

"Well, it doesn't look good so far."

"What is it?"

"You are looking at several different charges. You're being charged with conspiracy to sell and distribute cocaine, armed robbery, unlawful use of a weapon, and second-degree murder for a man named, Terrance Smith."

Quinn's heart dropped. Terrance being dead was the last thing he'd expected to hear. He began to wonder what happened while he was on vacation. The last time he talked to Terrance, he was on the way to meet with Hugo and everything was good. *"Maybe something bad went down."* He thought to himself. Quinn didn't care who Hugo thought he was. If he was responsible for Terrance's death, he was going to make him pay.

"How is that possible? I'm being accused of murdering my best friend. That can't be right. There's no evidence linking me to the murder."

"Actually, they seemed to have gathered a significant amount of evidence. Usually, you don't see a discovery this early, but there is supposedly a gun that was found in your club that matches the murder weapon. I've already been looking into the case."

As soon as Quinn heard those words, his heart sank into the pit of his stomach. His mind flashed back to handing Lavere his gun. *Lavere set me up.* A man who he would have given his life for had dropped a dime on him. He had fallen for his whole get out of jail early story. *"That snitch killed Terrance."* Quinn's sickness then turned to rage. Inside he was screaming. He hung up the phone in his lawyer's face. His brain had to piece everything together. The only thing he could think of doing was killing Lavere as soon he was free. *"His bitch ass is probably somewhere in protection. That won't stop me. I'm going to kill him."*

Quinn stared into Naomi's hazel brown eyes as she leaned forward from him across the prison table. *"I love this beautiful woman,"* he thought. He hadn't heard from her since the day he was arrested.

"What are you being charged with?" was the first thing she asked. Ironically, that was the first thing he'd asked his lawyer.

"I can't speak to you about it in here. How are you though?"

"I'm just wishing you were home. I can't sleep not knowing what's going to happen to you. The fact that you are stuck in here and I don't know when you're going to get out is driving me crazy."

"Don't worry, Baby. I will be out soon. I just need you to pay my lawyer so I can post bail."

"Your bank accounts are frozen on top of that, they found all the money you had in the house." Quinn was pissed because he had a large fortune stashed in the attic. It would take him some time to make that money back. He'd always thought that one day a burglar or the feds could break in and find the stash in his home, so he kept more somewhere safe.

"I talked to your lawyer. You're being changed with some serious crimes. He didn't tell me what they were. He said he didn't want to disclose that information without your permission."

"I didn't do it baby. I promise."

"I believe you." Naomi said it but wasn't truly convinced.

"Don't worry. I have a plan."

"I'm sure hope you do," Naomi said with skepticism."

"Just trust me on this. Follow the instructions on this note." Quinn discretely nodded toward his hand as he slid it across the table. There was a tiny piece of paper hidden underneath it.

"Put your hand on top of mine," he instructed. She did as he said, "Keep it there."

Quinn slid his hand back so she could take the note. As the guard on duty watched their interaction, they resembled two lovers showing normal affection. He was oblivious to the exchange that was just made.

"What did you do, Baby? Just tell me why they have you in this place." Naomi shook her head. She didn't know how to deal with having a man in jail.

"I didn't do anything. I'm innocent. You believe me, right?"

"Yes."

"Like I said before, I can't speak on it while I'm in here. I'll call my lawyer and let him know he can discuss with you. He will explain exactly what needs to be done to get me out. He's the best lawyer in town. Once he gets on the case, I'll be out of here in no time. It's all a big misunderstanding, you'll see."

Naomi looked into Quinn's eyes, and she honestly believed him.

"I'm going to keep praying for you. You should do it too." Quinn thought about it for a second wondering if it would really help his situation. "When, you get out I want you to meet my Big Mama, she's been asking about you."

"You haven't told her about this situation, have you? Quinn lifted his eyebrow. "I don't want anyone thinking negatively about me before I get the chance to show them the type of person I really am."

"I haven't told anyone. My Big Mama isn't judgmental anyway."

"I'd love to meet your grandma. I know it means a lot to you. I do have one request as soon as I get out."

"Anything, Babe."

"I want you to cook my favorite meal, salmon and asparagus with the apple pie and vanilla ice cream. The food in here sucks."

Naomi smiled because she knew Quinn loved her cooking.

"I'll do you one better, I'll have my Big Mama cook for us. She taught me everything I know in the kitchen."

"Okay, that's a deal."

"Walters, your times up!" The guard motioned with his hand for Quinn to get up and go back to his cell.

"Whatever you need, I got you, Baby," Naomi spoke with tears in her eyes.

Quinn could tell she was holding back. His heart was heavy. He knew once she walked out the jail, she was going to break down with emotions. Naomi was scared for her man but he needed her to have his back so she would. Naomi feared what kind of trouble Quinn had gotten himself into. He had shared with her that he broke the law in his past, but just never explained what type of crimes he had done just that they were serious. Naomi didn't need to know any of the intricate details because everyone had secrets in their past and she wasn't one to judge anyone for their mistakes.

The feds had frozen Quinn's accounts, so she had no access to any of his funds. On top of that, he had two million dollars stashed in the walls of his attic that was seized in the raid of his home. That was a big chunk of all the money Quinn saved from hustling, but thankfully he knew better than to keep his whole stash where he lived or in a bank account. The rest of his savings were in a safe spot that no one would ever find unless they knew exactly where to look. It was the pretty penny he put away just in case he saw a rainy day. Right now, it was pouring, and he needed his umbrella.

"I need you to get to Twin Light Condos Floor 18 Suite 1812. The keys are under the doormat. Use it to get in then open the cherry wood cabinet located in the bedroom."

Naomi read Quinn's note then immediately went to follow his instructions. She arrived at the address he gave her and was in front of the nicest apartment building she had ever seen. There was an underground garage that the residents used for parking with elevators that led you up to your apartment. She took the fancy

258

elevator up to floor eighteen, and then stepped into the hall inside of the building. It looked like a five-star hotel. She was a little upset that he had a secret place that she didn't know anything about. She followed the arrows of the hallway to the door of #1812. Following the instructions on the note, she lifted the doormat to find a key.

"You definitely don't have to worry about leaving your key there in these bougie apartments", Naomi thought. She unlocked the door to a huge open space that contained a kitchen, living room and dining room area. The ceiling was at least twelve feet high. The only furniture inside was a pool table, sectional sofa and sixty something inch flat screen television mounted across from it on the wall. There were a set of steps that led to a bedroom and bathroom with a walk-in closet. There was no bed in the bedroom, so the apartment wasn't a place where he spent much time.

Naomi went to the closet and there weren't any clothes in the closet just a very large cherry wooden cabinet. She pulled the handles of the cabinet to open it. The cabinet was completely stocked with cash money. It was more than double the amount of money that was stashed in Quinn's attic. She was easily looking at a few million dollars.

She ran back up the steps to the kitchen then opened the cabinet under the sink. There were a couple bottles of cleaner and a box of trash bags. She grabbed the box of trash bags then went back to the cherry wood cabinet. By the time she cleared out the cabinet, she had two full trash bags. After Naomi locked up the apartment, she rushed to her car to transfer all the money into the trunk. She went straight home. It was still a total mess from the raid of police officers who had rummaged through. Naomi couldn't fix herself to clean up, still in shock of what happened.

"I really have to be careful with all this cash," she thought to herself while carrying the bags of money into the house. Naomi phoned Quinn's attorney and left him a voicemail about her plan to drop off a payment to him first thing in the morning. She went to the living room and plopped down on the sofa then turned on the television and flipped through the channels until she reached the first news station.

It was seven o'clock pm and the top stories of the day were about to be reported. Naomi was stunned when the reporter began introducing the top story of the hour. The news station showed a video of Club Live with several of its employees being escorted out of the building by officers.

"Oh my God."

Naomi pressed up on the remote's volume button so she could hear the reporter.

"A man who has been identified as Quinten Walters was indicted for murder, drug trafficking, and robbery. Quinten Walters, owner of Club Live, a popular nightclub in the city is believed to have used illegal money to fund the business. Money, he stole from a series of bank robberies including the notorious, Community City Bank robbery that resulted in the death of a security guard.

Terrance Smith, a former member of Quinten's gang, is the man Quinten is accused of killing. Police are also looking for another man, Devante Richards. Police say he is also linked to these crimes. If anyone has information on his whereabouts, we urge you to call our tips hotline. We will have more information on this story as it becomes available."

Seeing the picture of Michael on the news as a victim who died the day of the robbery brought back old grief. Worst of all, Naomi had discovered a tormenting revelation. She couldn't hold back the tears. Quinn was responsible for the death of her high school sweetheart. She looked at the four trash bags full of money. It was it was all stolen or drug money. She was torn on what to do with it. She knew Quinn needed her help, but she was hurt.

Although he never lied to her about whom he was, he never told her the complete truth either. The whole time they had been together, she had no idea who he really was. The ache in her heart was unexplainable. She had so many mixed emotions and questions. She wanted to confront him, but how? How could she look him in his face knowing he killed Michael? How could she live with herself knowing that she was sleeping with the enemy?

Naomi still loved Michael and even though she was no longer in love with him, she had enough respect not to piss on his grave. A part of her didn't want see Quinten ever again.

Somehow, another part of her was missing him. He needed to hurt and to pay for what he'd done. Naomi contemplated what to do with the money. There was no way in hell she would turn it in to the cops. If she kept it, she would have to get away fast without being noticed. She was in possession of millions of dollars of illegal money that belonged to a man who was in jail depending on her to bail him out. In her heart, she felt wrong to take his fortune and abandon him in his time of need.

"Should I give him a chance to explain?" she thought to herself. *"What is there to explain? He would never know how much pain he's caused me."* In Naomi's head, it didn't matter what he had to say, he was a murderer. *"How can I be with someone like that? Hell no, that's just crazy."* Quinn wasn't just a career criminal and killer which was bad enough, he was responsible for one of the darkest moments in her life.

Guilty Until Proven Innocent

Quinn stood before the judge for the first time since he had been arrested.

"Have you been provided a copy of the complaint against you?" the judge asked Quinn.

"Yes."

"Do you need the complaint read to you or do you deny reading."

"I do not need it read to me. I understand what my charges are."

"Would you like the court to appoint you counsel, or can you afford your own?"

"I will pay for my own lawyer." Quinn stood nervously in his bail hearing with just him the prosecutor and judge. Without a lawyer, he felt completely defenseless.

"Do you currently have an attorney?"

"I don't have one as of the moment. I'm still working on it."

"If you cannot come up with an attorney the court will assign you a public defender. Are you certain you do not need help obtaining representation?"

"No, your Honor, I have some people on the outside working on getting me an attorney. I just need a little more time."

"I'm giving you thirty days. If you do not have an attorney by then, the court will assign someone to your case. What is the prosecution's position on bail?"

"Your Honor, I would like to request that bail be denied for the defendant for the duration of the trial," Alfred chimed.

"And what is your reasoning for the defendant being held without bond?"

"Your honor, considering the nature of the crimes the defendant faces, the prosecution believes this man poses a greater threat to the community on the streets rather than behind bars. Quinten Walters is dangerous and his return to the streets will result in a spike in violent crime. This man is a monster who killed his own friend over money. I think that should say enough about the type of person he is."

"Judge, those statements are completely false and last time that I checked, the law states that the defendant is innocent until proven guilty. I would like to request bond in any amount. Whatever it is, I'll pay it." Quinn stately confidently.

"You can't buy your way out of trouble, Quinten. Your Honor, this man is a greedy, selfish, cowardly killer who shot his own friend in the head."

"Sir, this man is lying on my name. You don't know me or my friend who was killed." Quinn couldn't help but mug the prosecutor who was speaking so abysmally about him."

"Your Honor, there is nothing false about my claims. This man is a monster. You'd be better off freeing the apes in the zoo."

"Fuck you pussy! You ain't shit but a pig, you know that?"

Quinn's anger boiled over the top and he couldn't restrain himself from going off. If he didn't have cuffs around his wrists, he'd have his hands around the prosecutor's throat. Quinn had just played right into Alfred's plan.

"Order! I've heard enough! I will not allow my courtroom to be turned into a name calling contest. As of now, I'm siding with the prosecution. Bail will be denied for the defendant until further notice." Judge McGowan banged his gavel ending Quinn's hearing.

The next day Quinn stood anxiously at the bars of his cell.

"It is recreation time, and you got one hour! That's sixty minutes, not a second longer. Everyone must be back in their cell at one o'clock sharply! If anyone is late, that person will lose his hour of freedom for the next thirty days!" The guard announced.

The sound of numerous cell locks clicking opened echoed throughout the prison. After being on twenty-three-hour lockdown for weeks, his patience had run thin. The faint lines creased in his forehead revealed his stress. He needed to see why the hell he was still locked up and without his lawyer's representation. Soon as the cell bars slid open, he headed straight to the phones. His current mission was to call Naomi and confirm that she dropped money off to his lawyer. The phone rang, she didn't answer. After several tries, he was blocked and being sent straight to voicemail. He called his attorney hoping he'd get some good news.

"Good afternoon. Perkins law office?" the receptionist greeted.

"Can I be directed to Patrick Perkins?"

"Yes, one moment please."

"Hello, this is Patrick Perkins."

"Patrick, its Quinten.

"Hello Quinten, how are you?

"I'd be better the sooner I get out this joint, you feel me. Has Naomi been by your office to drop off my deposit?"

"No, I'm afraid she hasn't. She left a voicemail about a week ago. She said she'd be by to drop it off first thing in the morning, but she never showed, and I need a deposit in order to get to work on your case."

"Listen, I'll get you the money soon. For now, can you just get me approved for bail, I need you to request it at my court date coming up."

"I'm sorry, Quinten. I would like to help you out, but I can't enter my name into your case unless I receive payment first. It's just business."

"You know I'm good for it. I'll even pay you extra. Just help me post my bail and I guarantee you'll get your money."

"I have a lot of high paying clients who need my service Quinten. Under no circumstances do I work for free. I see a lot of guys like you who don't save their money then can't afford good representation. If you can't come up with the funds you may want to consider a public defender."

Click!

His lawyer hung up in his face.

Quinn slammed the receiver down. He had no lawyer to work on his case and was not trying to settle for a public defender. He picked the receiver back up and called Naomi at least ten times. Each time it went straight to voicemail. Quinn was confused and hurt at the same time. He wondered if Naomi had run off with his bread and if that was the reason why she wasn't answering his calls. As much as he didn't want to believe it, he felt as if it was the truth. *"Why else would she be avoiding me?"*

At that point, Quinn was worried that maybe something horrific had happened to her. If so, surely someone would have answered her phone to let him know. Deep down he knew that wasn't the case. Naomi was purposely ignoring his calls, and Quinn was feeling like a fool to have ever trusted her. She was the one woman who he had decided to give his heart and his trust and now he was regretting it.

Quinn went out to the basketball court where there was a game already going.

"Aye big homie, you got game you can take my spot."

The man offering Quinn a spot on the court was older than Quinn but due to Quinn's status, he was given respect of an OG. Upon his arrival in the joint, Quinn was shown much love from the other inmates on lockdown.

His reputation from the streets had followed him to jail. Several saw getting in good graces with Quinn as an opportunity to come up. The Mafia was street royalty and to be a member of the crew came with benefits. For the same reason that the convicts hailed Quinn the prison guards despised him.

"The game just started."

"Yeah, I'll jump in." Quinn figured a game of hoops would help relieve some of his stress and tension. "Who all on my squad?"

"Everybody with shirts on."

"Okay bet. I'll run point," Quinn said to his other teammates.

He checked the ball to his opponent then they began to run their game of scrimmage. Quinn finished with half of his team's points and slam dunk to seal the game by two points.

After his rec time ended, Quinn entered the cell and the bottom bunk was occupied as usual by his cellmate, Armando. His cellmate's sandals were at the bottom of the bunk. Quinn pushed his shoes to the side and climbed to the top bunk.

"I'm going to say this one time, don't touch my shit."

Quinn didn't respond, just grinned and laid his head back onto his pillow. He didn't care about the man he was sharing a cell with. He was focused on one thing and that was getting out of prison.

Little did Quinn know; he was sharing a cell with the man who held the key to his freedom. Sitting in a quiet cell for hours was boring. Quinn wasn't much of a talker himself, but the long periods of silence and inactivity were driving him crazy. He needed to talk to someone to at least keep himself from going insane.

"So, what you in here for man?" Quinn figured if he had to share a cell with a man, they may as well get along.

"That's not important, but I know what you're in here for. The media loves you."

"The media can stay off my nuts and keep my name out their mouths."

"You know it's a shame, I would have thought a man like you would have more options. If you had the right connections, you'd be released by now."

"You don't know what I got going on. I'll be out of here in no time, just watch."

"You remind me of my brother, he never admits when his back is against the wall, he would like you."

"If you have such heavy connections, why are you still in here?"

"I was arrested as I arrived in America off a plane from Mexico my homeland. They bring me here to this prison and charge me with crimes. I get denied bail and no court date until next year. They think if I sit in here long enough, I will turn on my family. They don't know that I'll never rat on my family. I rather die than be a disgrace."

Quinn could relate. He would never let his integrity be tarnished by becoming a Narc like Lavere. The more Quinn talked with Armando; he took a liking to him. His story was fascinating how he came from the mud to be one of the richest men in the world. Quinn ended up learning that Armando's family was the notorious, Mendez Cartel, one of the most powerful drug organizations in the world. Given Quinn's reputation, Armando was willing, even persuading him to work with his brother Jose in exchange for a ticket out of federal prison. The way things were looking for Quinn, taking Armando's deal was the best option Quinn had.

Making a deal with one of the country's most powerful drug cartels held major responsibilities. A few years ago, for Quinn it would have been the deal of a lifetime, but Quinn knew that the game was not all glitz and glamour. It had an ugly face and could deal you the worst pain you'd ever felt. Although its highs came with glory, the temporary bliss wasn't worth the permanent destruction. The death of his mother was his constant reminder. He knew he was making a deal with the devil but if he wanted to see the outside of a cell, he was going to need the Mendez Cartel's help.

Just a few days passed. Armando and Quinn had talked extensively. "Meal service!" the guard's voice blared through the speaker in Quinn's cell alerting him that the prison breakfast was now being served.

The loud echo of his cell door clicked indicating it was unlocked and he was free to make his way down to the cafeteria line. The hours and days were all a blur. Each day, the sun rose and set eventually Quinn had lost track of the days. They were all the same and he couldn't tell yesterday from two weeks ago.

The boring routine of prison was driving Quinn to do anything to help the time pass quickly, but it never did. Every minute that passed felt as if it were the length of an hour. Quinn paced his cell back and forth over a thousand times a day. Anxiety set in. He had concluded that he would rather beat his head against a wall than be on lockdown. There was nothing to do but sit and think, his time was being wasted as days turned into a few months.

Then an uncommon early morning came. He was summoned from his cell and sent to a private room. A pretty sophisticated young attorney entered. They locked eyes as she pulled out a seat and set across from him. Her expression read serious.

"Hello Quinten, my name is Angela Starks, your new court appointed attorney and I'll be representing you throughout your trial."

"What kind of time am I looking at?" Quinn asked, ready to get straight to the point. He had so many questions about his case that only his lawyer could answer, and he hadn't been able to get any answers until now.

"I'm going to be honest with you, Quinten. If convicted, you could spend the rest of your life behind bars but try not to think negatively. You do have some options, you can either take a plea for a lesser punishment or plead not guilty, but I must advise you that if you plead not guilty, it is up to the judge to determine your sentence. If you take a deal with the prosecution, it will definitely be less punishment. However, you will have to do some time because of the nature of the charges."

"I'm not taking a deal. I'm not guilty."

"That's your decision, Quinten. However, you still have time to think over your options. First, we need to try to get you approved for bail. We can get the government to unfreeze your accounts if there is reason to believe that the money was not the result of illegal business."

"I have an accountant who has invoice records of every transaction I make from my club and restaurant and the deposit amounts that go into my bank account." The truth was that Quinn had hired an expert in finance to adjust the numbers to mask the drug profits he deposited.

"If I can get you to obtain copies of those financial statements, there's a possibility you can bail yourself out."

That was music to Quinn's ears if only he had contact to the outside world. Naomi had his cell phone which contained all of his important contacts. He had no resources. There was no one who could oversee his club or restaurant. His businesses had been completely shut down.

"Mr. Walters, I am going to represent you in this case but in order for me to help you, I need you to be honest with me at all times. I need to know everything you know that way I can help you the best that I can. I know who you are and that doesn't matter. I'm here to represent you, right or wrong."

"You think you know who I am," Quinn said looking the public defender he was assigned directly into her pupils.

It was clear that she assumed he was guilty just like everyone else who watched the news and believed the lies and stories that they tried to paint of him being a monster.

"I have done my research and I found out that you operate one of the largest drug operations in the city. I also found that the charges filed against you date back to a slew of bank robberies."

"If that's all that you know about me, then you don't know me."

"The prosecution has an acquaintance of yours turning informant to bring you down. His identity is being protected. Is there anything I need to know about this confidential informant who is working with the prosecution? Is there anyone you suspect that may have turned against you?"

"I don't know who you could be talking about."

"I'm sure you know you've been set up. You can tell me who it is."

"I don't snitch. I have money if you can win this case, I will pay you after the trial. A hundred thousand dollars' cash will be yours."

"I can't promise that you'll win your case."

"But you can be my source to access the outside world."

"I'm not going to commit crime for you Quinten."

"All I need is for you to communicate with my people. Right now, I have no link between me and any of my outside associates."

"One of your associates is a fugitive. If I get caught, I can face felony charges."

"I'll offer you ten thousand dollars every week until I'm a free man. All I need is for you to relay messages back and forth." Quinn didn't know if he could trust her, but he needed to get her to bite the bait on this. He had to have something on her because if there was one thing he knew for sure, it was that people worked better with something at stake.

"Ok you have a deal."

"Give me a pen and some paper."

Angela reached into her briefcase and retrieved a pen and notepad. She slid them both in front of Quinn who began jotting words on the paper. When he finished Quinn slid the pen and pad back over to Angela.

"On that paper are two things. The first is the name Roc. The second is the address where you can find him. You must only go there at night and make sure no one follows you there. Let him know who you are and that I sent you there. When you meet with him, I need to you to inform him of all my court dates, the times, and locations.

I will write letters to communicate with him and you will hand them to him when you see him. Whatever letters he has for me you will hand to me when we meet. That's all you have to do for ten thousand a week. He will give you the money, cold hard cash in your hand."

"What about the informant? Who is he and what information might this man have that could incriminate you?"

Although Quinn had offered his public defender a bribe, he still didn't trust her, so he surely was not going to incriminate himself.

"Just do what I said and don't ask me anymore bullshit questions. In case you didn't know by now, I ain't snitch."

"How does the defendant like to plea?"

"Your Honor, I would like to set this case for trial. The defendant is pleading not guilty. Also, I would like to request bond for immediate release of the defendant. He has been incarcerated for months now."

"What is the prosecution's argument for keeping the defendant in custody?"

"As I stated at the first hearing, we believe the defendant is more dangerous on the streets. In order to protect victims and witnesses of this case, it is in the courts best interest that he remains in custody."

"Your Honor, my client is a law-abiding citizen who runs several legitimate businesses that he would like to tend to."

"Those are businesses that were funded by stolen and drug money."

"Those are accusations yet to be proven."

"Your Honor, the facts are that several kilos of cocaine along with a murder weapon were found stashed inside the club office."

"Okay, I've heard enough. Quinten, you will remain in custody. If you are found innocent, you will be released from custody. The trial will begin in ninety days."

"This is just a battle. We still have to fight the war," Angela whispered to Quinn.

"It's a war I'm going to win." He assured her.

Running From The Law

Alfred Pennington wanted to capitalize on the recognition he was gaining as a fierce, no nonsense prosecutor of the law. In reality, he was a cold-hearted corrupt man out for self-gain. It had been nearly ten years since he had lost a case.

Getting to where he had now established himself wasn't easy. He had spent countless nights away from home causing a divorce with his wife and missed time with his two kids. He was always working late until the crack of dawn to convict worthless scum bags just like Quinten Walters. Alfred made his way to the prosecutor's bench. Today, he walked with swagger and an increased amount of confidence than he ever had before.

Before reaching his seat, he made it a point to make eye contact with Quinn. His gaze was met with a cold blank stare. He honestly could not read Quinn's facial expression. He had no idea what the man was thinking with his sharp poker face. He was sure that Quinn was worried about the fate of his future. Quinn's pretend indifference didn't fool him.

"He's no different from any of those other black bastards. They act as if they're all tough with that bullshit thug persona. When I put the pressure on him, he'll bust like a loose pipe." Alfred thought.

Today marked the start of a trial for the biggest case of Alfred's career. Not to mention, the high amount of media attention the case was already receiving. As soon as the indictment was released, it made the top headline of every local news station. There was even an article in a major newspaper that read, **"Criminal Mastermind Set to Go to Trial."**

Alfred knew as the trial proceeded, its attention from the public would only gain. A win would give Alfred all the exposure he needed. He had been following the Midwest Connection's previous leaders for years but could never penetrate their organization. Quinten had eliminated his chance to convict them. He wanted to be the one to seal their fate and for that, he hated Quinn even more.

Alfred had the witness that prosecutors dreamt of. After he won this case, his reputation would increase, and his level of income would soon follow. He planned to run for congress and this case would help boost his resume. Alfred's mind began to wonder, and he thought about all the pussy he would attract with his newfound success. Suddenly, his penis began to stiffen, and he returned his focus to the courtroom. As Alfred reached his seat, he placed his briefcase on the bench table then glanced down at his crotch to ensure he wasn't embarrassing himself. *Good thing I wore briefs today,* Alfred thought then took his seat.

Why is this prick staring so hard? Quinn thought as he returned a sinister mug to the prosecutor

Other than that, he hardly looked at anyone in the courtroom. He scanned the crowd hoping he'd see Naomi, but she was nowhere to be found. Quinn kept his eyes focused on the podium, but everyone else's eyes were on him.

When the bailiff led him into the courtroom, he noticed evil glares from everyone around him. He also noticed how when he entered the courtroom, the atmosphere went from silent to a cadence of whispers and harsh remarks that echoed off all four walls. He couldn't believe how some people who didn't know the first thing about him could have so much hatred and envy.

Suddenly, Quinn's attorney barged into the courtroom right on time. Angela Starks was focused and ready to handle business. Out of everyone in the room, she was the most serious. Like Alfred, today also marked the start of the biggest case of her career. She needed a win to boost her reputation as a credible defense attorney.

As a black woman, Angela had to work twice as hard and be twice as sharp to be respected among the most prestigious lawyers in the city. After the trial was over, she would get the respect she deserved. She had caught a break with this case. High profile clients were hard to come by and they were usually taken by attorneys with big reputations. With this case she was taking a small risk that would reap much larger rewards. She was public defender so working as hard as she'd been on such a time-consuming case was unusual for a court appointed attorney.

Angela was being paid under the table, but she had a larger goal in mind. Angela's dream had always been to open her own law firm independently from the ground up since the day she began law school. In the next few years, she planned to be the most sought-after defense attorney in the city. Her sights were set on the top and this was her opportunity that she couldn't let slip away.

Detective Stephens slipped inside the courtroom just as court was about to begin taking a quick seat on the back row. He had spent so much time trying to solve the crimes Quinn had committed. There was no way he could miss watching Quinn get a life sentence.

"All rise! I present to you the Honorable Judge Samuel McAdams. Court is now in session. You may be seated."

Judge McAdams entered the courtroom then took a seat in his lawfully given position of prestige.

"I now present to you case seven, five, U, A, nine, three, two Walters vs. The United States of America. Without any further delay Attorney Pennington, you may present your opening arguments."

"Thank you, Your Honor."

Alfred rose to his feet and faced the large audience in attendance. "Ladies and Gentlemen, especially those of the jury, today you have been given an opportunity and placed with a vital responsibility."

Alfred made eye contact with every person on the jury panel. The jury was split between men and women with an equal number of jurors representing each gender. The nationalities were mostly white with three minorities.

"Let's start with the opportunity that has been awarded to you. Our city streets have been infected with the plague. Our neighborhoods are becoming more infested each day. The distribution of drugs, robberies and gang violence has seen a steady incline over the past ten years. Right now, as we speak, crime has reached its highest peak in the history of our city. The past three years have consecutively set a record for the highest annual homicide total in the history of this city. Numbers like these don't just appear out of nowhere, there is a root cause, a bad apple causing the entire tree to rot. This man, Ladies and Gentlemen is the plague in our city streets." Alfred pointed directly at Quinn.

"Several lives have been lost at the hands of this man and numerous families have suffered without any repercussions. This special jury has the opportunity to clean our streets from drugs and violence and to bring justice to countless families. It all starts by removing Quinten Walters from our streets. Now your responsibility is to capitalize on the opportunity that has been given to you. For years this man has been wreaking havoc throughout our city blocks and we haven't been able to capture him until now," he earnestly spoke.

"This may be our only chance to change the fate of our youth and prevent them from going down a road of destruction. Remember that the youth are always our responsibility, a safe future and clean streets are our responsibility. Protecting elderly who can't defend themselves against the gang members and drug dealers is our responsibility! Throughout this trial no matter what information is presented to you, I want you to always remember it is your responsibility to keep our streets safe and clean by removing the criminals who are causing the destruction and turmoil."

The entire courtroom gave a slight hand clap after Alfred's somewhat heartfelt speech. His plan with his opening speech had worked. He wanted to start off by getting into the jury's heads and let them know that no matter what arguments the defense presented, Quinten was a low-down, murdering, drug lord who needed to be thrown in deepest darkest cell and locked away forever. Quinn could clearly see Alfred's intentions to paint him as a monster.

"Some people are influenced by anything they hear." Quinn thought, referring to the courtroom audience. Unlike Alfred, Quinn was no stranger to the streets. He learned a long time ago that you can believe none of what you hear and half of what you see.

"I bet he's never even seen these streets he's talking about, probably never spent one night in the hood." Though his lips were shut, Quinn's mind had a lot to say. *"He couldn't last one night on my block without getting robbed, or one week without getting killed. But he's so sure that I'm the reason for all the violence. Like one person can be the cause of every problem in the hood? The streets been fucked up way before I stepped one foot on them."*

"Your Honor, my client has never been in any trouble and in fact, he has a squeaky-clean criminal record. He is a leader in the community and businessman. He has been wrongly accused and framed. Do we want to be a broken justice system? It's supposed to be innocent until proven guilty, not guilty until proven innocent," Angela stated.

"Yes, my client comes from a rough background, but he was able to overcome it. He should be looked at as an inspiration for those young kids from the inner city who wonder if one day they'll make it out. The prosecution doesn't have a legitimate case. There are too many holes in their story, and I will highlight those as we maneuver through this trial."

"Your Honor, the first person I would like to call to the stand is the defendant."

Alfred was ready to present his case and felt there was no better way to start than by putting Quinn on the stand then getting under his skin.

"Mr. Walters, you may approach the stand," the judge ordered. Quinn got up and sat at the testimony podium.

The bailiff approached Quinn with the Holy Bible in hand. The book meant nothing to Quinn. It damn sure wouldn't stop him from lying.

"Do you swear to tell the truth the whole truth and nothing but the truth, so help you God?"

"I do."

"Mr. Walters, where were you on the night of August fifteenth two thousand and ten when Terrence Smith was murdered?"

"I was on vacation."

"We found the murder weapon with your prints inside of your club the same night of the crime. Can you explain that Mr. Walters?"

"That does not prove that I committed any crime."

Alfred chuckled at Quinn's nonchalant attitude.

"Let's get this right someone else had a weapon that belongs to you, that is registered in your name and was found inside your club at the crime scene. If you were not in possession of the weapon, then tell me who was?"

"I don't know."

"You were supposed to purchase drugs from your supplier that day, right?"

"I have no idea what you're talking about."

"Of course you do. You and Terrance Smith went to purchase drugs from your distributor. After you two received the drugs, you got into a disagreement over each other's cut, it escalated, and you shot and killed him. Your own greed led you to murder your friend. That's why your fingerprints were on the gun that was raided from your nightclub which matches the same weapon that was used to kill Terrance Smith. That places you at the crime scene. Therefore, there's no one who could have shot and killed Terrance Smith but you!"

Quinn knew what the prosecutor was trying to do. He was trying to make him angry again and get an aggressive reaction. Quinn kept calm amongst the prosecutor's accusations.

"Are you done?" Quinn remarked sarcastically.

"Quinn knew who shot T, but he wasn't a rat. He would never get on a stand and drop a dime, even if it was to expose a rat.

"I was on my way in town at the time. I don't know who killed my friend, Terrance. If I did, I would tell you."

"If you were out of town at the time, where's your proof? Any plane ticket receipts, hotel receipts? You don't have any of that so why should we believe you?"

"I actually don't have access to it from prison."

Not having Naomi as an aid had hurt Quinn badly. She had access to all the evidence he needed to help his case. She was the only alibi he had besides Roc and he was somewhere lying low right now as he should.

"I wasn't there, and I don't know what happened and that's all."

Angela shook her head, upset that Quinn was purposely withholding information but there was one thing Quinn would never be in his life and that was a snitch.

"No further questions, Your Honor."

"The defendant may return to the bench." The bailiff directed Quinn back to his seat.

"Your Honor, I would like to call my next witness to the stand, Lavere Collins." Quinn turned his head to see Lavere entering the courtroom.

"This snake," Quinn thought to himself. Lavere had had a pitiful look on his face as he approached the testimony podium.

"Do you swear to tell the truth, the whole truth and nothing but the truth so help you God?"

Lavere placed his hand on the bible before saying. "I do."

"Lavere Collins, you know the defendant very well, am I right?"

"Yes, I do sir."

"Can you identify him in this courtroom?"

"Yes, he is seated right there." Lavere said as he pointed in Quinn's direction.

"For about how long have you known Mr. Walters?"

"I've known him for a long time, since we were kids."

"On the night that Terrance Smith was murdered, do you know who went with him to purchase drugs?"

"Quinn did."

"So, the last person who was seen with Terrance was Quinten?"

"Yes, as far as I know they were going to meet the connect."

"Mr. Collins, in the past, did you commit crimes with Quinten?"

"Yes."

"Do any of those crimes include robbery?"

"Yes."

"Is it true that Quinten Walters was the mastermind behind the crimes you committed?"

"Yes."

"Can you explain how Quinten Walters was the orchestrator of these illegal doings?"

"He came up with the schemes and convinced me to join him."

"On the day of the Community City Bank robbery, you and Quinten and three other accomplices set off to orchestrate a bank heist. Can you tell me exactly what happened that day and during the other robberies that were committed?"

Quinn watched with amazement as Lavere told a mix of lies and truths, giving intricate details of how they planned each robbery to how they pulled them off.

"I can't believe this nigga putting on a show like this. He deserves an Oscar." Quinn was thinking.

The whole courtroom was silent as they listened to Lavere's testimony. It was so vivid that everyone could envision the stories as if they were being played on a projector screen for everyone to see.

"Thank you, Mr. Collins. You may return to your seat."

Quinn watched Lavere closely as he walked past him. Lavere's head was lowered. He didn't even look at Quinn once the whole time he was on the stand. He avoided making eye contact. Aside from being a certified snitch, Quinn was more annoyed at how much of a coward Lavere was.

"Your Honor, I'd like to call Lavere Collins back to the stand." Angela was going to counter Alfred by using his very own star witness against him.

"That was a great little performance you put on in front of our courtroom just a moment ago. Now let's cut the theatrics and get down to the real facts. You just testified to save your own ass, am I right?"

"I object," Alfred interrupted.

"Angela, watch your language." Judge McAdams intervened.

"Yes, Your Honor, I apologize."

"You are testifying to save yourself some time, am I right?"

"Your Honor, my client does not have to disclose our deal."

"Exactly, you and the district attorney made a deal to in order to incriminate my client. We all know that those deals consist of less jail time in exchange for the conviction of another party."

"Angela, please get to your point," the judge butted in.

"Is it true that you are jealous of Quinten's success and want to bring him down to your level?"

"No, I just wanted to come clean and do what's right."

Angela laughed loudly. She had to admit, Lavere could put on a good front.

"You killed Terrance Smith and framed this entire case in order to save yourself."

Lavere was nervous and sweat began to drip from his forehead like whenever he was feeling pressured.

"Your Honor, my witness has an alibi for where he was during the night of Terrance Smith's murder. He couldn't have possibly set up the defendant," Alfred butted in.

"Can you explain your whereabouts, Lavere?" Judge McGowan questioned.

"I was umm…I…"

"We had a meeting that night," Alfred chimed in again.

"I think the witness can speak for himself," Judge McAdams stated.

"Yeah we umm…had a meeting."

"About what? How you two were going to setup up my client."

"Your Honor, the details of our meeting are confidential," Alfred interrupted.

"Alfred this will be the last interruption I tolerate from you. I think the witness can answer for himself."

"I met with Alfred and Detective Stephens to give them evidence that I had."

"I'm going to guess that you had been wearing a wire."

"Yes."

"No further questions your honor."

"Okay Angela, if you do not have any more questions for the witness, I'm ordering a two-hour recess.

"At this time, we would like to proceed with the trail. Does the prosecution set forth any evidence against the defendant?"

"The prosecution would like to present audio evidence of Quinten conspiring to distribute narcotics."

The tape-recorded voices of the Mafia members discussing their illegal business were played for the jurors to hear. The prosecution's next set of evidence was video evidence of the defendant handling the drugs.

Lavere had secretly planted hidden cameras inside the club office. Angela's argument was that the faces and voices on the tapes could not be made out to be Quinten. After that the first day of trial was over.

Two days later the trial resumed where it left off. The prosecution presented their physical evidence. The last major piece of evidence the prosecution presented was the murder weapon matching Quinn's firearm registration. With Quinn's name attached to the murder weapon, it was hard to argue that he wasn't at the crime scene. However, of all the club's video recordings there were none with Quinn the week leading up to Terrance's death which checked out with his alibi of being out of town.

It was up to the jury to make the determination based on their belief. The decision of whether Quinn would be found innocent or be sentenced to an amount of time that could place him in a cell for the rest of his life was up to twelve strangers.

"Before we dismiss the jury to deliberate their decision, I'm going to allow both parties to present their closing arguments. We will start with you, Angela," Judge McAdams stated.

"Your Honor, my client is an innocent man being framed. Why would someone want to frame him? I'll tell you why. Jealousy can drive a person to unusual extents. Quinten Walters is a young business owner from an impoverished area who has made a way for himself. As far as the law is concerned, he has a squeaky clean record and has never been in any trouble with the law. The statements that the prosecution presented are falsehoods and should be taken as mere hearsay. Their entire case is built upon lies of a jealous associate. There is reasonable doubt that my client committed any of the acts alleged. You should find my client not guilty of all charges."

Alfred waited for Angela to take her seat next to Quinn at the defense table before he arose and walked to the front of the courtroom. He cleared his throat to assure he had everyone's attention.

"Ladies and Gentlemen, during this trial you have been presented facts that point to the defendant's guilt. You have been presented with witnesses who stated out of their own mouth that the defendant is guilty. If you will remember when we started this trial, I advised you that you have a responsibility. As you deliberate and make your decision, I ask that you remember that responsibility."

The view outside every window of Naomi's two-story condo was breathtaking. She was surrounded by sand, palm trees, the ocean and mountains. Los Angeles had the best of both worlds, and she was happy to have relocated. She had purchased her new place for well over a million dollars and imported new furniture. She had movers bring it in and set it up for her along with the exquisite African artwork that graced most of the condo's walls. Her new place was equipped with the latest state of the art appliances, new light fixtures, hardwood floors and granite countertops. She had bought everything with Quinn's money which had totaled up to seven million dollars.

Naomi planned to use the money to open her own financial planning and accounting firm once she received her degree. She had enrolled and got accepted into Southern California University where she would finish her last two years of school. Naomi was using the website of one of Kansas City's local news stations to watch a live feed on Quinn's trial. Her eyes were glued to the television as the results of the deliberation were about to be announced.

After several hours of debating the verdict, the jury had come to an agreement. The jury was about to make the final decision on Quinn's guilt. No matter what they decided, he knew his fate lay in his own hands never in anyone else's. The jury came out ready to reveal their deliberation.

"Everyone be seated," stated the judge after banging his gabble. The room was completely silent as everyone waited with anticipation. "Has the jury come to a verdict?"

"Yes, Your Honor," said the main juror. "We the jury find the defendant guilty of all charges."

Mixed emotions filled the sound of the crowd but most cheered in favor of the judge's decision.

"Order!"

Bang! Bang! Judge McGowan banged his gavel forcefully.

"Order in this courtroom!" The courtroom quickly silenced themselves to hear the judge's sentence.

"Quinten Walters, you are sentenced to serve life in prison without the possibility of parole," Judge McAdams stated.

"I'm sorry, Quinten," Angela said disappointed in the result of the trial. She had given her best effort to present a strong case in defense of her client. She was even more upset that she didn't get the career changing win that she had hoped for.

Alfred got up celebrating his victory pumping his fist as he walked toward the front of the courthouse to brag about his victory to the awaiting media. He was still undefeated, and this victory was the best yet. He looked back at Quinn who tried to portray that he was unaffected by his loss in court. *"I bet that look will change when he's rotting in a cell knowing he'll never get out."* He left the courtroom.

The bailiff began escorting Quinn out of the courtroom. As the bailiff was leading Quinn to be escorted back to the jail, Detective Stephens walked up and stopped right in front of Quinten.

"I think you'll become quite fond of that orange jumpsuit."

Stephens chuckled to himself then patted Quinn's shoulder before walking to the front of the courthouse so he could catch up with Alfred and the reporters. Quinn said nothing just nodded and gave Stephens his trademark grin.

Guilty on all charges was the jury's decision and Naomi knew it was coming since she had been following the trial. The prosecution's arguments were overall stronger than the defense. Quinn's face displayed a blank face during the announcement of the verdict. It amazed her that he was not breaking a sweat or showing any type of emotion. That was one of the things she loved about him, he was always strong and holding it together.

Prison would make most people go crazy, but Naomi didn't doubt that Quinn would be okay. If only he had chosen a different path, and they had met some other way she wished. Quinn was about to go away for a long time, and she would never see him again. It was a bittersweet moment watching the man who had brought her the most pleasure and the most pain, get sentenced to a long life behind bars. She couldn't help the tears as they fell from her eyes. As much as she hated him for what he had done, he was still the love of her life.

Quinn nodded slightly to the officer standing by the back doors of the prison transport van. The officer was hired by the Mendez Cartel and in disguise. The judge, jury, and everyone else thought he was being led to captivity but in reality, he was being led to freedom; last night would be his last night in a cell. Quinn wasn't going back to prison ever again. Before he ever let the cops get a hold of him again, they would have to put him in a wooden box. He was going to be transported to the private airport where Armando's brother Jose had set up a private plane to take him to Los Angeles.

As soon Quinn touched down in California, he was going to meet with his new plug and start a bigger, stronger organization. Quinn was officially saying goodbye to the unpredictable Midwest and hello to the steady sunshine and palm trees of the west coast. The undercover officer opened the door of the van and Quinn stepped inside. He closed the door and went to get in the driver's seat but was stopped by the sheriff and his deputy before he could get inside the vehicle.

"Don't worry about transporting this asshole, I want to escort him to his cell my damned self." The sheriff stated.

"I've been assigned to transport the inmate; I just want to do my job." The undercover officer needed to be the one to transport Quinn or else Quinn really would be going to prison.

"It is also your job to take orders from a higher up, now stand down."

The undercover officer stepped off and gave the sheriff his key.

"Rick, you sit back there and keep an eye on that piece of shit," the sheriff said to his deputy.

"Shit!" the undercover mumbled to himself. A major kink had been thrown in their nearly perfect plan. He pulled out his wallet looking for the phone number he was given to call if anything went wrong.

"Hello." Roc answered

"There's a change of plan, the sheriff is taking the inmate to the correctional facility now."

"Man, what?! I don't have time for this! Why aren't you driving that van?!"

"Look man I tried, but the muthafucka just insisted. I can't blow my cover."

"I don't have time for excuses. You had one job!"

"I'll give the money back for the job if that's what you want."

"That's not my problem, take that up with the Cartel, they hired you. I'm not taking responsibility for your fuck up. You hear me muthafucka!"

"Bro, what's going on?" Tank asked. He could tell something was on Roc's mind by the change of his demeanor.

"We have a change of plans. The officer who is supposed to be transporting Quinn got mixed up now the sheriff is taking him to the prison himself."

Roc sat up in his Cadillac, completely hidden behind his presidential tinted windows. He was outside of the building of the Federal Judicial Court. There were a ton of police cars parked in the back of the courthouse. After a couple of minutes, he spotted the paddy wagon driving off. Roc started his SUV and began to trail the paddy wagon, leaving a three-car distance between them. He kept trailing as they merged onto the highway, he continued to stay a couple cars behind in attempt to blend in with traffic.

"How does it feel to finally get what you deserve?" asked the guard sitting across from Quinn in the paddy wagon that was heading to the Missouri State Penitentiary. He had a sarcastic smirk on his face. "Don't worry, Buddy. I think you'll get used to your new home. You have plenty of time to think about what you did." The cop began to chuckle as if he had amused himself. "It amazes me how you animals think you can beat the law."

"You animals, huh? What is that supposed to mean?" Quinn questioned while turning his nose up.

"Oh, you know exactly what I mean."

"You don't know me, Bro." Quinn looked the officer up and down and concluded that he was nothing more than a racist pig.

"Oh, I know who you are. The whole city and half the state know who you are. You're a low life con man who thought you could cheat the system and get away with it. Guess what buddy, your luck finally ran out." The deputy laughed hysterically.

"Fuck the police. Who said I didn't get away with it?" Quinn mumbled to himself.

Quinn grinned slightly. *"As soon as this paddy wagon stops, and these back doors open, Roc or Tank is going to put a bullet in this prick's head. He got no idea he's breathing his last minutes of air. Dummy."*

Quinn could not see the front seats of the transport van and had no clue that the man be driving the paddy wagon was not the undercover hired by the Mendez Cartel. Quinn grinned even wider then chuckled to himself.

"Something funny boy?" The deputy inquired harshly.

"Nope, nothing at all." Quinn responded with politeness.

"Watch your mouth boy or you're going to have a long miserable time in prison. I know the warden and I'll tell him to put you on his shit list."

Quinn grinned at his weak threat knowing the only two things allowing him to keep breathing a little longer were the cuffs around his ankles and wrist.

It wasn't until the paddy wagon exited on old country highway, a two-lane interstate that led to the middle of nowhere that it became much harder for Roc to disguise himself. Few cars were on the interstate and the further they traveled; they were the only two left on the highway.

The sheriff driving the paddy wagon noticed a black Escalade trailing him in his side mirror. It had been behind them since they'd left the courthouse. He sped up and switched lanes a few times to see if the Escalade would keep up with him and it did. Once they were, they only two cars on the road, he knew without a doubt he was being followed.

"Damn, they're onto us," Roc said after noticing the sheriff's unusual driving.

The sheriff switched lanes to the right of the Cadillac then he slowed until he was on the side of the passenger door. "Pull over your vehicle!" yelled the sheriff after rolling down his window.

"We're going to have to pop his tire?" Roc said.

"Just stay on the side of him and I'll handle it," Tank said while rolling down the passenger window of the SUV.

The sheriff was just about to reach for his radio to call back up and report the suspicious SUV when he saw a man hanging out the windows, with his rifle aimed. Tank squeezed the trigger of his automatic and fired a shot into the paddy wagon's back tire of the driver's side.

In an attempt to stop the criminals, the sheriff swerved the paddy wagon in the direction of the SUV.

Boom! The collision caused Roc to nearly lose control of the wheel.

"This muthafucka is crazy!" Roc yelled.

The sheriff returned fire while swerving toward him again. Roc's passenger window shattered.

Boom!

Roc swerved wildly almost losing control again.

"Shoot that son of a bitch!"

The sheriff sent more shots. Roc and Tank both ducked then Tank raised up to let off a rainstorm of shots.

Pow! Pow! Pow! Pow! Pow! Pow!

One bullet hit the cop in the neck and the others tore through the side of the paddy wagon. Roc watched as the paddy wagon spun into a three sixty, then veered off the road colliding into the guardrail before flipping over into a ditch.

It all had happened so fast. Quinn was being knocked around the back of the paddy wagon then he heard the cascade of shots right before the bullets ripped thru the truck frame. He tried desperately to duck but there was no use, bullets had already ripped open the side of his belly. He held his stomach and grimaced as the blood leaked all over his hands then dripped onto the floor.

The burning of the bullets was eating out his insides. His breath became short and the harder he tried to breathe, the more he tasted blood. He could feel death creeping upon him. This wasn't part of the plan. It wasn't supposed to go down like this at all. He was supposed to make it out.

The paddy wagon's tires screeched loudly then it tumbled over serval times. All four windows shattered spewing tiny pieces of glass everywhere. Specs of glass cut Quinn's arms and hands. As the vehicle was tumbling over, his body was thrown against the walls. The rapid turning caused him to be banged around several times and right before the van finally came to a halt, his head violently smacked the floor. While in his unconscious state of being, all he could see was pitch black.

"This is it. I lived by the gun, now I'm gon' die by it."

His life was slowly fading. He was putting up his best fight, but it was too hard. He didn't have the strength. In his short, twenty-two years of life, he had been through more than the average human being. Since the day his mother pushed him out, he had been fighting through life and now he was exhausted.

He shut his eyelids and began to rest when suddenly his vision became clear, and he witnessed the moment that everyone talks about. His life flashed before his eyes. In a split second, he saw everything, the good and bad. It began with memories of his pops playing with him as a little baby, embracing his mother on his graduation day, all the crimes he had committed, the bodies he had caught. Then there was Naomi and the fear in her eyes shook his soul. He shoved the gun in her face as he robbed the Community City Bank. It wasn't until that moment that he realized who she really was."

"I'm sorry baby. I love you." Suddenly his urge to fight was rejuvenated. His love for his woman gave him a reason to live.

"I never believed there was a God but if there is one, I hope you can hear me. Prove to me that you're real." Quinn wasn't ready to go just yet. He had to see Naomi again, he needed her to forgive him.

"God, if you can hear me save me. Give me a chance to make things right." Quinn knew in his heart that he had committed too many sins. He didn't deserve mercy, but he hoped God would grant it to him anyway.

His watched above his body where the shadow of the devil was hovering over him. He knew this was it; it was his time to go. Looking in the eyes of death, he began to fear the torment that was waiting for him in hell. After this day, he would be remembered forever as legend, one of the best to ever do it. Like many legends from his hood, his time had come at a young age. He had seen more in his youth than most people would see in a lifetime. He took one final breath.

Three Years Later

There was the steady beat of an IV monitor echoing loudly. The room was dark, and he couldn't see anyone. Other than the machine yelling out every time his heart beat the room was completely silent. He tried to move his body but was extremely weak. Much more desperately he tried to move his limbs but still nothing happened.

"Why can't I move my body!" he thought to himself. *"Ok, just stay calm don't panic."* After taking a few deep breaths he finally calmed himself completely down, then he began to think about what had happened to him that would land him in the hospital. He dug into his memory bank but couldn't find anything. *"Think Quinn! Well shit, at least I remember my name."* If he could remember that there was hope that he could remember the rest of his past. He closed his eyes and began to think as hard as he could. He focused harder, using all the concentration he could muster then his memory began to resurrect itself.

It had been buried in a coma for nearly three years. That's when his dream had come back. He thought he had died. His life had flashed before his eyes and that was it. He had been sentenced to life in prison and died in an attempt to break out but somehow, he didn't die, and he wasn't in prison.

"Or am I?" Maybe he was in a hospital waiting to be rejuvenated so he could be taken back to the hell hole called a cell.

"Hell no!" His mind yelled to him. He wasn't doing that again, he had to move his body. He had to escape if that was indeed the case. He would rather have died than go back to prison.

"Ok just try to wiggle your toe like Uma did." He had seen Uma move her body from temporary paralysis but that was just a movie. Would it really work for him in real life? He figured he'd might as well try it. After several minutes of trying to move, his body made no attempt to move on its own. Quinn was starting to think the worst. *"Am I paralyzed? Hell no, I can't be no liability."* He had to stand on his own two feet. *"Ok just concentrate. If my memory can come back with concentration so can my body movement."* Again, Quinn closed his eyes and focused as hard as he could. This time he put

all his effort into moving his hand. His arm began to twitch slightly, and he knew there was some hope. Quinn kept his eyes closed and focused even harder. His arm shot up and the pain was excruciating.

After applying the same amount of focus and concentration to the rest of his limbs, Quinn was able to gain a small amount of feeling in the rest of body. The pain was excruciating, and movement felt so unnatural. *"Damn, how long I been like this."*

Lifting the cover off his body was like moving a boulder. Quinn got up and stood to his feet. He almost collapsed to the floor, but he was determined to move. He began to shake trying to keep his balance and had to hold onto the bed for support. He looked around the room he was in and realized it was not a hospital. He was inside someone's house. That's when even more confusion set in.

There was a small glimmer of light coming from one end of the room and he could tell it was a window being covered by a large curtain. Slowly but surely, he made his way over to the window gaining more strength as he continued to move his body. After walking several feet, Quinn felt like he had just walked a mile. He pulled back the curtain and it continued to retract much further than he expected.

Quinn's eyes were filled with amazement. The ocean, mountains, and beautiful sand. He looked to his right and saw a large estate in the distance and another one equally as large when he looked to his left. The more he assessed his surroundings the more confused he was. He looked around the room now that there was light from the window giving him a clearer vision. The bed that he had been lying in was large a king-sized bed. There wasn't anything else in the room besides it and the heart monitor. He walked out the room and found himself in the coldest mansion he'd ever seen. He remembered having major paper, but he wasn't balling this hard.

Quinn walked through a long hallway and passed three other rooms before coming to a glass elevator. As he rode the elevator down, he overlooked the house, and it was marvelous. Crystal chandeliers hung from the ceiling. Windows were all around with breathtaking views, marble floors, and artwork that should have been inside a museum. In the living room he noticed Roc and Vanilla. They both looked up with astonishment realizing the day that Quinn would awake again had finally come.

To Be Continued...

Thank you for reading! To stay connected with me, turn back to the copyrights page and follow my social media accounts. If you enjoyed the book, please visit amazon.com and leave a review.

www.ingramcontent.com/pod-product-compliance
Lightning Source LLC
Chambersburg PA
CBHW031202020726
47499CB00002B/457